I0712689

NOTES FROM EXILE

By
Sabina Baral

Sabina Baral
Notes from Exile

Edition I

Typesetting Robert Błaszak

ISBN
979-8-89778-233-8(Ebook)
979-8-899778-230-7(Paperback)
979-8-89778-232-1(Hardcover)

I wrote this book for myself,
for You,
and as a warning.
It is a piece of my life,
But not only.
It is my Yizkor.[1]

For my Daughters

---

[1] *Yizkor, in Hebrew „Remember," is the first word of the prayer for a departed parent or closest family, with an overall theme of keeping their memory alive.*

Both the prayer and practice took on a new meaning after WWII, where entire families and communities perished, leaving no one to honor them with a prayer. Survivors of such com- munities wrote, first spontaneously and then as part of a movement, entire books recording every detail they could recall about their murdered brethren. Those that could not write, dictated. Those that could, wrote in whatever language they knew, longhand, creating an unprecedented record of a world that disappeared. Over 2,000 Yizkor books have been written.

Table of Contents

FOREWORD

*They say that time heals all wounds, but we
never live long enough to test that theory.*

José Saramago, *The Cave*

1968 slipped into the pages of history without much thunder—yet it was a monumental year. Martin Luther King and Robert Kennedy were assassinated. North Vietnam launched the Tet Offensive, which arguably turned the tides of the Vietnam War, and protests against the draft and the war itself erupted not only throughout the United States but also in Paris, Berlin, London, and Rome. The showcase trial of the Chicago Seven highlighted the profound division that this war brought to America. The Democratic Party Convention in Chicago opened amidst bloody riots. A manned Apollo spacecraft circled the moon. Two U.S. Olympians on the podium bowed their heads and raised black-gloved fists during "The Star-Spangled Banner," a now-recognized salute to the Black Power movement. In Europe, the Prague Spring erupted and was squashed within months by the invasion of "friendly" Soviet Bloc armed forces. Student protests against dictatorships swept the globe; in France up to ten million workers joined in.

And in Poland, then ruled by the puppet government under the authoritarian thumb of Moscow, 1968 was the year of the

March Events. Student protests sparked a wave of massive, government-incited antisemitic repressions that, over time, forced the exile of the majority of Polish Jews — all Holocaust survivors — and their families. **This is my story**. Older parents—good, quiet, simple people who lost everything except for their lives during the Holocaust—and their only child, a twenty-year-old daughter. **This is my story**.

The first act took place in the summer of 1967 when Israel emerged victorious in the Six-Day War against the Moscow-supported coalition of Jordan, Syria, and Egypt. Ties with the USSR made the Polish authorities consider themselves party to this distant conflict. They allied with the Arab countries and broke off diplomatic relations with Israel. Coincidentally, in March of 1968, student protests erupted against the communist regime, first in Warsaw but soon also in other academic centers of the country. Street conflicts with the police, beatings, and arrests followed. The government needed an internal enemy on whom to blame this unrest, and the recent war in Israel became very convenient. In carefully staged public displays of party-line support, factory workers across Poland assembled to denounce Zionism. A massive media campaign unfolded. Soon, a racial twist was added, and the enemy was relabeled simply as Jews. Masses were mobilized, hate sessions organized, and a public purge began, resulting in a wave of mass emigration. Observers called it "the largest antisemitic campaign in Europe since the fall of the Third Reich."

Now, fifty-plus years later, the exile of Polish Jews caused by the March Events is a subject that lies somewhere between taboo and *tabula rasa* — in that dark, frozen space reserved for ugly secrets deeply buried by its perpetrators. Systematically erased from Polish history and barely known elsewhere, the facts struggle for air, haunted only by the regretful—no, shameful—ignorance of the Polish post-war generations. The pain inflicted on my parents—on all of our parents—is now largely unknown. Twenty-three years after the unimaginable losses of the Holocaust, its survivors were once again excluded from the social landscape of the country of their birth and isolated into the lonely enclave of the shamed and unwanted. Jews. They once again lost their homes and the privilege of living in the only world they knew and understood. In the middle of Europe, they were once again declared enemies of yet another system.

They left.

They left behind twelve hundred Jewish cemeteries and the ashes of six million. They took with them the biggest treasure of the post-Holocaust nation: their children. Or they sent the children out of Poland alone.

And so, out of the need of my heart, **NOTES FROM EXILE** was born.

Maybe you've heard such stories; maybe they concern you or previous generations of your family. Maybe they pertain to other countries, other journeys, and other injustices. Or maybe you are among the lucky ones—born in a good place, among good people, and in good times—and have had the luxury of never giving it a thought.

This story happened to me and to thousands like me; it is my page in the history of Polish Jews—my *Yizkor*—and it took me many years to find the strength to write it. "Silence encourages the tormentor, never the tormented," said Elie Wiesel in *Night*. This is my effort to break the silence.

This story is especially true today, when 80 million refugees circle the globe seeking safety, water, and dignity; when antisemitism has erupted full force again, and when fascism and xenophobia are both thriving and protested at historic levels.

When "NEVER AGAIN" was butchered on October 7, 2023 and the world was silent.

* * *

I bow my head to the shadows of my parents.

ix

WHY AGAINST THE JEWS?

THE ANTI-ZIONIST CAMPAIGN OF 1968

by Prof. Dariusz Stola

Dariusz Stola is a historian, professor at the Institute of Political Studies, Polish Academy of Sciences, and fellow at the Center for Migration Research, Warsaw University. **From 2014 to 2019, he was the director of the POLIN Museum of the History of Polish Jews.** He published ten books and more than a hundred articles on the history of Polish Jewish relations, the communist regime in Poland and on international migrations in the 20th century, including *Nadzieja i zagłada* (Hope and Destruction), 1995; *Kampania antysyjonistyczna w Polsce 1967-1968* (The Anti-Zionist Campaign in Poland, 1967–1968), 2000; *Patterns of Migration in Central Europe* (2001, with C. Wallace); *Kraj bez wyjścia? Mi-gracje z Polski 1948-1989* (A country with no way out? Migrations from Poland 1948-1949), 2010; *PZPR jako machina władzy* (PZPR as an instrument of power), 2012, with K. Persak).

In Polish historiography, the dramatic events of spring 1968 are often simply referred to as *March*, and for many, the term is synonymous with an anti-Jewish witch hunt with an official name: *"anti-Zionist* campaign." I place the terms Zionism and Zionists in italics as in Poland of 1968, they belong neither to Polish nor English but to another language: the Orwellian newspeak of the communist party. They were not used to refer to a particular variety of nationalism but were substitutes for *Jew* and *Jewish*, including cases where the person referred to as a Zionist was neither Jewish nor pro-Israeli.[2]

The hate campaign that began in March 1968 included aggressive antisemitic propaganda, barely covered with the fig leaf of anti-Zionism; mass mobilization against "the enemies of socialist Poland," among whom the *Zionists* stood prominently; expulsion of Jews from the party, government posts, and other positions; the destruction or drastic restriction of Jewish institutions and organizations; and discrimination against and harassment of individuals for being Jewish. Last but not least, the wave of Jewish emigration that followed the campaign (encouraged, induced, and sometimes simply forced by the authorities) reduced the Jewish population in Poland by half and brought organized Jewish life to the edge of extinction.

The anti-Zionist campaign followed the main chapter of the March Events: a youth rebellion and its pacification by the authorities. Street riots broke out when police and groups of communist party activists armed with clubs brutally attacked a peaceful student rally at Warsaw University on the 8th of March. In the following days, in Warsaw and other academic centers, there were numerous protest meetings, student strikes, and street riots, to which the authorities responded with clubs, arrests, expulsions from the universities, and conscription into the army. While students were the primary agents of the rebellion, protests also took place in cities without academic institutions in more than a hundred localities across Poland and involved many young workers and secondary school students. By the 27th of March, the police arrested 2,591 people, including 597 students, while more than 600 students had been drafted

---

[2] For a more extensive analysis of the anti-Zionist campaign see D. Stola, *The hate campaign of March 1968. How did it become anti-Jewish?*, Polin: Studies in Polish Jewry, vol. 21 (2009).

into the army and sent to distant garrisons. Many more people were beaten, removed from universities, blacklisted by the secret police, and subjected to other forms of harassment.

Concurrently, an attack against dissident intellectuals unfolded, including the persecution of independent-minded writers (favored targets were the Catholic writers Paweł Jasienica and Stefan Kisielewski), scholars, and artists, which evolved into a wider campaign of intimidation of the intelligentsia. Thus, the *Zionists* were under fire in a peculiar company of student rebels, young rioters, Catholic intellectuals, and independent artists. The third current, least visible but key for the developing events, was a power struggle between party factions, groups, and leaders that went on behind the scenes. To make sure, no proof of any Zionist conspiracy behind the youth rebellion of 1968 or the faction struggle has been ever found. The claim was one of the factors endowing the campaign with its grotesque character.

On the eve of the campaign, Polish Jews wore a small relic of the once-great Polish Jewry. There were approximately 25,000–30,000 Jews among Poland's 32 million inhabitants (i.e., no more than 0.01 percent). The group was aging, and its Yiddish culture and religion were in retreat. The group's education levels were well above the rest of the population, which meant that they were strongly overrepresented among the intelligentsia. This and other factors, such as the selective nature of emigration, which took especially those who preferred to live elsewhere than in communist Poland, made the group overrepresented, as it seems, in the Communist Party and state administration, their upper strata in particular. Moreover, popular perception tended to exaggerate the extent of this participation to frequently paranoid proportions, following the well-rooted prejudice of *żydokomuna*[3].

The real and imaginary Jews made part of the faction struggle inside the communist party. In the previous political crisis in Poland in 1956, the leadership of the Polish United Workers' Party (PZPR) was divided into two factions. The relatively reformist group included leading Jewish communists; the more conservative faction put the blame for Stalin-era crimes on the Jews. Władysław Gomułka, who, after a few years of isolation, returned to the top position in the party's Politburo, only to gradually marginalize its leaders and put his own people in key positions. In the 1960s, a new force appeared on the political scene, the Partisans, a rather loose group of party leaders and lower-level activists united by political backgrounds often shaped in wartime underground (hence the name), unappeased ambitions, and a world view combining chauvinism and communism. Their leader was General Mieczysław Moczar, the head of the Ministry of Internal Affairs (MSW) and its powerful Security Service (SB).

Zionists and Zionism had been the target of communist hate propaganda for a long time. At least since the Slansky show trial in Czechoslovakia in 1952, the terms had become code names for Jews and Jewish. After the Israeli-Arab Six-Day War of June 1967, when the Soviet Bloc states broke relations with Israel, the terms acquired a new dimension. MSW leaders realized that the opportunity to hit the Zionists was near at hand. Speaking to the ministry directors on 28 June 1967, General Moczar defined Polish Jews as infected with dangerous Zionism, indicated them as a collective object for particular scrutiny, and gave priority to the struggle against Zionism thus understood. Preparations for a purge were well advanced when the ferment

---

[3] *Żydokomuna* means Jewish communism.

among students and intellectuals intensified in early 1968 and could easily be connected to it. Sources originating within the MSW began to spread a theory of Jewish conspiracy behind the dissent.

The theme of Zionism was initially absent at the onset of riots on March 8. But three days later, two articles gave the signal and direction for a propaganda offensive. Meanwhile, the 'Jewish explanation' of the youth protests became part of the MSW secret reports to the Politburo. Taking them as a basis and side-tracking members who opposed antisemitic initiatives in the past, Gomułka gave the green light to intense attacks against Zionism, which snowballed in the media and in public speeches. As head of the party, Press Bureau Olszowski proudly explained, these followed the party order for a "Press campaign against the instigators and the bankrupt politicians, to reveal their political background—reactionary, revisionist, and Zionist forces."

The communist party controlled virtually all the mass media. Olszowski noted with satisfaction that in just the first ten days of the campaign, 250 relevant articles had appeared in the press. A significant portion of this propaganda barrage contained more or less openly antisemitic content. The 1968 campaign was also the first hate campaign in communist Poland to exploit the power of television, a new medium that had just become widespread. But most of the party energy went into the organization of rallies against the Zionists and other enemies of socialist Poland. Some were huge undertakings, with 100,000 people bused in from a whole province, but more people took part in smaller, local meetings: factory and department rallies, meetings of basic party organizations, sessions of county, city, and district party committees, meetings of the party satellite and 'transmission belt' organizations, such as trade unions, youth, and women's organizations, etc. In

Warsaw alone, and in only the first two weeks of the campaign, there were more than 1,900 basic party meetings, nearly 400 rallies, 700 meetings of the core, and 600 meetings of various party groups.

The slogans and banners at the gatherings were strikingly similar, following the guidelines of the party headquarters. Thousands of meetings passed resolutions and sent letters to the party leadership in an increasingly radical tone. "We swear in memory of those who died for power to the people that we will clean from Polish soil, with our workers' fists, all the instigators and leaders of the coup against the workers' and peasants' government. We will not permit revisionist and Zionist rioters to accuse us of antisemitism," wrote the workers from the Polfer factories, while the workers from the Baildon steel works demanded "a purge of Zionist elements from party ranks, removal from their positions, and the refusal to permit their children to continue further university studies."

Simultaneously grew a wave of dismissals from the party and jobs. It began with Roman Zambrowski, once a powerful member of the Politburo and Secretary of the Party Central Committee. He was attacked in absentia, denied any chance to defend himself, and removed from the party and his government position. News of the dismissal, broadcasted immediately, sent a clear message: if such a prominent figure was defenseless, any *Zionist* could be freely attacked. The dismissals descended from top government officials and editors-in-chief of major newspapers to university professors, bookkeepers in cooperatives, teachers in elementary schools, and factory foremen. Top-down instructions unleashed the social dynamics of the purge, fuelled by the settling of personal accounts, the desire to take someone's position, popular resentment against the establishment, and, last but not least, the hatred of Jews.

A key moment of the campaign was March 19, when 3,000 party activists gathered in the Congress Hall in Warsaw to listen to Gomułka. They filled the hall holding banners such as 'Down with the Agents of Imperialism and Reactionary Zionism!' and 'We Demand a Complete Unmasking and Punishment of the Political Instigators.' The meeting was broadcast on TV and radio. Gomułka tried to appear moderate, devoting only a minor part of his speech to Zionism and denying it was a real danger for Poland. There was, however—he claimed—a problem with those Jewish citizens of Poland who were more loyal to Israel than to Poland. "I presume that Jews in this category will sooner or later leave our country," he prophesied, adding: "We are ready to give emigration passports to those who consider Israel their Fatherland." His speech contrasted with the audience's behavior, especially of the members of the Volunteer Reserve Militia (ORMO) in the gallery, who at that moment became excited and, holding anti-Zionist banners, and encouraging the speaker "Bolder, bolder," "Go ahead Wiesław, give names."

Gomułka's prophecy was self-fulfilling. Soon, hundreds and then thousands of people submitted applications for emigration permits. A condition to get the permit was to renounce Polish citizenship. Consequently, the emigrants were leaving with a 'travel document,' which made clear that "the bearer of this document is not a citizen of the People's Republic of Poland." It was a one-way ticket with no return. The emigration wave culminated in 1969 and took almost 14,000 people, i.e., half of all the Jews in Poland.

It is not easy to find evidence for the specific motives of the officials and officers who made Zionists the target of the campaign. In the campaign of 1968, lies were a key pillar of the regime.

First, the anti-Zionist campaign was a reaction to the student protests and dissent among intellectuals. It was a tool for fighting the youth rebellion by compromising its alleged instigators, leaders, and goals as aliens. The anti-Zionist propaganda also provided a smokescreen to hide the true targets of police brutality. The symbolic anti-Jewish violence that filled the media blurred the fact that non-Jewish students and workers were the great majority of those beaten, arrested, and otherwise repressed.

Second, anti-Zionism was used to prevent the rebellion from spreading beyond the universities and youth to broader groups, industrial workers in particular. This seems to be the most important motive for the aggressive and demagogic campaign. At least since the autumn of 1967, when a series of strikes followed a rise in food prices, the party leaders had been seriously concerned about the possible eruption of popular unrest. Portraying the dissident students and intellectuals as *aliens*—Jews, bloodstained Stalinists or their sons, arrogant members of the establishment, and so forth—certainly contributed to alienating them from the masses. Jewish communists seem to have been the best scapegoat available, against whom the party could direct popular frustration and anger for its past crimes, recent misdeeds, and constant absurdities of the regime. Pointing at Jewish communists, their Polish (ex-) comrades could absolve themselves and imply that after the purge, a better, purely Polish socialism would come.

The third objective of the campaign was to change the political balance in the party leadership. The attack on Zionists revitalized the conflict that had been ripening in the Politburo for a few years and gave its proponents a strategic advantage over their adversaries. Within a few weeks, the latter realized their defeat. The campaign enabled Gomułka to reconsolidate the party leadership on his terms and maintain his authoritarian rule for another two years.

Last but not least, we need to stress motivations of a different nature. Explaining why the Jews should not reduce the initiators and participants in the campaign to rational agents and their motivation to a calculated pursuit of interests. At least for some of them, attacking the Jews was a primary goal in itself, not just an instrument of other goals. Poland in the spring of 1968 was the scene of innumerable expressions of irrational anti-Jewish resentments and prejudices. They are well visible in the recorded words and deeds of the excited participants in the hate meetings, as well as some of the officials and officers at the upper levels of the state–party power structure. Making the *Zionists* a key target of the campaign served both the political interests and dark emotions rooted in prejudice and paranoid worldview.

*Our lives begin to end the day we become
silent about things that matter.*

Martin Luther King

DECEMBER 1968, SÜDBAHNHOF, VIENNA

Everyone recognizes misery.
It makes a person defenseless.

Albert Camus, *The Stranger*

Vienna was cold, white, and festive. Store windows, like old-fashioned Christmas cards, twinkled with tiny lights and tempted with beautiful wooden toys, perfume and cognac, a plaid cashmere scarf, and a velvet dress with an impossibly large bow on the shoulder… the Viennese knew how to do store windows. Christmas carols shimmered in the background: familiar tunes sung in German, somehow out of place so early in the day. Distinguished, silver-haired ladies enjoyed a leisurely morning stroll with their well-groomed dogs. The dogs were well dressed; some wore coats of Astrakhan fur, and some ladies did as well. They matched. The smell of coffee and cinnamon whiffed from a café we pass by. Holiday cheer and the elegant Viennese atmosphere surrounded us without touching. We don't fit in here; after a night on the train, we are disheveled and feel dirty. At the Wien Südbahnhof railroad station, someone read our names from a list—they expected us here, and this calmed a bit of my frayed, chaotic thoughts.

On December 20, *Chopin*, the pride of Polish State Railways, sweated out the final chapter of our Polish lives on the route from Katowice to Vienna as if fulfilling its namesake's legacy of forced emigration and exile. The journey lasted only a few hours, but it was fatefully significant; we left home forever. Much time will pass before another place on Earth becomes "home" to us.

The Peoples Republic of Poland was sealed; leaving was a rare and celebrated privilege. But there was no joy among the Jewish passengers of *Chopin*. Suitcases, bags and packages, tears, eyes full of uncertainty, fingers intertwined. Jewish families from different cities settled into this journey to exile in nearly every compartment. We said goodbye to some of them at the Wien Südbahnhof; they would go to Israel. Goodbye. Take care. Have a good life. A scene from *Fiddler on the Roof* after the pogrom.

I am embarrassed by the broken heels of my boots; the humiliating parting gift from Polish customs officers at the border. I limp on my tiptoes with an awkward gait through the elegant streets of Vienna in a feeble attempt to compensate and pretend all is normal. I keep checking my reflection in the gleaming windows, hoping no one will notice. No one does, even if it's noticeable. No one cares.

We arrive at a tired-looking, modest hotel. We put down our bags and suitcases in the simple room assigned to us. It occurs to me for the first time that we have become people who live out of suitcases. I take off the boots with broken heels. Mama looks at me—she guesses what is coming—and urges me not to throw them away. *"They are almost new"*, she pleads heatedly. *"We will fix them somehow…"*

But I don't want them anymore. They embody humiliation. I shove them into the wastebasket, but they don't fit. The basket is too small; the wicker bulges, hisses and deforms. Still, I am determined. I am done with these boots. It takes some force, but I win. The eventual demise of the boots (and the basket) alleviates, for a moment, some of my helpless anger.

Strangely enough, I don't even regret the loss. I don't want to remember how many months of math tutoring they cost and what a victory it was to find them in a city full of empty shelves. I should have thrown them out of the window of the train while we were still in Poland, before we crossed the border.

Sounds of a Slavic conversation reach us from the hallway. Two Czech girls — they each left for Israel some months ago and have now returned to Vienna to meet their families, whose permits to leave the country were, for some reason, delayed. They will be reunited any day now.

The obvious hits me — this is a hotel for emigrants. Of course, it is. We are now emigrants.

Another family from Wrocław is here — the Srebrniks. Neatly dressed parents of impressive proportions; their beautiful daughter, Stella, with a storm of unruly, curly hair; and their son, Boris, whom I vaguely remember from some Jewish summer camp. Stella's hair makes her appear wildly and pleasantly uncontained, whereas Boris is tidy, clean, and completely put together. He wears a well-fitting, elaborately trimmed coat with straps, hooks, epaulets, leather buttons, and even a slim collar of gray astrakhan. He fits in well — a coat-and-collar match to the best-dressed Viennese ladies and their dogs.

The Srebrniks have another daughter, their eldest, who married a man from Montreal a few years earlier and has lived there since, eager for her family to join her.

Unlike most, the Srebrniks are, therefore, wanted and awaited; someone is making joyous preparations for their arrival. For them, this journey is simply the "in-between." But they, too, had to leave their Polish lives behind–they were no longer theirs–and the exit was ugly and humiliating.

Our situation is different—we are not even sure where our journey will end. Tata has some cousins in America, but they have never met; in fact, they didn't even know of each other's existence. Their father, Tata's uncle, emigrated from Poland to America during the interwar period, escaping antisemitism and searching for work. All that connects Tata with these new cousins are letters, photos, and a shared last name: Binder.

The Srebrniks and us instinctively cling to each other—the only familiar souls—and all of us feel reassured when we land in adjacent hotel rooms. Before long, Mrs. Srebrnik knocks on our door, asking if Vienna is in the same time zone as Wrocław. This must be a pretext; she just wants to make sure we are here and that they aren't alone. Because, really, what difference does it make what time it is? As of now, none of us have any appointments or plans; our calendars are empty. Our lives are empty, filled only with anxiety.

It is unclear how long we will be in Vienna or, for that matter, in that hotel. This is awkward: should we unpack all the suitcases or just leave them open and dig as needed? We reassembled the contents hastily on the train after the customs inspection at the border. We now dig in this mess to find pajamas, toothbrushes, tea bags, and a few other trivial symbols of normality. In the spartan hotel bathroom, the shower is luxuriously hot; it soothes the outer layers of anxiety. What now? Mama pulls a *grzałka* out of her bag; it's a thick metal coil connected via an electric cord with a plug on the opposing end. She discovered this ugly contraption in the Siberian labor camp during the war, but in my childhood, many homes in Poland had a *grzałka*—the practical *accoutrement* of a post-war tea-making ceremony. With the coil in a cup, water boils in minutes, and, voilà, we have tea. There is only one cup in the room, so we take turns drinking the tea we had brought from home. I imagined our first encounter with the West quite differently. The great free world I anticipated had not revealed itself as yet, not on the first day, anyway. I will clearly have to wait longer.

The rest of the day is slow and uneventful. It must have gotten a bit warmer because the snow on the streets turned to yucky slush. It does not befit Christmas; it does not even befit Vienna. We eat a tasteless dinner in the drab hotel restaurant and turn in early—too early—perhaps to avoid conversation.

Days pass without content. Both of my parents are fluent in German and get around the city without much trouble, but they are quiet. We don't really talk to each other except for practicalities: "Are you hungry?" or "I wonder if we can borrow an iron here" is the extent of our conversations. The three of us do a bit of sightseeing. Vienna is impressive—my favorite is perhaps the Schönbrunn Palace or maybe the elegant storefronts on Kärntnerstrasse. We freeze to the bone, listening to Christmas organ music in front of the famous Stephanskirche, the 800-year-old mother church of Roman Catholics.

I am curious what lies ahead, strangely carefree and unanchored, as if floating in a Chagall painting. When I forget for a moment how and why we got here, that we live out of suitcases and *are homeless*, I feel as though we are at the onset of an extraordinary adventure I hadn't yet understood or learned to enjoy. Then I remember. This Viennese interlude is both a painful ending and a new beginning. But the beginning of what? When and where will this "beginning" start? The "Travel

Document" in our pockets burns like a brand, declaring: "The bearer of this document is not a citizen of Poland." We have no right of return — they don't want us there. They pushed us out and shut the door. Nor do we have the right to enter any other country except Israel. Austria allowed us in only as transit passengers, en route to Israel.

After a few days, we learned that they didn't want us in Vienna either. Our uncertain and possibly lengthy path to the United States will lead through Rome. After all, we don't have American visas, which is a major obstacle. We don't have Italian visas either, but that somehow escapes my attention. I also don't notice that no one asks us to buy train tickets to Rome or that there is no bill for the hotel in Vienna. Thankfully, because we really have no money. But Rome is unexpected.

One day, a note appears in our hotel room — an invitation to Shabbat at the Jewish Congregation. Celebrating Shabbat has never been our thing, but I hope it will be a social opportunity, a moment to feel human, lighthearted, and maybe even joyous. My parents don't want to go; they have consistently declined all possibilities of social encounters — but I lobby hard. There will be lots of people, I argue, maybe someone they know — what harm can it do?

In the end, they agree. There is indeed a crowd seated at a long table, many, like us, newly arrived from Poland, but no one we know — they seem to all be from different cities. Dinner is preceded by a short prayer. We aren't quite sure what to do with ourselves once the meal is over — when is it appropriate to leave?

A pleasant man approaches Tata and takes him aside. After a short conversation, a commotion. Tata rises abruptly, clearly upset. "Let's go," he hisses, putting on his coat in flight, without pausing, struggling with the sleeve because his scarf is in it, practically running out the door. Mama and I follow. In an extravagant gesture so unlike him, Tata hails a taxi and gives the driver the address of our hotel. I idiotically wonder how much it will cost. In an agitated voice, Tata explains that the gentleman at the Congregation asked if we needed anything and offered him money. Apparently, in a well-intended gesture, the Austrian Jews thought we were poor refugees in need of a handout. *Humiliating!*

And a scary thought: Is this the impression we now make?

On New Year's Eve, I spent a while with my parents, wanting to sound joyous and upbeat and to wish them a Happy New Year. In the end, we just hugged. I then went out to Stephansplatz, where a few of us young ones agreed to meet in front of the church. It's terribly cold; the church is full; since the demise of my boots, I don't even have proper winter shoes. We are not sure what to do with ourselves; I spent the previous New Year's Eve with Jacek and a bunch of friends in a flimsy lace dress made just for the occasion and hair in a fancy updo. Surely, most of us have similar memories. Here, in Vienna, I am bundled up in layers upon layers of every warm piece of clothing in my suitcase – not very festive. Someone brought a bottle of alcohol – it was the Polish "Pejsachówka," allegedly for Passover, certified as Kosher with a signature of Poland's chief rabbi stamped on every bottle. One of the items rumored to be all the rage in the West. Clinging to each other in a tight circle, holding plastic cups filled with harsh liquor in freezing hands, at midnight, we welcome the New Year 1969.

ZIONISTS! YOUR PLACE IS IN ISRAEL!

We are prepared to give emigration passports to all those who consider Israel their homeland.

Władysław Gomułka, leader of the Communist Party of Poland, March 19, 1968.

The famous-infamous gathering of the core of the Polish United Workers' Party (PZPR) in the Congress Hall in Warsaw chants enthusiastic support for the speaker, "Comrade Wiesław" Gomułka, the party's First Secretary and, de facto, leader of Poland. It's a long speech. He carefully enunciates the Jewish names of the instigators of recent riots at the University of Warsaw as if the names alone were both an indictment and proof of their implied guilt. The crowd hears the coded innuendo and understands him well—he has just named the enemy.

In 1936, when the reactionary Polish government similarly encouraged antisemites, Romain Rolland, the famous French novelist, sent a letter to a Warsaw magazine, "Oblicze Dnia" *The Face of the Day*. He wrote: "I really regret that I am not a Jew, for I am ashamed of my brother Christians." Three years later came the war in which the Nazis annihilated six million Jews. And twenty-three years after the war, Gomułka encouraged antisemites once again. Looking for an internal enemy and scapegoating the Jews was a time-honored Polish tradition.

* * *

I was a second-year student at the Wrocław University of Science and Technology. On that fateful day, our professor stepped up to the lectern and turned on the radio. In silence and disbelief, instead of a lecture, we listened to the live transmission of Gomułka's speech. Many of our professors were among the surviving Polish intelligentsia of Lviv, the formerly Polish city incorporated into the Soviet Union. To them, the USSR was the aggressor that occupied eastern Poland. They were quite skeptical of the party-run government and the socialist system it enforced.

In case anyone missed the essence of Gomułka's speech, Prime Minister Józef Cyrankiewicz spelled it out without ambiguity. "Some Polish citizens of Jewish ethnicity carry nationalistic, Zionist, and therefore pro-Israeli beliefs. In the current political climate created by the state of Israel, these people find themselves in a quandary." And t h e n , a diagnosis that dispelled all doubt: "Simultaneous loyalty toward socialist Poland and imperialist Israel is not possible."

"Zionists to Dayan!"

"Kikes to Israel!"

Warsaw students took to the streets, and in the next few days, the student strikes spread like wildfire countrywide. I regarded the moment as lofty and noble, historically important; I looked forward to joining the strike in defense of our Polish cause. It hadn't occurred to me, not yet, anyway, that the erupting events intended to draw a demarcation line between me, a Jew, and my Polish home and friends, even between the Jewish and Polish parts of me which, thus far, coexisted seamlessly and in harmony. I was also too naïve to understand the political maneuver these speeches heralded, that the insults hurled at Israel were thinly veiled attacks on all Polish Jews, and that we were witnessing the staging of a newly invented, modern version of a pogrom. Not bloody, but effective, with similar, dramatic consequences. Gomułka never even mentioned the word "Jew." He didn't have to; his minions understood:

Jews – OUT!

It was an organized and well-prepared action. Historian David Engel of the YIVO Institute wrote in "Poland": "The Ministry of Internal Affairs compiled a card index of all Polish citizens with Jewish roots..." (!!!) The very fact that they kept track of the ethnic ancestry of Polish citizens is both scary and disgusting. Subsequently, on June 29, 1967, the Ministry repeated its previously ignored request to ban Jewish organizations from receiving support funds from the American Jewish Joint Distribution Committee. On October 2, 1967, the request was adopted by the party's Central Committee. Could there be another purpose of such a ban except to punitively choke Jewish social, educational, and cultural life? These organizations, cautiously developed after the war by the handful of survivors, were now doomed to close: Jewish schools and youth clubs, vocational training programs, Jewish cooperatives where many of our parents worked, summer camps for children, aid and food distribution for the needy, matza for Passover, care for cemeteries, etc. Only institutions carefully chosen to project an image of a tolerant Poland remained and were supported by the government: the Yiddish-language newspaper *Folks-Sztyme* (*Voice of the People*), which, for lack of readership, shrunk after 1968 to a weekly, the conformist Social and Cultural Association of Jews in Poland (TSKŻ); and the Jewish Theater in Warsaw, which continued to operate without its star, guiding spirit, and leader, Ida Kaminska. Ida also emigrated, first to Israel and, eventually, to New York.

*   *   *

A few months and many sleepless nights later, as the government scenario of *Judenrein* unfolded, *nolens volens*, we, too, gave them what they wanted and applied for permission to leave. Since the application had to be accompanied by the promise of a visa to Israel, it branded us as Zionists—also according to plan. Soon, we found ourselves not just accused but also sentenced and convicted, with three weeks to liquidate our lives and leave—unconditionally, stripped of Polish citizenship, with no return. The formal framework was not a passport but a government-issued "Travel Document" for stateless persons, and in it, like a lifeline, a lonely visa to Israel.

At the onset of the Six-Day War, Poland, like the rest of the Soviet Bloc except Romania, broke off diplomatic relations with Israel. With no Israeli representation, promises of our visas—and the visas themselves—were issued by the embassy of the neutral Netherlands.

Now, in Vienna, we had to somehow resolve the matter of the Israeli visas we did not intend to use. A meeting was scheduled with *Sochnut*, the Israeli organization responsible for absorption, whose charter is to "inspire Jews throughout the world to connect with their People, heritage, and homeland, and empower them to build a thriving Jewish life in Israel." We had no idea what to expect.

The gentlemen of *Sochnut* tried to convince us that going anywhere but Israel was a mistake. They applied some pressure

("Israel needs you"), then a dose of Jewish guilt ("Do you really want to go from one diaspora to another?"), and, finally, threats ("Israel is the only place where you are welcome and will be safe"). All of it was reasonable and, most likely, true—but our minds were made up. Truthfully, we listened to what they said but didn't process it; we just waited for them to finish.

At the end of an exhausting day, they understood that Mama was in poor health that both parents had concerns about the Israeli climate, and, above all, they feared another war. And the biggest argument any Jew could have is family. There is some family in the US. With this understanding, Sochnut gave up on us and annulled the visas. It was at once a great relief and a scary, pyrrhic victory – we now had no visas whatsoever. We just declined the only option, which truly, enthusiastically wanted to receive us and give us shelter. A new destination emerged and a new stamp on our fate – Rome; if we were to get to the US, it would have to be through there. Our only home, the threadbare Viennese hotel, seemed particularly drab that evening. I am overcome by childish fear that no one will ever want us, that we will forever be poor and live in dowdy hotel rooms.

Rome is a new development in the evolving methodology of our exile. Until now, people have applied for various destination visas in Vienna. But the number of Jewish exiles from Poland and, even more to the point, the number of applications to leave grew dramatically with each passing week, just as the Polish government planned. The Austrian authorities realized that they lacked the capacity to handle this *exodus*, and from now on, Vienna will serve only as a stopover point. In a few months, other routes will open—a ferry from the Polish port of Świnoujście to Ystad, Sweden, a train to Copenhagen, and some air routes as well. For now, however, the only option was the train from Poland (Warsaw, via

Katowice to Vienna) — and then either Israel or Rome.

Mama asks about our "lift" – the wooden crate that contained all our worldly possessions. We could use some lighter clothes; the sheepskin coats and heavy sweaters we packed for the Viennese winter wouldn't be of much use in Rome. The officials simply don't know what to tell us. Rome was not on the agenda until recently; we would be among the first, and procedures haven't been worked out as yet. Buying anything was out of the question: we simply had no money. We were allowed to take only five dollars per person from Poland, so our family fortune consisted of fifteen dollars, and Tata said it was for a "dark hour." I hope the "dark hour" has discounted pricing.

It's OK; somehow, we will manage.

"Rome" sounds magical to me.

WROCŁAW, A CITY RISEN FROM GERMAN RUBBLE

This is the lesson: never give in, never give in, never, never, never, never — in nothing, great or small, large or petty — never give in except to convictions of honor and good sense. Never yield to force; never yield to the apparently overwhelming might of the enemy.

Winston Churchill, *Harrow School, 29 October 1941*

Breslau is the German name of the city where I was born. Originally part of Poland for its first 350 years, it was incorporated into the Kingdom of Bohemia in 1335 and remained, under various rulers, one of Germany's prides for the next six centuries. In 1937 Hitler boldly promised to his nation Nazi victory in a speech delivered from Breslau, from the central balcony of the opulent Hotel Monopol where, at various times, Greta Garbo, Marlene Dietrich and Pablo Picasso luxuriated as guests. As it turned out, Hitler couldn't keep his promise. In August 1944, facing the barrage advance of the Soviets, he declared Breslau a closed military fortress (*Festung Breslau*) to be defended at all costs. With most of the civilian population trapped inside, the city endured an epic 82-day siege, which turned it into a heap of rubble; unbelievably, 90%

was destroyed. Tens of thousands died. Not much was left of the thirteenth-century City Hall in perfect Gothic, or the elegant Baroque mansions, or the university which bore ten Nobel prize winners (*https://www.Wrocław.pl/en/nobel-prize-winners-from-Wrocław*). The jewel-box opera house and the red brick Gothic churches barely stood. A few months later, planes full of escaping high military command and the last surviving civilians took off from runways made of city rubble, flying over the smoldering splendor of the thousand-year-old Gothic cathedral. Unbelievably, they even cut its taller tower to facilitate take-offs.

Hitler committed suicide on April 30, 1945. Absurdly and with maniacal stubbornness, while his generals were negotiating terms of surrender, *Festung Breslau* continued to fight and claimed another score of lives before it finally fell. With nothing left to defend, not even pride, the German armed forces surrendered unconditionally on May 8, 1945. War in Europe was over. When the victors divided the spoils, Breslau became part of Poland and was renamed Wrocław. This is where I was born a few years later. My luck.

My parents, Esther Goldman and Zygmunt Binder, came to Wrocław in early 1946, separately, and not knowing each other. They were both natives of Galicia, which was, since the end of WWI, part of Poland and, until then, part of the Austro-Hungarian Empire – such was the war-shaped mish-mash of Eastern Europe. Tata's family lived once in Yavoriv, outside of Lviv, which Russia claimed among its prizes at the end of WWII. He went to Yavoriv when the fighting was over and looked for his family home; there was nothing but ashes. He left. Mama's home and the beautiful fields and orchards amidst which she grew up remained part of Poland. But there was so much devastation there, so much tragedy and death, and so much hostility from former neighbors that she and her two surviving brothers didn't stay either.

Esther and Zygmunt married in 1947 and, a year later, miraculously, got their first apartment on 40 Ruska Street, in the heart of Old Town. One hundred forty thousand former residents of Lviv and its environs resettled to Wrocław so as not to be stuck in the Soviet Union. All of them, and the countless thousands of former soldiers, looked for a place to live. Any space with four walls and a ceiling was a rare and luxurious find; even three walls were prized. After a wild period of squatting and finders-keepers, a Housing Commission was hastily formed by the new Polish Russian socialist government, corrupt and imminently bribable. Tata offered to them the only item of value he had – his leather coat from the army – and the young couple got an apartment to live in!

In the apartment, they found an unexpected prize: an oversized ugly oak dining set and a few *landschaft* paintings in washed-out colors. This post-German lot moved with us to 25 Włodkowica Street a few years later and witnessed my entire Polish life.

In the voluminous belly of the huge two-tier credenza, behind ironed and carefully folded sheets and tablecloths, lay for years my beloved doll, Małgorzata. I did have two other dolls, but it was Małgorzata I coveted. A few doors down the street from us, on Włodkowica 21, was a cottage cooperative, "Plecionka," which, among an array of stuffed animals, also produced ragdolls – for export, not to be sold on the domestic market. But Pani Irka, our neighbor on the third floor, worked in "Plecionka" and helped my parents buy two imperceptibly flawed and suitably discounted dolls judged to be unsuitable for export. Stuffed with sawdust, these dolls had brightly painted celluloid faces, impossibly blue eyes, and orange-red cheeks. Years of use and abuse left their mark; their faces were

Esther and Zygmunt Binder with their daughter Sabina, Wrocław (1948)

In the Market Square (1951)

a bit scratched, and their bodies fatigued and disfigured, coming apart in seams, with bits of sawdust stuffing missing here and there, one leg thinner and longer than the other. They looked deformed. As a child, I was somehow convinced that they were victims of Heine-Medina – that's how childhood polio was called in Poland – the most deforming disease in my medical repertoire. Also, the dolls from Plecionka were sewn together entirely in one piece, with no detachable parts. Clothes and hair were factory-attached onto their bodies, so I couldn't comb or undress them, which was a big flaw in a doll. I loved them nevertheless, the more so because they were crippled by an incurable disease.

But Małgorzata… Małgorzata was perfect, and I cherished her.

Safely placed out of my reach behind the mountain of folded whites, she was different: her head and limbs were made of porcelain, she had hair and eyelashes, and her eyelids moved so she could open and close her eyes. And she had real clothes! I was an only child, and we never had pets, so Małgorzata was the love of my childhood, the one I longed to cuddle and sleep with. I imagined playing with her and suffered at the thought of her lonely years in the credenza.

But Mama was firm and unwavering in her conviction that I was not old enough to play with her, *such* a doll, a *sleeping* doll.

When I finally reached the previously unspecified suitable age, dolls did not interest me. Mama, triumphant that Małgorzata survived my childhood unscathed, reassured me: "You will give her someday to your own children." But Małgorzata didn't survive emigration; I don't know what happened to her. In fact, it didn't really matter; my daughters preferred computer games to dolls, and Małgorzata would surely end up in some American credenza, alone once again, sentenced to loneliness and endless aging without old age.

32

With uncle Janek and his son, Henry (1953)

Summer Vacation (1954)

PRE-DEPARTURE HARASSMENT PART ONE: WHAT ARE WE ALLOWED TO TAKE?

*There is a theory which states that if ever anyone discovers
exactly what the Universe is for and why it is here,
it will instantly disappear and be replaced by something
even more bizarre and inexplicable.
There is another theory which states that this has already happened.*

Douglas Adams, *The Hitchhiker's Guide to the Galaxy*

Except for a few pieces of hand luggage, the belongings of every departing family were packed for emigration in wooden crates mysteriously called "lifts." Since the final destination of most families was unknown, the address was generic and binary in nature: "ISRAEL" for those who intended to go there and "VIENNA" for everyone else. In the Viennese purgatory, a new address would be written on our lift; we hoped it would be "UNITED STATES." Now, it turns out that purgatory will have two stops. Our lift will first go to Rome, and then, who knows.

Inside was everything we owned — our entire lives. It wasn't much. Our Wrocław belongings amounted to old, clunky, post-German furniture and tired bric-à-brac. According to my parents, the furniture was not suitable for emigration and, for different reasons – the authorities agreed. There were regulations regarding apartments vacated by Jews: they had to be empty, clean, and in good repair for the new tenants, so each family struggled to sell whatever they could, often at ridiculously low prices. It was a buyer's paradise. Some of the stuff was outright given away just so the old bed or wardrobe was no longer in the way. On the flip side, every last penny we had had to be spent since the only money we were permitted to take with us was five dollars per person. Consequently, it was of utmost importance that we try to buy and bring with us stuff we could use in our new life or sell to support it, whenever and wherever it starts. That, in turn, created a paradise of opportunities for stores or, to be precise, for store personnel. Whichever way you look at it, neither the selling nor the buying was good for the Jews.

We all struggled with the same issues: how to prepare, even in the smallest measure, for the unknown life ahead. And the double quandary of "how to sell what you have" and "what and where to buy" was further complicated by the unexpected, complex, and non-trivial issue: "What are we allowed to take?" That last question troubled me retroactively for years. I didn't recall and couldn't find in books or on the internet any documents defining what a Jewish family leaving Poland in the wave of '68 was allowed to take with them. I did remember, however, the worried looks on my parents' faces, rushed preparations, and a prolonged and humiliating customs inspection focused on finding whatever we were NOT allowed to take. I also remember many hushed conversations my parents had with other Jews in Wrocław, equally troubled and confused.

Is a violin allowed? How about an embroidered tablecloth? A pair of candleholders? Coffee? Flour and sugar? No one had answers.

While writing this book, I combed through the Internet looking for customs regulations from those times and, empty-handed, I turned to my exiled colleagues: "What do you remember on the subject of our baggage?" A floodgate opened; joint recollections of hundreds of people formed a picture of greed, shameless opportunism, and lawless harassment.

The portly credenza that was, for years, Małgorzata's luxurious prison, along with the remainder of our furniture, was not allowed to leave Poland. Anything made prior to 1945 required special, costly permissions from various institutions, museums, and even ministries. It's actually amazing how much bureaucratic energy Poland invested into limiting our options on what to do with the precious little accumulated during the post-war years. Rules pertaining to antiques, art, old books, and even old photographs were especially strict. Media pounded on the theme that Jews not only robbed Polish national treasures while they lived in Poland, but they now plotted to take it all out of the country. Our furniture was far from valuable antiques – it was just old. And certainly not Polish; the pieces sat in the apartment for many German years, and then, one day, as *Festung Breslau* collapsed, they found themselves surrounded by Poland. However, on the occasion of Jewish emigration, their status rose from old junk to valuable antiques, so they had to remain in their new Polish homeland. We sold them for pennies, thrilled that there was a buyer.

Our paintings, sappy, candy-colored landscapes, also had to stay. They, too, were German leftovers and adorned the apartment on 40 Ruska Street when my parents entered it in 1947. Their previous owners left them; even if they survived the siege, they surely had other worries trying to escape the crumbling *Festung*. And we weren't allowed to take them since they were painted before 1945, and they have now become part of the Polish National Art Treasury. *Rightfully* so, I thought. Keep them. I was glad they stayed behind; I had never liked them. In America, I dreamed I would fill my walls with fantastic, modern art.

Pani Krysia, the neighborhood seamstress who generously referred to us as "Jews but nice," inherited our bulky Russian refrigerator. Its brand was ZIL: **Z**avod **I**menya **L**enina (Lenin's Factory Works). Those ZILs were among the few brands of kitchen appliances available in Poland, maybe the only ones. My parents bought this refrigerator when they planned to emigrate to Israel in 1957. At the end of the heart-wrenching, prolonged go-don't-go episode, we didn't leave but stayed in Poland as owners of a Russian refrigerator we didn't need, couldn't afford, and had no room for. It appeared larger on the outside than it was on the inside and took up a lot of space in our tiny kitchen. In Israel, it would have been a necessity, but here, in Poland. Most people still cooled their food in pantries of our thick-walled post-German buildings or, in the winter, on the outside window ledge, but we had a refrigerator! And now Pani Krysia had it.

Our washing machine, the '60s miracle of technology ridiculously clad in chipper blue-speckled enamel, sold in no time. Before we owned the washing machine, laundry was a huge undertaking that had been planned for days. The principal equipment was medieval: a large, oval, deep metal tub, the same one in which I was bathed as a child, a corrugated metal washboard, and a huge caldron pot for boiling whites. Our apartment had no running water, but there was a cold-water-only faucet in the staircase hallway. Laundry started by refurnishing the apartment the night before. The kitchen table was moved to the center of the room, making it almost impossible to move around. In its place against the wall, on two chairs, landed the tub, which usually hung from the ceiling of our pantry. The caldron, which also lived in the pantry, landed on top of our old-fashioned wood-and-coal stove; this is how we heated the kitchen in the winter. At other times of the year, the stove was stoked only on laundry days. Wood and coal were brought in buckets two stories up from the basement – a huge task. After the fire was made in the stove, it was time to fill the cauldron with water from the hallway, also carried in buckets. It took a few hours for the water in the cauldron to heat, after which it was poured into the tub, and the bucket-caldron-tub ritual was repeated a couple more times until the tub was filled. The last batch of heated water remained in the cauldron for boiling white bedding. The rest of the day was spent washing (on the washboard), rinsing (yes, more buckets of water), and sweating in the heat of the fire and in laundry fumes. In short, laundry was not a spontaneous operation. The hallway plumbing froze in the winter because the pipes were exposed – an afterthought installed on the surface of the impenetrable three-foot-thick walls; on those days, we had no water whatsoever. We carried a few buckets a day from the nearby fire station – just enough for cooking and personal hygiene, but laundry on these frozen days was given away to Pani Jadzia, a neighborhood woman who supported herself by doing laundry for others. Her services didn't cost much, but still, it was a luxury for us. In contrast, the washing machine, hooked up by a hose to the hallway faucet, was a miracle. An extra luxury attachment was a crank-operated mangle, which squeezed the water out of the laundry by passing it between two rubber rollers – another clever and ingenious miracle! In many Old City apartments, laundry was still done by means of tub, washboard, and cauldron, and washing machines were hard to come by, so ours sold quickly.

Part of the pre-departure bureaucracy was also the infamous "run around" – obtaining stamps that certified that we'd returned all the library books (separately from the local library and separately from the frequently used University Library), that we had no unpaid loans (who in the world had loans in Poland?!) and are current with payments for rent, coal, and other utilities. Finally, something about military service forced Tata to stand in a few more lines, pay a few more fees, and collect a few more stamps. If anyone in the West was interested in designs of Polish stamps, we could help with an impressive collection.

One day, Mama came home particularly agitated. In order to receive the next required stamp, this one from the Building Administration, they requested her to pay rent and utilities (water, gas, electricity, and coal) for our apartment in advance until the end of the month. We were departing on the 20th. It was winter. The water was frozen. Coal was expensive.

"Thieves!" Mama repeated in a bout of helpless anger. "Thieves!"

There was little success in my efforts to calm her. For years, we pleaded with the administration to cover the exposed water pipes to fix the winter freeze issue… and now, when we had no running water at all, they asked to be paid for it even beyond our departure date! For Mama, this demand was the proverbial straw that broke the camel's back; one stamp, one humiliation too many. Each of us, sooner or later, reached such a breaking point. But this was the wrong time to fall apart. More lines awaited, more fees to pay and stamps to affix, and time was running short – our drop-dead date of departure was mercilessly approaching. We still needed to get rid of some things in the apartment and arrange for cleaning. We still had to get passports at the police station, I still had to go to Warsaw to get the mandatory Israeli visas, and we still had money that had to be spent.

I now see a comic element in the latter, but then, anyone going abroad was allowed to exchange in a specially designated bank enough Polish zlotys to receive five dollars per person, regardless of whether the planned trip was a week-long vacation in Bulgaria's Golden Sands, a hard-won family visit abroad, or emigration.

FIVE DOLLARS PER PERSON.

"Even that was uncertain," recalls Róża Goldfarb Holmgren. "They searched my sister's purse and took away her five dollars. The rule applied to Polish citizens, not to stateless nobodies like us."

They did with us whatever they wanted.

Some of this changed over time with word-of-mouth experience. Jurek Wajda (George Celler) recalls that a year later:

"We knew where to go for various approvals, what documents were needed, how much we should pay, which company would pack *the lift*, etc. We also collected trivial knowledge, like the dimensions of pillows suitable for nothing.

Since my family was planning to go to Australia, we took only the basics: clothes, books, and some kitchen utensils. We gave away all the furniture. My parents had a very large set of silverware acquired in Wałbrzych, surely post-German. It weighed more than we were allowed to take, so about half of it was left with Polish friends.

Eventually, not according to plan, my parents settled in Vienna. And once in a while, for many years, various visitors from Poland brought a fork or a spoon from the set."

And another story that amazes and moves me deeply. Shmuel Zelman Szwalbnest and his wife Miriam locked their fully furnished apartment in Gliwice, gave the keys to the neighbor, and just left. The contents of their Polish lives did not interest them. "No regrets," says their daughter Zosia, who happily lives in San Diego.

At a Jewish seaside student camp (Ostrowo near Jastrzębia Góra), the last one before exile (1967).

PRE-DEPARTURE HARASSMENT PART TWO: ALL THE RAGE IN THE WEST!

No frogs can sing as well as Polish ones.

Adam Mickiewicz, widely regarded as Poland's greatest poet
Pan Tadeusz, Poland's national epic

And now emerged an unexpected, new dilemma, farcical on the surface but humiliating and painful in practice: what to do with that little bit of money that would have remained after we sold everything, paid all the requisite fees and anticipated expenses, set aside the five dollars per person – our allowed safety funds, and created a reserve for the yet to be dispensed bribes which paved our way to departure?

Years later, a bottomlessly sad realization: by spending this money, we squandered years of shy, modest, unspoken, trauma-laced dreams my parents may have had in their grey post-war existence. Two Holocaust survivors who never dared to speak of dreams. And now, after years of painstaking denial, of darning socks, mending clothes, using threadbare towels, soldering pots, and wearing the same pair of fatigued shoes yet another year, they spent sleepless nights thinking of reasonable ways to spend their meager savings.

And a farse: is there anything in Poland, anything at all, that could be of use or value in the West? So during the days, our twenty-one days, when not in line to collect stamps or meeting potential buyers of our bed or frying pan, they frenetically ran around stores and paid ridiculous bribes to buy something, anything, which could be useful at the unspecified other end of our upcoming journey. The shelves in Wrocław stores were habitually empty; anything resembling desirable merchandise, actually, anything resembling altogether, was hidden under the counters. The dusty shelves were stale and grey, and the personnel disinterested in anything approximating service. But the Jewish exile energized the scene. Like in Charlie Chaplin's *"Modern Times,"* the bright-lipsticked salesladies now pouted an air of importance and secret knowledge as they dispensed from under-the-counter china, bedding, or sugar unseen by mere mortals. And collected bribes. Nothing was accomplished without bribes.

Ma'am... How much? We will gladly reward... When should we come?

It was rumored that the small towns nearby offer more buying opportunities – with fewer Jews, the competition for goods was lesser. Tata made several such excursions. He once came home with a valuable bounty – a transistor-powered radio named "Szarotka" – Edelweiss. It was cute, this Edelweiss, in red bakelite; people said that these Edelweisses are all the rage in the West; Americans pay fortunes for them. I eagerly examined transistor radios held by Frankie Avalon and Annette Funicello as they danced in American beach movies of the era, but none resembled our Edelweiss. Perhaps Edelweisses post-dated the movies?

Another time, Tata scored a contraption called "prodiż" – an electric cake baker reputed to be the appliance of choice in every modern American home. I wasn't convinced. But, I had to admit that my sample data based on American films distributed in Poland was flawed. There were few culinary details in the plethora of John Wayne or Kirk Douglas westerns or in the beautiful epic adaptations of *War and Peace* or *Gone with the Wind*. The cowboys, the Indians, Countess Natasha, or Scarlett O'Hara simply didn't bake cakes. Embarrassingly, none of us thought then about the fundamental reason why this cake baker was not the perfect accessory for export: even the plug didn't fit the 120V electric network in the US.

Meanwhile, like a ticking bomb, every day brought us closer to departure. Perhaps a day spent chasing a prodiż would have been better used arranging for having our apartment repainted for the subsequent, ethnically appropriate, tenants?

Hartwig, the company in charge of transporting our belongings, came to weigh and measure what we had. "One small lift will suffice," concluded the representative. The lift was prepaid, ordered, and built, and people to pack it were hired for a specific date. Uncle Zacharje spent days at our kitchen table surrounded by rolls of hard-to-get toilet paper, wrapping cups and dishes to protect them from chipping during their upcoming journey. The meager baggage was packed, and we completed the required customs declaration, listing each bookmark, each pair of underwear, and each pot. In triplicate, I think.

The most dreaded formality still awaited us. The awareness that it is coming weighed on us greatly. By appointment, the three of us went to the local police station where, in a seedy office, we each copied in our own handwriting the supplied text: "I hereby renounce the citizenship…." I somehow couldn't stop looking at the half-eaten sandwich on the desk of the uniformed functionary. There were so many Jews to strip of citizenship that he did not have time for a proper midday meal. He collected our government issue identifications, put them in a file cabinet behind, and in return handed us Travel Documents where, in several languages, right in the front, it declared: "The bearer of this document is not a citizen of Poland." We knew it was coming, but the moment was overwhelming. No return from here. No drumbeat. Just THE END.

The fee collected for this privilege was audaciously high – five thousand zlotys per person, an equivalent of two-and-a-half months average salary. That's what each Jew paid Poland to lose their home and country. I am reminded of a story from the Holocaust when, in the town of Czortków, the Germans ordered each Jew to pay for the bullets used to shoot them. Our story is not nearly as dramatic, but the devious minds that invented it were of similar ilk.

A few days later, I traveled to Warsaw by plane, which was the first flight of my life. There, at the Dutch Embassy, our Travel Documents received the required visas to Israel. Jacek, my Polish boyfriend of two years, accompanied me on this journey. On each of our two evenings in Warsaw, we went to the theatre. Rescuing shreds of civility amidst a mudstorm. Last moments together.

With the visas in our Travel Documents, we can now buy train tickets to Vienna.

Next on the agenda was the customs inspection.

- 7 -

1	2	3	4	5
234	Chustki do nosa	szt	10	
235	Płaszcze letnie	"	2	
236	Czapka	"	1	
237	Szaliki	szt	3	
238	Wanienka	szt	1	
239	Kasza gryczana	kg	4	
240	Cukier	"	3	
241	Mąka	"	2	
242	Serwis porcelanowy 6 - cioosobowy	szt	1	obiadowy
243	Kasza manna	kg	0,5	
244	Ryż	"	0,5	
245	Beczułka do kiszenia ogórków	szt	1	
246	Ogórki konserwowe	opak.	1	
247	Mikrofony	szt	3	
248	Staniczki	szt	3	
249	Rękawiczki	par	3	
250	Materiał na spodenki	mtr	1,5	
251	materiał na sukienkę	"	1,5	
252	materiał na sukienk ę	"	1,5	
253	Jawox	pud.	2	
254	Sznury do żelazka	szt	3	
255	Przedłużacze	"	4	
256	Okulary słoneczne	"	4	
257	Piłka do metalu	szt	1	
258	Przesszczoty	"	4	
259	wtyczki elektryczne	"	3	
260	elementy elektroniczne /opory,kondensatory./	"	1300	
261	" " /gniazdka,wtyczki,bananki/	"	200	
262	lupa	"	1	
263	Pincety	"	2	
264	Podstawka do mikrofonu	"	1	
265	Wkręty do drzewa	"	2	
266	Przełączniki przechylne i różne	"	25	
267	Suwmiarka	"	1	
268	Podstawki pod palniki do kuchenki gazowej	"	4	
269	Krawaty	"	2	
270	Gąbki do mycia naczyń	"	4	
271	Druciki " "	"	4	
272				

This barely legible scan is one of the multi-page customs declarations of Szymek and Małgosia Fisz (Simon and Malka Fish), emigrating to Denmark. Among others, itemized items are porridge and rice for the children, a jar of pickles (!), four mugs, two frying pans, and four dishwashing sponges. Szymek had two ties.

PRE-DEPARTURE HARASSMENT PART THREE: AT THE CUSTOMS – OUR COLLECTIVE MEMORY

Nothing discloses real character like the use of power.
If you wish to know what a man really is, give him power.
This is the supreme test.

Robert G. Ingersoll, about Abraham Lincoln

Motley and Monarch, The North American Review, December 1885

On the scheduled day, our packed lift with its lid still detached was delivered by Hartwig to the Customs Office hidden in the for-official-use-only depths of the Wrocław Main Railway Station. The thorough and thoroughly humiliating procedure lasted several days. It was December; the hall was cold like a morgue. The customs officers, warmly clad in government issue stitched parkas, had a complex assignment: first, they looked for administrative discrepancies in our previously completed declaration, hoping to find something that is not listed, or listed incorrectly, like our 46 long-playing vinyl records entered as one line item; we were reprimanded that they should have been listed individually, by title. This was the prelude – just to warm us up to the idea that they can and they will. Secondly, and perhaps more importantly, the officers looked for transgressions: items we did declare but are not allowed to take. In any event, their most evident task was to convey to my poor parents that the list of problems in either category was so extensive and serious that the only solution was a bribe – the customs inspection was a free-for-all bribe generator of unknown scope and amount.

The longer the list, the bigger the expected offsetting "financial argument," so the digging in our lift was a diligent, self-serving hunt.

The implied scenario was that we, the Zionists, are the greedy and dishonest abusers, and they, the patriotic officers, dutifully defend the interests and goods of Poland. Their job was to uncover the scope of our abuse, prohibit it, and punish us for the attempt. And the disgusting catch: the officers themselves were the sole beneficiaries of this punishment. It was not an official government fee, fine, or tax determined by documented rules. Instead, it was a personal reward—an arbitrary bribe paid directly to the 'finder,' with no receipt, no accountability, and no limits. They worked methodically and conscientiously, wreaked havoc, and rejected whatever they pleased. *Not allowed*. After collecting a bribe, they rejected less but made a bigger mess, probably for show but also perhaps to alleviate any pangs of conscience that they are letting us off too easily. Or, likely, to make it clear that the inspection is not over. Of strategic importance was the precise moment when to hand over the bribe. It had to be early enough to prevent the whole lift from being turned upside down, but it couldn't be too early because there was nothing preventing them from deciding a few hours later, or the next day, that another bribe could be extracted. They could also decide that the offered bribe is insufficient and continue the process until satisfied.

Take, for example, our "samovar," which they found in the depth of the lift and presented for all to see as if it were a priceless, hunted treasure. It wasn't at all a samovar; it was our old, pot-bellied electric kettle in the shape of a samovar, its years of service marked by numerous scratches and burn marks. Not at all pretty and certainly not valuable. *A samovar?!* His high-pitched voice conveys the grave significance of this discovery. And where is the permit?!

This truly was unexpected. In our customs declaration, we listed the item truthfully as an electric kettle. Tata tried to explain that we had no idea a permit was required; it's a worthless item we've had for years. But the officer doesn't listen; he senses blood and makes annoyed faces to show that any argumentation on our part is a waste of time. I whisper: "Let him reject it; why do we need it, anyway?!" Mama's solution is even more pragmatic: "Give it to him." But Tata is exhausted and exasperated; all of a sudden, the stupid samovar turns into a matter of honor; emigrating without the samovar simply makes no sense whatsoever. Yet another bribe ends the incident. I was furious. And, to add salt to injury, at the end of our journey, it turned out that the samovar, like the prodiż and all other electrical gadgetry, could not even be plugged into the American electric network. Of course.

They tortured us only a bit longer because, truthfully, we had nothing. They rejected something for the sake of decent loyalty towards their employer and let us go because, surely, more could be gained faster from the next Jewish family with appointments lined up after us. Time really was money.

When they were done with us, they told us to repack the lift, after which it would be nailed shut under the inspector's watchful eye. They rushed us along. "Hurry, hurry." Uncle Zacharje packed everything with stoic patience: things fit together like a puzzle: medicine bottles in my shoes, crystal – the famous ugly Polish crystal – was wrapped in sweaters and bedding; and each china cup, each handle, was securely wrapped in layers of toilet paper. They ordered us to unwrap some of the cups for the inspection, looking for treasures hidden under the cover of the toilet paper. Money, I guess. Or jewels. We had neither. Now everything was helter-skelter. Sheets, pillows, the stupid samovar, books, Tata's suits, my sweaters, a simple ceramic vase for cut flowers we hoped to enjoy in our new life somewhere – all in a heap. The floor was covered with a pile of wrinkled, torn papers. And, off to the side, a precarious stack of poor, completely naked porcelain cups. Repacking with reasonable care was simply out of the question – only speed mattered now. The search could take any amount of time, but repacking had to be in express tempo; our executioners were impatient. Faster! One even mumbled: "Do you want us to start the search over again?" Is he angling for another bribe? "Faster! We can't be here all night!" The next family, the next bribe, is waiting.

In a fleeting, searing pang, I imagined Jews being rushed along railroad ramps during the war. A similar, inhuman air of undeserved superiority and empowerment prevailed.

The customs inspection proceeded according to rules and regulations known only to them, and they were the sole arbiters of alleged applicable law and propriety. Nothing was transparent; nothing was published or spelled out—yet their authority was unquestionable, and judgment was delivered with an air implying that everything should be obvious; only the stupid or the abstinent would not get it.

"Handwritten materials not allowed!" – they barked at my old girlish diary.

What harm to Poland could it be to allow me to take my teenagers' diary? And where was it stated that "handwritten materials not allowed!"? The rule evidently pertained not just to Jewish handwriting because the notebook where I collected autographs was also rejected. On the first page was Marino Marini, who was certainly not a Jew. I was probably fourteen then; I still remember the teenage frenzy when Ludka Kurcer and I stood for hours in front of the famous Hotel Monopol along with fifty other hopefuls trembling with excitement, waiting for HIS appearance and the coveted signature. Martha Argerich, who in 1965 won the Chopin Piano Competition, gave me her autograph following a post-competition recital in the tiny auditorium of the Electronics Building on Prusa Street. Not a Jew. Another page bore the signature of Marlena Dietrich, who gave two concerts in Wrocław's Hala Ludowa (now Centennial Hall) in 1966. She was clearly moved; she said how gratifying it was to perform in Polish Wrocław. She, too, was not a Jew. Her concert was a solemn moment for me, a proud daughter of Wrocław. Tickets cost a fortune, but what the heck, I could always do more tutoring – it was worth it. On another page was Ida Kamińska, the Grand Dame of Jewish Theatre. Jewish. My biggest treasure – the autograph of Mieczysława Ćwiklińska, who, after the performance of *Trees Die Standing Tall* by Alejandro Cahona, wrote: "For beautiful Sabinka, wishing a grand future." Non-Jew. She was almost a hundred years old then. To me, this gracious wish had the power of a prophecy. But handwritten materials were disallowed.

And then, the grapevine whirred:

"Samovars require a special permit."

"And where do they give such permits?"

"I don't know."

There were rumors that Polish carpets produced in Kowary were greatly valued in the West – they were the BEST, the modern version of prized Persian rugs, simply treasures. But, according to those who have already cleared customs, only used carpets were allowed, one per room of our apartments. Most of us didn't have Kowary carpets in our homes; people bought them only for emigration. H.J.'s family attached old fringe to newly bought carpets – maybe they won't notice? Basia Rzepkowicz (Leaffer) remembers farewell dance parties in Warsaw each Saturday. "We wandered from one home to another in dirty shoes, stomping and trampling on the carpets, trying to make them look used." But even that did not suffice. During the Rzepkowicz family customs control at the Gdański Train Station in Warsaw, the officers demanded a document from the Building Administration stating that the two carpets in the Rzepkowicz lift correspond in size and shape to the rooms of their modest 500 sq. ft. apartment. The officers didn't know the apartment where the family lived but stated with aplomb that the carpets looked "suspiciously large." Basia, 17 years old then and scared to death because the carpets were indeed newly bought without consideration of size, was sent to extract the required document. The whole inspection could have been delayed for days, and the carpets could have been rejected and readmitted only with a hefty bribe. Thankfully, the lady in Administration was busy, didn't pay attention, and missed an opportunity for a bribe, and Basia returned to the customs hall with the required certificate.

Teresa Pollin: "After a prolonged search—crowned by a hefty bribe—my mother proudly dragged home a Kowary carpet. New, of course. Too new for the circumstance. I was tasked with making it look used. For days, I walked on it, the dirtier my shoes, the better. I felt proud and victorious when the carpet passed the customs inspection."

After we arrived in Israel, I was given the opposite task: 'Now wash the carpet and restore it to its original clean glory so it can be sold.' On all fours, armed with a scrub brush, soap, and water, I scrubbed for hours… and then—tragedy! As I worked, the beautiful colors and patterns vanished, replaced by large, shapeless stains of an indistinct hue. My mother had been cheated—the carpet was a worthless, colored fake, not from Kowary at all."

The parents of Klara Samsonowicz (Sigvardsson), exhausted by life and losses of the Holocaust, didn't have the strength to start over yet one more time. It was the father's second family – the first one perished in the Holocaust. Like some others in those dreadful times, they decided to save the children. Klara, a student of Russian Philology at the University of Łódź, was to leave Poland without them, with an aunt and uncle who lived in Wrocław. She presented herself alone for the customs inspection in Łódź, and it was clear she had no money for bribes. "No gain, no pain" must have been the officer's motto. They didn't even bother to open Klara's lift, but using long metal rods in fencer-like moves, they pierced the wooden sides of the crate. A game – as if this "inspection" technique allowed them to examine the contents. Klara watched helplessly. Inside, pierced, were her beloved books, bedding, and clothes. This is one of the few stories I heard of pure intent to damage.

Money not allowed, new not allowed, old not allowed – the only elements of our Polish lives we were allowed to take with us were those produced between 1945 and 1968 – and used. And even that with exceptions. And not without ill will. A lot of ill will.

Klara Sigvardsson still has this leather-bound edition of Mayakovsky's poetry pierced with metal rods by Polish Customs.

H.J.: "The lift containing books, my sister's piano, and my skis, with which I simply couldn't part, arrived in Israel a few months after us. An unusual stench enveloped us when we opened the lid. Many of the books were destroyed because someone – most likely several someone – pissed on them." A farewell gift from Poland to family J. Six months prior to the March Events, Dr. J. was decorated with the Medal of the Golden Cross of Merit for scientific achievements in medicine. After the March Events, she was thrown out of work, and her books were pissed on.

M.T., a researcher who left Poland on November 29, 1968, was ordered to pay back his November salary. He was also ordered to pay for the renovations of his family's Warsaw apartment to suit the needs of the new tenants.

Inga Karliner was an outstanding student at the Department of Physics at Warsaw University—a star. To recognize her achievements in her fourth year of studies, the department granted her a merit scholarship of 1,000 zł per month. After March, when she informed the department that she would be emigrating to Israel, she was ordered to repay the received scholarship funds – 10,000 zł in total. She did.

Marek Pelc: "I had to pass an exam for a bicycle card because we had a bicycle in the luggage." Evidently, this "bicycle card" was a permit required to ride a bicycle on public roads. None of us had a bicycle card while living in Poland; I never even heard of one.

Victoria Lernell had to cut out from newspapers her husband's obituaries because newspapers were not allowed. He died recently in a mountain climbing accident; they've been married only for 18 months. She was leaving alone—and was saved from committing the "crime" of departing with a couple of newspapers containing his obituaries.

G.N.: "Customs ordered us to sew something on our sewing machine to show that we know how. Sewing machines were allowed for personal use only."

Szymek Fisz (Simon Fish): "They insisted that our cheaply painted glasses were made of silver. After the bribe, it suddenly became clear that everything was ordinary colored glass. My monthly salary was 1,000 zł – and that's how much we paid that day in bribes."

H.J.: "We couldn't take our furniture. The suitable pieces were all classified as antiques and, as such, disallowed. My parents gave the furniture away to friends, who were supposed to remove everything from our apartment as soon as we left. And only the piano...."

Simon Fish clarifies: "Musical instruments were allowed only with credentials from music school or conservatory." But even that often did not suffice. Piszczyk—Ludwig Kahane, whom we all called "Squeeky"— studied at the Warsaw Conservatory of Music in the trumpet and percussion class. "To obtain permission for my beloved trumpet, the one I played from the beginning, I was sent to the National Museum in Warsaw (first fee and permit #1), from there to the Ministry of Culture (second fee and permit #2), and finally to the custodian of musical instruments at the Warsaw Opera House (third fee, and permit #3, of course). All this to make sure that allowing my trumpet to leave Poland did not represent a loss to Polish national culture."

Ewa Bober (Eva Fromm) studied at the College for Dental Technicians in Wrocław. She was leaving with her older sister and brother-in-law. Her belongings—clothes, shoes, and books—barely filled one suitcase. "I wanted to take my pillow, but it was not allowed," says Eva, "because I never worked in Poland." Evidently, only people who had previously worked were allowed a pillow. "My sister did work in Poland for several years and tried to take my pillow for me, but that, too, was disallowed." The officer asked for an "exception permit."

"Without such a permit, only one pillow per person is allowed," he declared. Bandits.

Karol Zmijewski (Carl Fromm) tells the only story I heard where the family customs inspection ended without a bribe. "We had nothing in the lift except for books, bedding, and my Mother's fur," Karol knew about the expectation for bribes but considered it a matter of honor not to pay. "What should we have paid for?!" he fumed. Reasonable, but not practical – in December 1968, reason was not in vogue. The inspection took place in an unheated hall; all officers wore heavy government-issue stitched parkas. "The one in charge made himself comfortable in the only chair; Mother and I stood in front of him. He took the first book and began flipping through its pages methodically, calmly, with no rush, from the beginning, one page at a time, all the while throwing us meaningful looks. He finished the first book, tossed it aside, and took another. There were about two hundred books; he flipped, one by one, every page in each book. It took several days – and Mother and I just stood there..." After all these years, Carl choked up: "...Mother and I just stood there..."

Leon Szyfer says that in Szczecin – perhaps only in Szczecin – it was possible to apply for a privileged alternative procedure and clear customs at home, in the courtyard (most old buildings had one). The application itself was costly, and if approved, the fees for the inspection were suitably higher. But, reportedly, everything went easier at home. In addition to preparing envelopes appropriately stuffed with cash, it was advisable to also set the table with cold cuts and vodka.

Jurek Wajda (George Celler): "We packed a lot of hand

luggage, for the months we would not see our lift. My father was always generous with tips, but the porter at the Gdański Railroad Station in Warsaw demanded a ridiculous sum, and my father refused. The porter retaliated with a loud scene and threatened to denounce us to the customs. I guess the charge would be a refusal to pay the demanded tip – after all, so many people were getting rich during the Jewish exile. Why would the porter not get his share? In the end, nothing happened."

In 1955-56 and again in 1959-1963, H.T.'s father, a historian, was a member of the Commission for Supervision and Control of the United Nations in Vietnam and Laos. There, he began collecting figurines of Buddha and similar items, which he brought with him to Poland and declared meticulously at the end of each tour of duty. After March, Dr. T. was kicked out of work. The family also lost their apartment since it was connected with his work. Their older daughter, an honor college graduate, was turned down wherever she applied for work. The younger daughter was not accepted at the university after taking the entrance exams. Leaving was the only option. The family obtained all the required permissions to take their Buddha collection with them, and yet many pieces were rejected by customs.

One of the officers attempted to steal a silver dagger. "He did it quite brazenly," says H.T. "When my Dad asked about the missing dagger, the officer unbuttoned his coat and shamelessly showed the dagger in his inside pocket. He gave it back upon request. "Also missing at customs – and never found – was a rare and beautiful English edition of the Kama Sutra."

The customs clearance of family T. was used as an opportunity for staging a hideous propaganda film. H.T. wrote to me: "All of our luggage was filmed, with a particular focus on the Buddha collection. Among the featured pieces were items already rejected by Customs, and some which were rejected after the filming, in an apparent change of heart. In the background, behind the belongings, the director of the film placed a lift with Israel stenciled in large letters as the destination. This charade was meant to document the loss of Polish national treasures illegally carried by Zionists to Israel." The shameless truth is that family T. was emigrating to another country, not to Israel, and the Israel lift belonged to someone else, unrelated and not connected... And the Buddha collection had nothing whatsoever to do with Polish culture, and it had spent only a few of its hundreds of years in Poland.

PRE-DEPARTURE HARASSMENT PART FOUR: THE ABUSIVE POWER OF DOCUMENTS

It seems to be a fact that man, tortured by his demons, avenges himself blindly on his fellow man.

Franz Kafka, *Letters to Milena*

Disallowed were also personal documents, which was a huge issue. I still fume at this punitive, ill-willed audacity. How do you start a new life without certificates, diplomas, dissertations, and publications—without any proof of who you are, or rather, who you have been?

H.J.: "Our parents smuggled my mother's scientific publications and our school diplomas between sheets of music hidden in the piano." H.J.'s sister was a music school graduate, which allowed the family to bring her piano.

Adam Gryniewicz: "I hid mine and my wife's documents under my shirt."

Rysiek (Rami) Weiler: "I had no difficulties with the transcript of my grades and high school diplomas, but that was hard to predict. Both had to be certified by the Ministry of Education and, altogether a surprise, by the Ministry of Foreign Affairs. (Note: high school diplomas had to be certified by the Ministry of Foreign Affairs). To be safe, I notarized a copy of the more important papers and mailed a set to our family in Israel. An unexpected difficulty arose with a copy of an exam paper I wrote at the end of my third year at the University of Science and Technology Studies; it was an analysis of a fictional electric installation in a factory. "Out of the question; no scientific papers are allowed." It didn't help explaining that there is no scientific value in this student paper. It's all fictional, and the factory doesn't even exist. NO. I didn't give up and smuggled the paper into our lift, hoping they wouldn't notice. They noticed. I still did not give up. I put it in the suitcase, and that worked."

After the 1967 Six-Day War, following the tune from Moscow, Poland also allied with Israel's Arab adversaries and broke off diplomatic relations with Israel. Since then, all Israeli affairs, including the issuance of promises and visas for the banished Jews, were conducted by the Dutch Embassy in Warsaw. While gathering these recollections, I heard a seemingly incredulous story – that the Dutch Embassy helped smuggle the disallowed personal documents and scientific papers. I asked our emigration friends in the Netherlands what they knew about it. In reply, I received photos of a gathering in the Amsterdam apartment of Asia Bilska. Among several of "our" women was an elegant man whom Asia introduced as Ted de Rijck van der Gracht. "From February 1968, he was the third or second secretary of the Dutch Embassy in Warsaw, twenty-seven years old then; it was his first diplomatic post. Smuggling Jewish documents in the official diplomatic mail was out of the question, but at sizeable risk, Ted carried what he could in his personal luggage."

My family had no trouble with documents, but it wasn't much of anything: mine and Mama's birth certificates (Tata didn't have one since all the archives in Yavoriv burnt during the war), my high school diploma, my parents' marriage certificate, and the transcript of my grades from the University of Science and Technology.

Another incredulous roadblock: each permitted document had to be authenticated by one or more designated institution(s). So our three weeks, the twenty-one days allowed to organize our affairs prior to departure, were, among other indignities, also spent on collecting authentication stamps on each document. Every day, along with other Jews, we lined up for hours at various ministries, courthouses, schools, the Department of Education, the administration for the building where we lived, and countless other offices. An award awaited at the end of each such line: in exchange for the prerequisite fee, our documents were adorned with coveted stamps nobody in the world cared about – indicating the blessing of Polish bureaucracy. Most of these documents already bore stamps affixed when issued – but such was the procedure: never too many stamps and, certainly, never too many fees. And that's not all. Each authenticated document had to, in turn, be translated into English (!) by a sworn translator from the approved list and, afterward, notarized by a similarly chosen notary public who affixed yet another stamp, in turn authenticating the translation. It was audacious, absurd, took forever, and cost a fortune. Mama declared "robbery," and she was right. Humiliation and robbery.

Ted de Rijck van der Gracht. (2004)

In 1968, as a lower-ranking employee of the Dutch Embassy in Warsaw, he helped exiled Jews smuggle out of Poland their personal documents and scientific papers.

Among the papers left by my parents, I discovered a stamped translation of their marriage certificate issued in Wrocław in 1947. On the reverse are thirteen (13) different stamps, some of which are further amplified by signatures or handwritten notes made by the officiating civil servant. The stamp in the upper right is from the sworn translator; the one to the left of it, from the President of the Voivodship Court, attests to the authenticity of the translator's stamp. There is a round stamp from the Chairman of the Regional Court, another from the Ministry of Justice, and yet another from the Ministry of Foreign Affairs. I amplify: two ministries needed to authenticate the English translation of a twenty-one-year-old marriage certificate of two Polish citizens. The whole thing screamed of abusive bureaucracy and shameless extortion. To obtain all these, my parents probably had to stand in thirteen different lines and pay thirteen different fees of up to 30 zlotys each. In 1968, the 30 zlotys could buy thirteen quarts of milk or eight loaves of bread. So the stamps on their now translated and validated-for-export marriage certificate were worth 100 loaves of bread.

There were also ubiquitous problems with photos.

Szymek Fisz (Simon Fish): "Pictures from before 1945 were not allowed." So if someone had such an extraordinary treasure as photos of dear ones who perished in the Holocaust, the cruel regulation required that these photos remain in Poland (in whose care?) or be smuggled in the hope that they would somehow go unnoticed. Or, one could try to "legalize" the photos via a bribe.

Michał Antopolski remembers that his photos from Boy Scouts ("even from Cub Scouts") were disallowed because "photographs in uniforms are forbidden." Wojtek (Jerry) Siegenfeld, who studied Customs Law in Poland, remembers

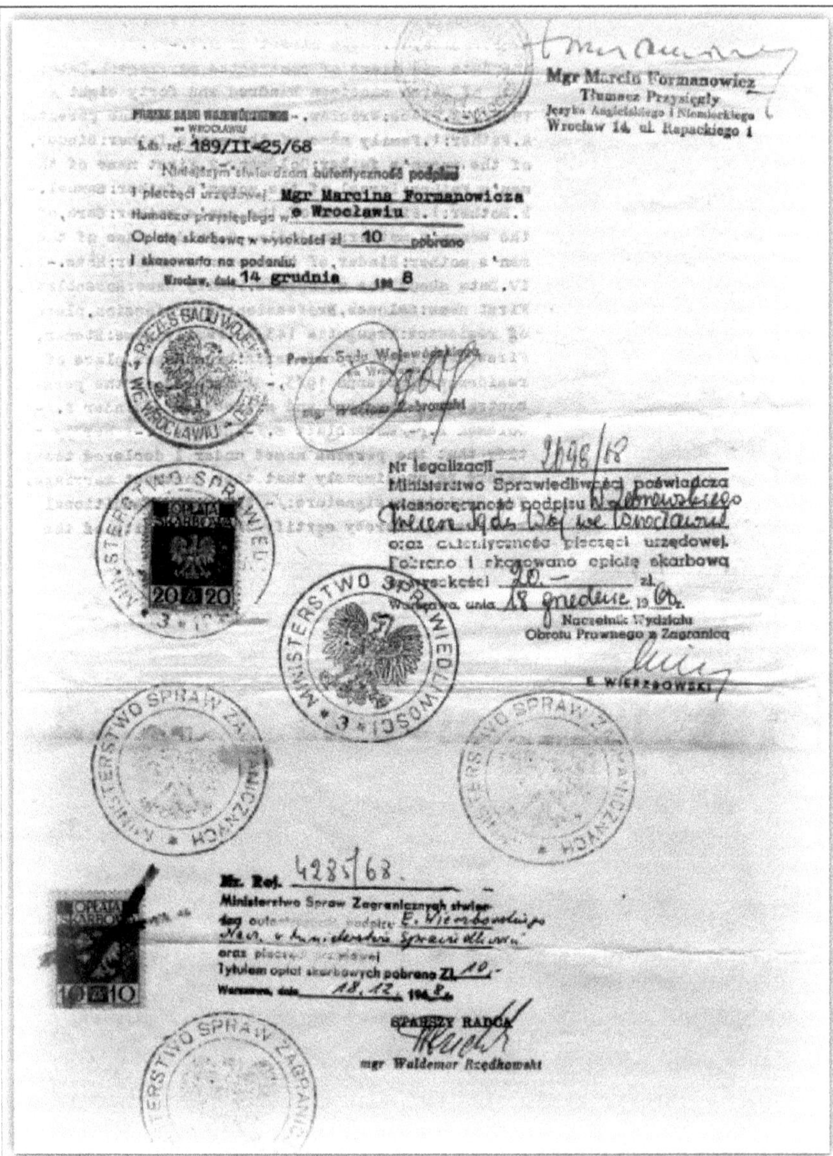

This is the reverse side of the translation of my parents' Marriage Certificate. The stamps and certifications of authenticity were obtained between the 14th and 18th of December, 1968.

such a decree; its intent was "not to facilitate copying of Polish military uniforms by the enemy." Evidently, there was a concern that some sinister foreign power may want to infiltrate the Boy Scouts.

Our family had concerns about photos as well. While no photos survived the Holocaust on Tata's side, Mama brought back several pre-war photographs from Siberia, some of which I include here. They were too precious to part with, even for a few months, so we didn't put them in the lift but had them with us in hand luggage. Thankfully, they didn't attract attention. The customs officers on the train were more interested in photos of me with Jacek.

They were shamelessly greedy, without precedent. The workers who packed our lifts instructed beforehand how much to give ("prepare several envelopes with cash") and to whom.

* * *

Our lift was labeled "Vienna" as a symbol of our uncertain future. We left with a few suitcases in hand; their content was specified in the customs declaration for the occasion of the next circus, at the border.

PRE-DEPARTURE HARASSMENT PART FIVE: THEIR LAST CHANCE – AT THE BORDER

How can we solve the Jewish question in Poland? [...]
The Zionist answer may seem the most radical:

let the Jews emigrate to Palestine and create a Jewish state there.
When the Zionists proposed this idea forty years earlier, Jewish
socialists understood immediately the reactionary content of this
postulate.

It boiled down to admitting that Jews are guests in the countries
where they live, that they should not and cannot feel like full -fledged
citizens there and that, potentially, today, they are already citizens
of Palestine.

And it was exactly this position that suited antisemites the best.
It is no accident that cultured Polish antisemites such as Prince
Radziwiłł and Count Rostworowski recently made this suggestion in
the Senate, supposedly in accordance with the interests of the Jewish
population as formulated by the Zionists.

Jewish socialist activist Viktor Alter, *On Antisemitism*, 1937

History repeats itself.

Zebrzydowice, the town and train station at the border between Poland and Czechoslovakia, became the demarcation line between our lives thus far and the future. An hour before the train pulled into the station, a group of uniformed customs officers piled into the cars — Poland's last bastion of defense against Jewish plunder. "Accompanying persons" in each compartment were asked to leave. For us, it was Jacek, my Polish boyfriend, and my uncles Janek and Zacharje, Mama's brothers. They will travel the rest of the way in a separate section of the train reserved for those who will not cross the border in Zebrzydowice.

The officers pointed methodically at one piece of luggage after another. First, they inspected the structure itself to see if we hid money, gold, or gems in the straps or locks or if there was perhaps a second bottom in one of the suitcases. They tapped, knocked, turned the suitcases over and upside down, twisted the handles, and carefully examined the frame and reinforcements. They worked nonchalantly, mechanically, with no sign of interest or passion. Since nothing was found in the structure, they proceeded to the contents.

I wondered about their orders. Were they looking for something specific? Did they have a list of items previously rejected from our lift? Or maybe their task was to destroy whatever they could. Or, simply, on this final occasion, to humiliate us as much as possible? Or, simpler yet — perhaps there were no top-down instructions; they just wanted to extract one more bribe for themselves. This would be a logistic and legal challenge since owning and showing more money than the permitted five dollars would be self-incriminating – was all this to extract the five dollars?

They opened my suitcase, flipped it upside down, and

unceremoniously dumped everything onto the worn velvet seats. Packed neatly among my folded warm sweaters for the Viennese winter were a few poetry books. The volumes were so precious to me that, like amulets, I wanted them near: poetry by Maria Pawlikowska-Jasnorzewska, *Market of Rhymes* by Julian Tuwim, and romantic poetry by Pablo Neruda in Polish translation. I knew most of it by heart. Everything was now a messy tangle. "It's all right," I kept calming myself. We are almost out of Poland; they are the last ones. I'll fix everything once they leave.

They took interest in the large envelope full of photos and examined them one by one, throwing each carelessly onto the pile as they were done with them. My uncles and Mama, me as a little girl on vacation in Kudowa Zdrój accessorized by a big white dog, friends whose names they brazenly demanded to know ("they are looking for Jews or Jew sympathizers," crossed my mind), my Grandfather Samuel Goldman who died in the Siberian labor camp, some of the murdered members of the Goldman family. My heart pounded because pre-1945 photographs were forbidden, but somehow, there were no comments. They paused at the photos of Jacek and me in the mountains.

Jacek was born and raised at the foot of the Tatras. He loved them, and knew them well. "I'll show you, and you will fall in love," he often repeated. We ran out of time.

They confiscated the city plan of Wrocław I bought in the travel section of the Ossoliński bookstore on the Old Market Square, declaring it "a government document." My diary had no luck again — first, it was rejected from the lift, and now from the suitcase. Influenced by *The Diary of Anne Frank,* I started writing it as an impressionable teenager. It was a memento of myself, of my inner thoughts and developing worldviews, even of my handwriting as it matured over the years — but they were not going to let me keep it. There was no one left to give it to. I imagined for a brief moment the officers reading it and laughing, making profane comments. I didn't even want them to touch it. Struggling, I tore the thick notebooks filled with pages and pages of scribbles, destroying the material evidence of my innocence, my Polish childhood, and my first kiss. I lingered over the task, making the pieces smaller and smaller, watching my words and stories disappear. I held back tears – or did I? Poland was safe now; my diary will not leave the country.

They aggressively fingered the stitching of my embroidered sheepskin coat.

Finally, they told me to take off my boots, examined the soles, and — *crack* — broke off both heels. It turned out we weren't smuggling anything inside; the heels weren't even hollow. I was in shock. I stood in stockinged feet on the worn compartment floor, speechless, motionless, as the heels and boots landed carelessly on the pile on the seat. The officers left. The inspection was over.

Eva Shpringer tells a similar story: "I came to Vienna barefoot; the customs officers tore apart the soles of my sandals. They found nothing, but the sandals were ruined. I had no money but in Vienna, Sochnut bought me another pair, so I didn't go to Israel barefooted."

Jacek tried to get back into our car in Zebrzydowice. Not that it mattered, but we hadn't even said goodbye. I heard him explaining feebly that he had to return my lighter, which accidentally stayed in his pocket when he was ordered out of the compartment. It was the coveted Ronson he gave me as a present for my twentieth birthday a few months earlier. I enjoyed using it so much to light a cigarette that I actually smoked more since I got it. But the officers didn't let him in; they simply returned the lighter to me.

We sat still, perhaps in shock, as the train rolled out. The last Polish station on our journey slowly moved past us and finally disappeared. It was hard to see anything – there was light in the compartment and dark outside… it was snowing, a scene from *Anna Karenina* or *Dr. Zhivago*. Through the steamed-up window, we briefly saw Mama's brothers. They stood side-by-side, also motionless, both in long coats and old-fashioned felt hats that I so much loved to try on. Their elongated silhouettes looked like figures from Magritte. I don't think they saw us because they did not return our desperate waving – but every window probably had people waving. "See you, bye-bye," we whispered feverishly to ourselves.

Twenty-three years earlier, as the war ended, these two uncles and Mama, their youngest sister, were released from the Siberian labor camp and returned to Poland. They buried their father in Siberia, and, as it turned out, no one else was left alive. The three of them were the only survivors of the once large, thriving family. The train trip from Barnaul near Novosibirsk to Przemyśl, the station nearest Nowosielce, took six weeks. And now they, too, were separating. Would they ever see each other again?

The train rolled slowly. I eagerly looked at their faces – last glances – and I saw or imagined that they cried, but the window was fogged up… in truth, I couldn't see much. We cried.

Jacek ran alongside the accelerating train until the end of the platform, still waving goodbye, still gesturing at his heart. Then he got smaller and smaller until he disappeared. I never saw him again. He was my tender, beautiful first love.

Róża Goldfarb (Holmgren) has different memories from

Zebrzydowice. It was late October when her family departed from Warsaw. There were two other Jewish families in their compartment. It truly was unexpected when the customs officers declared that their two suitcases apiece were too much to be inspected in a routine manner and ordered the whole group to get off in Zebrzydowice. "We thought they would get off with us, but they didn't. The train left, and we found ourselves alone on the deserted platform," recalls Róża. It was cold, and the station building was locked and dark. After prolonged, vigorous banging, a cleaning lady appeared and let the shaken group inside. It was a bare, empty room with not even a chair to sit on. The modest Customs Office in the corner of the building – a cubicle, really was also locked. They spent the night on the floor, shivering. Zebrzydowice rarely saw a lot of customs action in the past years: perhaps a merchant marine returning home by train and smuggling a pair of silk stockings for his girlfriend, or someone bringing a hard-to-explain new set of sheets from a vacation in Hungary... petty stuff. But on the occasion of the Jewish exile, it also gained importance.

The next train was scheduled to leave at eleven in the morning.

"The door of the Customs Office opened at eight, but no one seemed to share our sense of urgency:" continued Róża. "The officers looked at us disapprovingly. "Don't worry. If the inspection is not finished in time for the eleven o'clock train, we will certainly manage to get you onto the next one, around midnight," the same one we've been taken off the night before. The inspection started shortly after nine. My two suitcases were first. They took out every piece of clothing, carefully examined each picture, and squeezed the suitcase handles... I started crying. They looked at me with contempt; "Just doing our job, Miss." In the end, nothing was rejected. It was almost ten o'clock now.

The idea of spending a whole day at the station was overwhelming. No food to buy, no bench or chair to sit on. Taking a significant risk, the group scraped together some illegal, hidden money and handed it over. This is what they've been waiting for. The inspection was over.

At five minutes to eleven, we were on the platform. The train pulled in, but the conductor wanted nothing to do with us. Our tickets from the night before were no longer valid and, according to the conductor, there wasn't a seat left on this train. Sheer hysteria ensued: suitcases pushed onto the train through doors and windows, someone helping, someone else pushing them back out, the conductor screaming, my mother screaming, me screaming, a passenger on the train screaming that there is no space. At the conclusion of this dramatic and rather inelegant scene, we somehow got onto the train and left Poland." Goodbye.

An intriguing story: what would be the purpose of this incident if not to extract yet another bribe? The departing Jews were not allowed to have any money beyond the five dollars per person. Producing the bribe was self-incriminating; they could have been arrested. But if the recipients turned them in, the bribe would be lost. So, in a bold transgression greed won, and the customs officers extracted illegally carried money.

There were also frightening rumors that a certain Mr. and Mrs. Z. were arrested after being taken off the train in Zebrzydowice. They apparently hid something undeclared in their lift. The inspection was apparently completed, and the lift shut, yet, for whatever reason, it was opened once again. Years later, I heard a whispered story that the Z's smuggled a diamond in the freon compartment of their refrigerator, for which they both spent several years in a Polish prison. Whatever it was, it was their property, and the crime was that they dared to take it with them.

* * *

The March witch hunt, aimed to rid Poland of its Jews, was conducted from start to finish in an atmosphere of premeditated *humiliation*. Were these instructions from above? Today, as an American who believes in the law, I would have asked about the applicable paragraphs and tried to advocate for myself with truth and logic. Back then, the lawless law was on their side. We had no rights, not even a right to defend ourselves.

History repeats itself.

SCRATCHING THE ISSUE OF UNSETTLED ACCOUNTS

The inherent vice of capitalism is the unequal sharing of blessings.
The inherent virtue of socialism is the equal sharing of miseries.

Winston Churchill, *House of Commons*, 22 October 1945

As in the entire Eastern bloc of that era, education in Poland was free for all citizens. I don't remember anyone articulating it that way, but logically, future work for meager pay benefitted the socialist country and could have been seen as repayment for the studies. Since the exiled graduates fell short of fulfilling this implied *quid pro quo*, the government came up with another clever revenue generator: the departing Jews had to reimburse Poland for their finished studies, even though free education was a commonly understood and loudly touted citizenry benefit. The demanded sums were astronomical and seemed arbitrary, different for various faculties: thirty thousand zlotys for law and humanities (that's how much Wacek Szer (Mark Scher) paid for his law degree, and H.T.'s parents paid for philological studies of her sister), forty-five thousand for science and engineering (parents of Helena Stawska (Lindskog) paid such a sum for her studies at the Warsaw University of Science and Technology Institute, and Jurek Wajda (George Celler) paid for his degree in physics). My husband Edward's medical studies cost his Mother one hundred thousand zlotys. There was no way out of this quandary: no one hired Jews, and most of those who already worked lost their jobs. H.T.'s sister, a stellar student, did not get hired for any position for which she applied after graduation. And Michal Antopolski tells a bittersweet story of a friend who pleaded to be hired "at least for half-time since only one of her parents was a Jew."

Jurek Wajda (George Celler) from Warsaw remembers the thriller-like details: "Wacek Szer (Mark Scher) and I went together to the designated office on Karowa Street, around the corner from Hotel Bristol. We each carried a briefcase full of 100-zloty bills. I paid forty-five thousand for my diploma in physics," says Jurek, "while Wacek paid thirty thousand for his law degree." In cash.

The requested sums were simply unattainable for most families of this hand-to-mouth society. For some, it was all the money they got from liquidating their Polish households. Others couldn't even manage that. Adam Gryniewicz stayed in Poland for several years longer than he wanted until he finished the assigned work order, which "paid" for his education. Luckily, he could.

I don't know how many graduates paid for their education – perhaps 3,000? If the average fee was forty thousand zlotys, then cumulatively, the departing Jews delivered in various briefcases, suitcases, backpacks, and boxes 120 million zlotys in cash. The government that exiled them got the cash – the Jews left with education. It is not clear what Poland (or individual Polish beneficiaries) did with the cash. It is clear, however, that the Jews did well with their education. They published and patented, earned PhDs and professorships, and flourished in business. They grew families and educated their children. They became good and valued Swedes and Americans, Danes and Canadians, Israelis and Germans.

***

The five thousand zlotys per Travel Document extracted at the moment of "forfeiting" our Polish citizenship was also a major revenue generator. If the number of people departed was 13,000, then the collected fees would have added up to 65 million.

***

The flip side of the equation is the earned, yet never paid, pensions of the departed. According to the historian Dariusz Stola, "Against the background of emigration from Poland as a whole, or against the total Polish population, the post-March Jews were a remarkable group. What strikes immediately is a very high level of education: the percentage of people with higher education and students among them was eight times higher(!) than among the general Polish population," says Prof. Stola (*Post-March Emigration*, Warsaw 2000.) If only half of the emigrating adults belonged to the generation of our parents and worked in Poland for the twenty postwar years then, in round numbers, at the moment of their departure, they will have jointly worked in Poland ONE HUNDRED THOUSAND YEARS. And if this group of highly educated people were to earn only a meager pension of two thousand zlotys per month, less than the average salary, then the roughly calculated value of their unpaid pensions amounts to two billion four hundred million zlotys. Most pensions would likely be higher, reflecting education, years of service, academic achievements, military service during the war, supplements for merit or military decorations, loss-of-health-related benefits, etc. Was all this worth five billion zlotys? Ten billion? Pensions earned by Polish citizens and never paid. WHERE IS THAT MONEY?!?!

* * *

Nota bene: my mother-in-law, the one who "bought" for one hundred thousand zlotys the right for her son Edward to leave in 1969, emigrated as well, in 1973. If her monthly pension were to be only two thousand five hundred zlotys for almost thirty years, then Dr. Helena Baral, Chief Physician of the Pediatric Hospital in Bytom, left in Poland almost 870,000 zlotys in never collected pensions.

HELA

You make a life out of what you have, not what you're missing.

Kate Morton, *The Forgotten Garden*

My husband's father, also Edward, also Dr. Baral, is not buried in a grave. He was killed by the Germans in Ternopil, now Western Ukraine. His body was never found.

He left the bunker where they had been hiding to look for food. In the bunker, along with Edward, was his seven-month pregnant wife Hela and another family of five, the Ashkenazys. It was July of 1944, and fighting was fierce; Ternopil changed hands three times in the previous week. Knispel, the man who, for money, of course, but conscientiously and reliably, brought them food during their two years in the bunker, disappeared several days earlier – he may have been killed or may have run away. They haven't eaten since.

Edward spent many years in Ternopil. He knew the city well. He spoke German fluently. Admission to many Polish universities was governed in the 1930s by *numerus clausus*, then *numerus nullus* – a racist-driven administrative method of denying Jewish students access to universities and related institutions, which forced many Jews to study abroad. Edward enrolled at the Charles University in Prague as a German student; his medical degree was from there.

He was a surgeon, but in those horrible times, he was everything. A local farmer whose family he treated for years, often for free, sometimes for a chicken, recognized him and scored points with the passing German: "This is Dr. Baral, a Jew." Someone witnessed the scene and saw him taken away.

Hela waited in the bunker. The next day, with her big belly, she too came out of the bunker and started a search, aided by her best friend, Ruth Buczyńska. They still hadn't eaten, but they didn't look for food – they looked for Edward, then for his body…. Nothing. The Russians entered two days later for good, and that was the end of WWII in Ternopil.

Hela's son was born two months later, and she named him Edward. After the war, she, too, finished medical studies and became a pediatrician.

She was tall, very attractive, and glamorous. She was also talented. She played the piano, sang beautifully, laughed contagiously, and was a gifted storyteller. She was Hela, the sought-after pediatrician. Hela, the life of every party. Alone in the world, the sole survivor of the Zeiler family from Sambor — or so she thought. Hela, with a bleeding soul and a broken heart, raised her son alone and remained a widow for almost thirty years. A government work order required her to move from her beloved Krakow to Bytom, where she became Chief Physician at the Pediatric Hospital.

* * *

Years passed.

In 1969, her son Edward also graduated from medical school and left Poland for Sweden so he could live as a Jew with dignity. Hela, who lived through an escape from the Krakow ghetto and, later, from the camp in Płaszów, through years of the Ternopil bunker, through mourning her husband without burying him… In probably the toughest decision of her life, Dr. Helena Baral decided to let her only son go alone and stay behind. At forty-nine, she felt old and didn't want to become a burden to Edward.

DECEMBER 20. GOODBYE, POLAND

I observed the extermination of the Jews in Poland from two different viewpoints divided by an abysmal antinomy: as a Christian and as a Pole. As a Christian, I couldn't not feel compassion for my fellow human beings. I often thought what these wretched folk felt when they were herded into gas chambers [....]
As a Pole, however, I looked at these events differently.

In keeping with the philosophy of Dmowski, I regarded Jews as an internal occupant, one that is always hostile towards the country of diaspora. Therefore, I could not help feeling glad that we are getting rid of this occupant, and not with our own hands but with the hands of a third, external party [...]. I could not hide satisfaction when traveling through Jew-free towns. I saw that the hideous, slovenly Jewish hovels with an inseparable goat on the porch stopped marring our landscape. Asked by Thurm (a German bureaucrat with whom the author happened to then travel) „Sehen die Polen die Befreiung vom den Juden als ein Segnen an?"
– do the Poles see their liberation from the Jews as a blessing?" –
I answered „Gewiss" – sure – certain, that I express the opinion of the vast majority of my countrymen.

Nationalist activist Józef Górski, *At the turn of history,*
2006, 288-291

Most likely, the first Jews arrived in Poland in the 11th century, forging and following the European trade routes. In 1334, the Polish king Casimir the Great granted them fundamental rights and protection: freedom of faith, travel, and trade. In 1968, Casimir's promise was overtly broken. Crossing now the Polish border, not by choice but for lack of choice, irrevocably, I thought that we, the post-March exodus, represented the ultimate closure, the last chapter of Jewish history in Poland, perhaps the last Jews of Poland – this is what I thought when I could still think.

But now I couldn't. I couldn't think.

The wheels of the train clattered a soothing rhythm, which somehow, like a mantra, was in harmony with my heartbeat. I expected this to be a big moment filled with lofty and important thoughts – after all, my twenty years in Poland, my whole life thus far, was ending... but my mind was empty.

We've been exiled for being Jewish from the land where our predecessors lived and worked for nine centuries, from the land for which they fought and where they were buried. Towns and villages throughout Poland are filled with Jewish remnants....

I couldn't think about any of them: about Chasidim from Lublin, or Tzadik's from Galicia, fools from Chełm, or the heroes of the Warsaw ghetto uprising. I couldn't think about the mystics or the communists. I couldn't think about the exceptional Jewish Poles and couldn't find any meaning in the fact that Brzechwa, Leśmian, Słonimski, Wieniawski, Artur Rubinstein, Jerzy Toeplitz, Isaac Bashevis Singer, Aleksander Ford, Maurycy Gottlieb or Bruno Schulz were all Jews. Painters, musicians, scientists, economists, educators, and mathematicians – a spectacular array of people who were born in Poland, died in Poland, and enriched the Polish culture and

SABINA'S JOURNEY

Painting by Bożena Dusseau Labedz, a Cum Laude graduate of the Academy of Fine Arts in Krakow, Poland, in the class of the famous Duda-Gracz.

She now lives in the Netherlands. SABINA'S JOURNEY was inspired by NOTES FROM EXILE.

the Polish imprint in the world with everything they had. I also didn't think about the millions of simple people: cobblers, bakers and milkmen, farmers and tailors, klezmers, and soldiers who, for centuries, walked the Polish soil living their meager Jewish life. I didn't even think about Jacek; until recently, the two of us planned a future together; the only obstacles we saw were the likely objections of both families, which we hoped to overcome.

I was tired, I'd had enough, I wanted to be free of Poland. You won. No, we won. Actually, all of us lost. It's all the same. And if the creative output of any Polish Jew convinced me on that day, it is the poet Tuwim. Not *We, Polish Jews*, his 1944 tragic hymn of dual identity, of unrequited love, where he declares: "I am a Pole because I want to be. It's nobody's business but my own." It didn't work this way for us; the people on my train were here because we were denied the right to be Poles in Poland. Instead, I thought about Tuwim's clandestinely published satirical invective at the Polish society, *Kiss my arse, all of you*. WE ARE LEAVING. You will have Poland *Judenfrei, Judenrein*, your Poland, yours alone. And in a moment, as soon as we cross the border, your antisemitism will be only your problem, only your cross to bear, yours alone.

I fleetingly notice that Poland has become a "there" in the fog of my thoughts.

* * *

Until 1941, Poland was home to more than 3.5 million Jews, the largest community in Europe. No more than 10% survived the war.

The numbers are uncertain and differ in various historical accounts, but we know that the vast majority – perhaps as many as 280,000 - survived in the depths of the USSR: in Uzbekistan,

92

Kazakhstan, Siberia, or the far north. Most of them returned to Poland as soon as they could, among them Mama and her brothers.

Within the borders of German-occupied Poland, 200,000 to 300,000 escaped from ghettos and jumped from moving transport trains. Escaping was actually easier than surviving on the "Aryan" side. Only 30,000 survived, roughly 8,000 thanks to the heroic help of Righteous Poles. Perhaps a few thousand more were hidden by Poles who never admitted to helping Jews for fear of being denounced by their neighbors. The rest managed somehow on their own, eating bark and moss, living in holes in the ground, and sharing their hiding places with lice and rats. My Grandma Goldman was among those. After the war, they came out of fields and forests; some with false Ausweis Kartes and fake baptismal certificates, some hidden in monasteries, some were the almost-cadavers liberated from camps, and some, like Tata, returned with the Red Army, for fighting alongside the Russians allowed them to fight the Nazis. Eighty thousand left right away after finding nothing and nobody. Pogroms such as in Rzeszow in June 1945, in Krakow in August 1945, and the most well-known in Kielce in July 1946 hastened their departure.

Still, in early 1946, in the now reshaped, socialist Poland, 220,000 Jews cautiously registered with the newly created Jewish committees and, pained and injured, with souls that hurt and bled, in great fear and uncertainty, set about to restore life, hoping it could also be Jewish. That was the only thing they could give to their murdered families – to LIVE and TRY TO RESTORE THE NATION.

Post-war Poland, the home to which they so longingly returned, was by and large hostile towards them. The neighbors already divided Jewish possessions, and few were eager to return the beds, frying pans, tablecloths, or goats they grabbed after the Jews were deported. The assumption was that they would never return, so what harm could it do to take a few things from the cupboards or, for that matter, to move into the house or take over the cobbler shop?! I saw a short documentary clip in which a Polish peasant woman recalled how her Jewish neighbors in Lublin were being led out of their houses. She didn't comment on the drama; there was no mention of their tragedy, fear or dignity, no time was wasted on empathy. She talked about jewelry. "The daughters wore beautiful earrings," she recalled. "So I asked them to give me the earrings since they wouldn't need them anymore," continues the peasant with all righteousness of reason. "They didn't," she finishes, indignant at this lack of generosity and consideration.

The hastily passed restitution laws of 1946 favored the keeper, and "unclaimed" property devolved to the state in 1948. Instead of feeling welcome and greeted with a piece of bread, a kind word, or a warm smile, the returning Jews encountered hostility and danger. They rightfully feared for their lives. My Grandma Goldman was murdered by neighbors in hopes that no other Goldman would survive. Seventy thousand left after the Kielce pogrom, crossing the border illegally into Czechoslovakia while the government looked away.

Let them go.

In 1948, months after the founding of Israel, yet more left. More still, about 50,000, after Stalin's death (the "Gomulka emigration") in 1956–1959. We were what was left – *the last of the Mohicans*. I couldn't believe my parents stayed for so long. And now we, too, were leaving.

* * *

Our parents, the older generation of our emigration, were very diverse. Among them were Jewish Jews living Jewish lives. There were also Polish Jews—they believed that it was possible to be a Jew and a Pole simultaneously and without conflict. The post-war Polish Marranos hid their Jewish ancestry out of necessity, or fear, to protect their children, or simply because it was easier. For many, the dark secret of their Jewish roots was dragged out and made public in recent months as shameful deceit. Some of our parents were members of the Communist Party, and some were not, which was not easy; some were traditional and some very progressive, some educated and some very simple, believers and atheists. The Communist Party members could be idealists or opportunists, but most simply joined because that could have been the only way to get or keep their jobs or to get an apartment with running water. Some positions, and most military, required Polish-sounding names. Some families were mixed, Polish Jewish or Russian Jewish, married for love or out of gratitude for a saved life. Some spoke beautiful Polish, some colored their pronunciation with an Eastern lilt, and others yet spoke Polish with the accent of a Jewish shtetl and butchered the language. Some learned Hebrew in pre-war cheders. Yiddish, German, or Russian could be the *lingua franca* of their home. Their beloved writer could have been equally as well Sholem Aleichem, Isaac Bashevis Singer, Mickiewicz, Goethe, or Pushkin.

But all of them, ALL OF THEM, survived the recent Holocaust. The lucky-unlucky, tragically fortunate, unreasonably courageous, scared, with the endless will to live and hopes of rebuilding their tortured nation with injured, bleeding souls. They were the stunned objects, witnesses to the collapse of humanity. They suffered hunger, cold, disease, exhaustion, unimaginable losses and pain, terror in the face of the cruelty of their hunters and executioners, shock at the indifference of observers, horror of abandonment, and tragic loneliness. Actors in an unforgivable drama, victims of an inhuman experiment: how much suffering can you endure before going insane? Entire large families were murdered, entire villages. They often were the only ones left to say Kaddish or to remember and record the names of those who perished.

In spite of these differences, in 1968, our parents were equalized once again, just like in the times of the Nazis a couple of decades earlier.

When the propaganda said "Zionists," it meant "Jews." We became JEWS. Hounded. Excluded from the accepted social landscape. Struggling once again to maintain dignity with heads raised high. Because in the end we will cross the border, leave this swamp behind, and be human once again. Someplace else, we will be human again.

I have to admit that getting through it with my head raised high was not easy. I cried in spite of myself while tearing to shreds my girlish diary. And a while later, once again, looking at my motionless uncles standing on the snowy platform in Zebrzydowice and watching Jacek run helplessly alongside the train. I quietly cried the saddest cry. I choked.

* * *

After liberation, the survivors came out of the woods and wardrobes, barns and holes in the ground, attics and basements; they shuffled half dead from the liberated camps, blinded with light and drunk with air they crawled from the underground, they traveled for weeks by train from Siberia or Kazakhstan – home to Poland. What awaited them was often a cruel and difficult reality. The Germans were gone, but there seemed to be no place for them. Someone else lived in their homes now and wore their clothes; other babies slept in cribs they lovingly built and left behind, and there was now a Polish name on the marquee of their modest bakery or tailor shop. Some were killed just for showing up; some were thrown out of moving trains. Some died in pogroms. These acts of cruel violence were seldom punished. And while many Jews left Poland, our parents remained even though leaving was possible and perhaps prudent. To them, Poland was HOME, the only one they knew, where generations of their ancestors lived, died, and were buried, where their parents were born, and where we, their children, were born. After the gehenna of war, after years of torment, loss, and fear, they decided once again that Poland was their country. And these are the people whom Poland now expelled.

Among the manuscripts given to me since this book came out in Poland, there is one written by a friend's Mother, Rivka (Regina) Flaszner, who, as a young teenager, spent part of the war in a hole in the ground outside the village of Złotniki near Ternopil. She shared the hole with her older brother and their mother. The space was tight; the only way they fit there was to lay on their sides, front-to-back against each other, motionless. Only at night did they crawl out to relieve themselves and to search for something to eat. In the manuscript, Rivka does not complain of thirst or hunger. She talks about fear, the aching body, the discomfort of not moving, not making a sound, and not going to the bathroom for many hours each day, but she does not dwell on it. She does not even dwell on getting her first period in the hole; it's a miracle she got it, anyway, given her general exhaustion and malnutrition. Her biggest complaint was hundreds of lice in the seams of her clothes; she couldn't get rid of them.

She survived and stayed in Poland until '69. I met her in Sweden. She laughed often and made the best kutia: a

Ukrainian pudding from wheat, poppy seeds, and walnuts.

I also have the manuscript written by Mary Libling. We called her Aunt Mary, but in reality, she was aunt to Roman Polanski, the film director, whose real family name is Liebling. Mary had so-called good looks. She was blonde and blue-eyed. She survived in her city of birth, Krakow, carrying a fake ID of a Polish woman. With a perfect command of German, she worked in the German radio. She shuddered with fear each time one of her German bosses called her *"liebling"* (darling), thinking he had discovered her real name. It was very courageous, perhaps unreasonably so, for her to stay in Krakow, where many people knew her; she could be recognized and denounced at any moment. Her husband, Stefan, not blessed with good looks, was hiding in an attic of a bombed-out house, and Mary brought him food – so leaving Krakow was, for her, unthinkable.

Both of them survived and stayed in Poland. But I knew Mary in Melbourne, Australia. She was the closest friend of my mother-in-law, Hela.

* * *

In the face of this relentless, aggressive barrage, the decision to leave was no decision at all – there simply was no choice. Even if someone would be willing to endure the systemic and systematic humiliation, most lost their jobs and were left without means of support. And from the moment we applied for permission to leave until we actually crossed the border, nothing protected us. We were tried and convicted, and we finally confessed our guilt – with Israeli visas in our Travel Documents, we admitted to being Zionists. Aha!

"The anti-Zionist campaign of 1968" (title of a book by historian Dariusz Stola, 2000), which resulted in our exile, was

recorded in Polish social conscience and history books as a brainchild of a twisted, now-defunct political system. Yes, it was true. But this is not the whole truth. Too convenient and dishonest. It's a whitewash.

The system and methods of the People's Republic of Poland indeed oppressed and tormented all of us. Layers of convoluted lies, journalism and history treated as political sciences at the service of the ruling regime, where indoctrination is more important than facts. People were punished for daring to think differently; many went to prison, never having done anything; they served sentences for what they thought. Others believed in the ideological absurdities fed to us, and the majority simply kept quiet. In that sense, we all suffered. And it is also true that the country's leadership perfidiously masked this antisemitic campaign with anti-Israeli slogans.

Yet it is important to recognize and acknowledge that this campaign legitimized the just-under-the-surface antisemitism of the society as a whole, and many Poles, our neighbors, and acquaintances became willing participants and beneficiaries. Many of those who did not participate tried hard not to notice what was going on. The party's proposal to exclude Jews from the Polish social landscape was not opposed – and perhaps even welcome. Millions participated. Neighbors and former friends did not recognize Jews on the streets, and the phones stopped ringing. With no employment opportunities for the parents and no educational opportunities for their children, most Jews were abandoned by society and fearful of the future. And the media continued the hateful propaganda.

Our departure and its odious circumstances didn't generate any audible echo. Perhaps those who had the courage to say goodbye at the railroad station walked home wiping tears of helplessness or shame. Yet many others rejoiced at our humiliation and suffering, greedily counted recently extracted bribes, and enjoyed their new post-Jewish loot just like twenty-three years ago – property bought for next to nothing, vacated apartments, scientific appointments, and available positions at work.

It was easy to torment us because we were completely defenseless.

Nobody stood up for us.

* * *

And we, dizzy with the content and speed of events, are now in Vienna. I suddenly got a hair-brain idea to look for work here, and I succeeded. A charming, enterprising young man from Yugoslavia, a bit sweaty even in the cold of winter, operated a souvenir stand in the suburb of Grinzing. My job was to sell ballpoint pens. You flip the pen upside down, and the girl with straw-colored hair, pointy breasts, and an unreasonably tiny waist – a plebeian version of Jayne Mansfield – drops her bathing suit. I earned a few shillings a day, which, net of the bus fare, made no difference whatsoever in our budget – but I felt better. I was helping.

We spent three weeks in Vienna.

IT'S TIME TO MOVE AGAIN GOODBYE, VIENNA

Soon I'll be a stranger in a strange new land
Searching for an old familiar face
From Anatevka…

Sheldon Harnick, *Fiddler on the Roof, based on Tevye and his Daughters,* a book by Sholem Aleichem (Solomon Naumovich Rabinovich)

The mood on the train to Rome is almost upbeat; we are going into the unknown, but something is happening: a move forward. Again, a "Jewish train." There are many families whom we didn't see in Vienna; they lived in different hotels.

Where are you going?

To America.

–And you?

–To Germany. To Australia. To my sister...

Another surreal scene resembling that from *Fidler on the Roof,* which took place in 1905, some sixty years earlier. After the pogrom, the shocked, exiled Jews leave Anatevka. They push carts and carry bundles of their meager belongings.

"Where are you going?" Tevye asks Leyzor Wolf.

"To Chicago," answers the butcher, "I have a brother there. And you?"

"To New York."

"Oh, good, we'll be neighbors!"

However, on the train, in real-time, I also hear: "I don't know.

We have no one."

We traveled all night. The first part of the trip was through the Alps. I glued my nose to the window, looking for the dramatic, jagged, white landscapes I imagined the Alps to be, but I saw nothing, just a dark, flat plane of the window. "My future," I thought. "Dark and invisible…."

In the middle of the night, the train stopped in Venice. The name itself unleashed dreams of brocade gowns, heaps of gold coins transported in gondolas, Murano glass and Burano lace. "We'll be here for an hour," announced the conductor. An hour in Venice?! A few of us young ones decided to run out – perhaps we will see something? After all, none of us know how our lives will turn out; this could be our only chance to experience Venetian magic, the Rialto, the Bridge of Sighs, and the golden domes of St. Mark's Basilica?! To breathe the air of Titian and Canaletto. We jumped out of the train and found the exit from the railroad station… Which way should we go? We crossed the big plaza in front, one turn, another, wide, shallow steps, water everywhere, dark, cold, drizzly, slippery… We returned to the train earlier than necessary, out of breath, wet and cold, trying to hide our disappointment.

The others looked at us with envious amazement: we had been to Venice.

JANUARY 1969, STAZIONE TERMINI, ROME

Children and watches cannot be wound all the time,
you also have to give them time to work.

attributed to Jean-Paul Sartre

The main railway station in Rome is called Stazione Termini. Its name derives from the Diocletian Baths *(thermae)* across the piazza but also implies the final destination. Not for us – for us, it is the next stop. The station is huge, its cavernous main hall filled with shops, bars, restaurants, and offices of all varieties. An impressive bit of architecture, but other than sheer size, it makes a provincial and prosaic impression. The building opens onto an enormous sunlit square chaotically crowded with taxis and buses with a huge fountain in the distant left. It's morning, and we are in **Rome**.

Once again, pleasant strangers meet us here, shuffling pages of a list from which names are called. I listen intently, waiting for ours. It doesn't even cross my mind to wonder who these people are. The burning question is **what is next**.

We are divided into groups of several families each and led to a *pensione*: a large apartment barely adapted to its new multifamily function. Our suitcases get there separately via a small pickup. Randomly shaped and furnished small bedrooms and awkward shared spaces. There is a small, make-shift kitchen, inadequate at best, a living room proudly called *il soggiorno* with an impractical, theater-style, ornate sofa in the center, and a red dial phone on a side table. And, pathetically, one bathroom. As I later learned the secrets of the city, I understood that the *pensione*'s furnishings most likely came from open-air junk markets of Porta Portese. The Srebrniks, who talk often and proudly of their daughter in Montreal, are still with us. They are displeased; the room they were assigned is cramped and uncomfortable for four people. Of course. In Wrocław, they left a large apartment with a balcony, and they hoped for no less in Montreal. This is tough.

We, too, are cramped in our room. There is a large *letto matrimoniale* for my parents and a make-shift folding cot for me wedged between the large bed and the wall. The main piece of furniture, a surprising choice at best, is an imposing, huge wooden wardrobe placed diagonally in the corner. There isn't enough space for its ornate doors to fully open. They hit the bed. Our suitcases are also a problem. They don't fit under the bed. There is no room for them inside the wardrobe nor atop the wardrobe, which is not flat but adorned with elegant, decorative finials and other carved doo-dads. We place them helplessly against the walls, making the room smaller yet. Getting to my cot will require true acrobatics; I may need to get to it by climbing atop and across the large bed. There are no hangers in the wardrobe, and we have none either. We look at each other with consternation; Mama sighs. We don't want to complain, but we, too, hope that this living arrangement will not last long.

Thankfully, in a couple of days, it becomes clear that the *pensione* is a temporary solution meant only for the first few weeks. Meanwhile, each family should find and rent another place to live – a tall order since we don't know the city or the language. And, financial news: our first stop now is to be Joint, where we will receive some money, the first of our monthly allowances, which must suffice for rent, food, bus fare, and all other necessities. We don't know yet who or what Joint is. A benefactor? Maybe a bank? And, to help with the "scour Rome" assignment, we each receive a piece of paper: on one side are two addresses: one of the *pensione* so we won't get lost on the way back, and the other of Joint. On the other side is our first Italian word, *affittasi* – to rent, and all its conjugations. That's what we will look for.

The fact that the allowance is "monthly" frames our Roman timetable. It will take a while.

Life in the p*ensione* is complicated. Each of the ladies waits more or less impatiently for her turn in the kitchen to heat or to cook something on one of the four stove burners. The morning line to the bathroom stretches sometimes for a whole hour. The mood isn't always parliamentary: some of those waiting shout at each other – evidently someone tried to save a place in line for a friend who was still asleep, and the others considered this unfair, someone else pleaded that it is an emergency and may he please cut the line. Yes, any apartment, better or worse. We need to move as soon as possible. It is urgent.

ROOM WITHOUT A VIEW

Only in Rome is it possible to understand Rome.

Johann Wolfgang von Goethe

After crisscrossing the city on foot for a few days, we decided on a large room on the second floor of a building on Via Principe Amedeo 231, near *Stazione Termini* and next to a large produce market called *Mercato Esquilino*. The room is part of a spacious apartment with other rooms and tenants. Another blessing was that our landlady, Zoriza, was a native of Belgrade, where, as in Poland, Russian was part of the school curriculum, and we could communicate in Russian. She told us that her Italian husband, Mario, is the first choreographer at Opera di Roma. We haven't seen him yet; somehow, he was absent, and eventually, we understand that they don't live together and there is more to this juicy and complicated story.

Zoriza was a tall, handsome, broad-boned blonde. It is winter, so we can't appreciate her extravagant style. And it was A STYLE. She blossomed with even a hint of spring, dressed in chosen-for-attention dramatic, large-brimmed hats and bright, low-cut dresses in loud prints. She crossed busy streets recklessly, without bothering to check for oncoming traffic. Cars weren't ready for such an apparition; they swerved, screeched, honked, or stopped, but Zoriza was undisturbed. She waved and smiled at the terrified motorists like a celebrity, yelled at whoever dared to get in her way… queen of the neighborhood in a Fellini film. Her at-home manner was equally loud and explosive. She reacted to all twists and turns of fate with sincere, juicy laughter or with equally sincere, shameless screams and curses in several languages. A charming and rather impractical figure.

The building we lived in was nice. At the end of the well-maintained entry is a broad travertine staircase. It winds around a mesh well, inside which lords a large cage of intricate wrought iron – *ferro battuto* they call it – which once served as an elevator. The elevator was still there, but we were told that it was non-operational. Actually, the elevator is fine, but it needs a coin to coax it into motion, and coins, unfortunately, have disappeared from Italian monetary circulation. The cost of minting the elegant, beautifully designed 50- and 100-lira coins made of two concentric metals exceeded their face value. Some months later, a brilliant idea of a coin hung on a string next to the deposit box brought the elevator back to life. After the coin was inserted, the elevator whirred, hummed, gathered resolve, and moved heavily from floor to floor. At the destination, the coin was pulled out by the string and dangled again, ready for the next journey. I was impressed and amused by the simplicity of this solution and eventually discovered that many different pieces of equipment in Italy are operated by coin-and-string, even telephone tokens dangled next to payphones – proof of Italian good-natured ingenuity.

Just like Mario-the-absent-alleged-husband, Zoriza also worked at the *Opera di Roma;* she was an emergency seamstress. Sitting backstage during performances, she was responsible for fixing any developing wardrobe malfunctions. The pay, she said, was meager, but that didn't matter – she made good money renting rooms in her large apartment. Mario arranged for her this Opera job so they could spend more time together. It took several months before we understood their tangled history and only-in-Italy marital arrangement. Zoriza worked in the opera box office in Belgrade when Opera di Roma came on tour; that's how the two met. Love at first sight complicated their lives since Mario was married, and, in those days, divorces were not allowed in Italy. To complicate matters further, Zoriza could not immigrate to Italy without a family connection, even if the desirous party was the celebrated first choreographer of Opera di Roma. A clandestine, ingenious plot emerged: instead of Mario, Zoriza married Papa, Mario's father, who was a widower and the family's only eligible bachelor. She subsequently immigrated to Italy as her lover's stepmother. And Papa, in an ultimate gesture of male solidarity and dubious ethics, was the enabler of his sons' infidelity! I should have been upset by the deceit of Mario's wife, but instead, I was amused and inspired by this romance and by Mario's conjugal visits to our apartment. Never before and never after have I seen *in vivo* arguments so loud and screams so shamelessly unrestrained as between Zoriza and Mario. As in Fellini's films, they hurled at each other curses and framed photos, vases and plates. And then, unexpectedly, the mood changed; they kissed and made up and immediately closed the door. I loved this crazy drama; it was so passionate, so Italian, and so full of life. *Amore*!

On the ground floor of our building was a coffee bar. A huge, shiny machine hissed out fluffy *cappuccinos*, fragrant *espressos,* and beautiful *latte caldos* – frothed warm milk with or without a touch of coffee. The glass cabinetry tempted with *tramezzini* (triangular sandwiches made on white, crustless bread), croissants, and strange, tasty, crusty-crunchy rolls layered with slices of ham so thin that they were almost transparent. In any neighborhood bar such as this one, most customers were regular: the same people dropped in daily on their way to or from work, and they usually ordered the same things. Everyone knew each other, and their conversations – for they talked – were unrestrained and real. This warm familiarity was part of the texture of Italian life, which I, with time, learned to know, practice, and love.

Italians consume alcohol mostly in the latter parts of the day, but Zoriza had a different routine. She called the bar first thing each morning and, in a hoarse voice, with no introduction, announced: *due cognac*. The essence of the call was not who she was, what she ordered, or how much, because the order was always the same. The call simply announced that she was up and it was time to start the day. *Subito*, right away. The rest was a perfectly orchestrated, well-rehearsed, and well-timed operation. Immediately after she hung up the phone, Zoriza opened the front door and left it ajar. Moments later, a waiter in a starched white jacket appeared, carrying on a shiny tray two glasses filled to the brim with the amber liquid. He didn't even enter the apartment; no time was wasted on pleasantries. In her pajamas, with messy hair and a greasy face still awaiting the morning ministrations, Zoriza was at the door, her attire and demeanor in sharp contrast with the formally elegant waiter. She downed the cognac without ceremony, straight from the tray, one after the other, across the threshold, placing the empty glasses back on the tray. Perhaps she was a little embarrassed and thought we wouldn't notice, but most likely, she was simply too much in a hurry for those morning cognacs to waste time on form. She surely had an open account because I had never noticed any financial transactions accompanying the ritual.

And the market nearby, which made Mama so happy... It's winter, and we still can't imagine that it will stink during the warmer months. And how! Whatever didn't sell – vegetables, fruit, fish, crustaceans – was dumped onto a huge pile and rotted in the warm Roman air until it was hauled away at the crack of dawn the following morning. Sometimes, for example, during the surprisingly frequent *sciopero generale* – general strikes when all of Rome stood still – the market trash was not collected for days, and the stench was palpable even in our apartment.

There were other tenants in Zoriza's apartment. In the room adjacent to ours lived a family of Hungarian Jews, Eva and Ernesto, with a teenage son, Alex. They, too, wandered through Europe, hoping to get to America. During the first few days, I learned two phrases in Hungarian from them: *nem tudom* (I don't know) and *kis lábujj* (little toe). Saving on bus fare, Ernesto walked in new shoes that were a size too small; he shouldn't have bought them, but they were on sale, and there was a theory that they would stretch with prolonged use. Now his *kis lábujj* bled with an open wound, and he couldn't wear any shoes at all. After a few weeks, the Hungarians left, and Heniek Gwiazda from Łódź rented their room; I remembered him from some summer camps.

* * *

We don't speak Italian. It soon becomes painfully clear that it's hard to find anyone here with whom we can communicate in our existing repertoire of English, German, Polish, or Russian. Yiddish, the *lingua franca* on which my parents relied all of their lives, was also of no use. Roman Jews – a community of roughly 15,000 – speak a dialect known as Giudesco, similar to Hebrew. The foreign language of choice taught in Italian schools is French. In short, communication has become a challenge.

An important moment, clear only in retrospect – this was the beginning of linguistic isolation, which, for my parents and for many others, followed them in some form for the rest of their lives. We didn't know yet about idiomatic phrases, cultural isolation, and the soft borders of not understanding, even if you knew all the words. For now, it is clear that we need to study Italian quickly, *presto*; otherwise, we will not be able to function in Rome.

CHAPEAU BAS, HIAS AND JOINT. THANK YOU!

We provide services to Jewish immigrants and refugees, and others in need – without regard to their religion, nationality, or ethnic background.

We protect the most vulnerable ones, helping them build new lives and reuniting them with their families in safety and freedom.

We rescue people whose lives are in danger for being who they are. The Torah tells us that we must help the stranger among us. This, and our core belief that we must "repair the world" (tikkun olam, in Hebrew), are the driving principles behind our global work.

HIAS Global

I quickly and unexpectedly secured a job in Rome at HIAS, the Hebrew Immigrant Aid Society—the organization that had been the guiding force behind our immigration. Our caseworker, Mrs. Bottone, presented the opportunity. During my initial interview, we spoke English; then, someone in the waiting room needed help and spoke Yiddish, while someone else was searching for a Russian speaker to translate a document. I thought I was simply being helpful, but within half an hour, I had a job offer. It never occurred to me to ask about the terms of employment—mostly because I wouldn't have known what to ask, and, truth be told, I didn't care. I trusted they would be fair and, more importantly, I would be helping.

The HIAS task is to marginalize hatred by helping to resettle the oppressed from countries pervaded by racism and persecution to other, hospitable places. The organization started in 1881 in a modest storefront on the Lower East Side to provide comfort and aid to thousands of poor Jews fleeing waves of virulent antisemitism and often bloody pogroms in Eastern Europe. HIAS offered them shelter and meals, jobs, language, and civic training, helped locate families and friends throughout America, and offered railroad tickets at reduced prices to join them. By now, they helped over four and a half million people, from loaning them the $25 landing fee to those who washed up on Ellis Island in 1904 to serving survivors of gender-based violence in Uganda in the 2000s. In the current world where immigration and migration are the hope for life for so many, **"HIAS stands for a world in which refugees find welcome, safety, and freedom."** It now operates on the ground in over twenty countries in Africa, Europe, the Middle East, Latin America, and the United States. It helps over a million people annually.

During WWII, HIAS helped hundreds of Jews to escape from Europe to the US via passage from Marseille in occupied France, including the families of philosopher Hannah Arendt, painter Marc Chagall, and former Secretary of State Henry Kissinger. More recent well-known recipients of HIAS services include Jan Koum and Sergey Brin, who, along with their families and hundreds of thousands of others, escaped antisemitism in the Soviet Union. Koum was sixteen when he immigrated with his mother, a cleaning lady. He created WhatsApp and sold a majority stake to Facebook for $19.3 billion. Brin was six when he came to the US with his family of mathematicians; he later became the co-founder of Google, with a current net worth estimated by Forbes to exceed $150 billion. In 2009, Brin donated $1 million to HIAS. His mother Eugenia, a retired research scientist at NASA, has actively participated in HIAS's work as a board member, national chair for *myStory*, a project dedicated to documenting Jewish emigration to America, and headed the project of digitization of the HIAS archives.

In 1956, HIAS resettled Jews fleeing Hungary after the Soviet invasion and helped evacuate the Jewish community of Egypt. In 1959, they set up operations in Miami to assist Jews fleeing the Castro revolution in Cuba. In the 1960s, via its office in Naples, they rescued the Jewish communities of Algeria and Libya and arranged for the migration of Moroccan Jews. In 1968, it was us and Jews fleeing from Czechoslovakia after the fall of the "Prague Spring." In 1977 came the dramatic airlift of Ethiopian Jews straight to Israel. In 1979, after the fall of the Shah, HIAS helped hundreds of Iranian Jews with close family in the US to resettle here. Extraordinary work.

In 1975, the State Department asked HIAS to aid in resettling Vietnamese, Cambodian, and Laotian refugees. Not Jews. That year alone, HIAS resettled 3,600 of them. Afterward, HIAS expanded its resettlement work to non-Jewish refugees.

Our path unexpectedly crossed with other HIAS beneficiaries when, along with a number of other families than in Rome, HIAS invited us to a Passover Seder in Castellammare di Stabia, a small town in Campania on the coast of the Bay of Naples. I was puzzled – why there? How many Jews can there be in this Castellammare? I was surprised to find a huge gathering, several hundred people – Jews who shared our fate of exile after persecutions in Libya and Morocco. They came to Naples by boat and awaited passage to Israel, all thanks to HIAS. We didn't have a language in common, and our mimicked conversations lacked subtlety, but all of us knew the story of Passover as a struggle for freedom. Years later, I learned from books what these people went through before leaving their homes; they also left cemeteries behind. But there, in Castellammare, I looked at them with envy, amazed and delighted by their large, multigenerational families: parents and grandparents, brothers and sisters, aunts and uncles, and many children. The Holocaust didn't touch them. Our "Polish" families were so tiny in comparison.

All HIAS beneficiaries are treated with dignity and presented with clear expectations: to integrate into their new homelands, to study, work, and become valued members of society, and to eventually repay the expenses of their own passage for the benefit of others after them. Of course, I knew none of that when we arrived in Rome; I only knew how to pronounce the magic acronym "Hi-as." The abbreviation that was their first cable address and by which they became known worldwide.

The Roman office was on the second floor of an inconspicuous building on Via del Corso. I don't even recall a plaque on the front door. Inside, the space was sparse, functional, almost sterile—simple office furniture, no decorations or comforts, just the basics. The staff, about twenty people, was a Tower of Babel—a multinational mishmash. I assume we were all Jewish. Some colleagues I rarely encountered and don't even remember their names; others were part of my daily routine, our responsibilities closely interwoven.

There were four Italians: my supervisor, Sergio—stocky, plump, slightly balding; the warm, broad-smiled, maternal Mrs. Bottone; and two young women, Vicky and Marina, who worked in accounting. Vicky and I shared a special connection—we both loved an afternoon espresso. Most days, we stole away to the bar downstairs for a few minutes, enjoying a brief, quiet moment.

Jenny, a pretty, soft-spoken Englishwoman with long blond hair, worked with insurance companies, arranging coverage for the transit, storage, and contents of our lifts, as well as temporary health insurance for all of us. Suzy, a caseworker, was fluent in French, which proved helpful for some families.

Then there were the two American women—Mrs. Miller, jovial and wiry, a Chicago native with strong black-framed glasses and bold, op-art patterned sweaters, and the elegant, feminine Mrs. Dresner, who accessorized every outfit with a beautiful cashmere shawl. Mrs. Dresner liked me. She and her husband had season tickets to the symphony, and when he didn't attend, she occasionally invited me as a special treat.

The office's *lingua franca* was English. Mrs. Miller managed a rough Yiddish and sounded convincing, though my high school teacher, the unforgettable Pani Toporowska, would not have approved of her syntax or grammar.

Bottone, Miller, Dresner, and Suzy were caseworkers. Each of them guided a group of families through the tangles of the Roman process. During the original interviews, they established a path according to each family's wishes, then met periodically, answered questions, comforted, tried to alleviate concerns, held hands, wiped tears, and helped at every turn – a cross between a coach, a therapist, and a caring friend. Mrs. Bottone looked after our family.

There were several of us from Poland working in HIAS, all about the same age, all multilingual. Maja was Mrs. Miller's assistant; our American paths crossed later in Ann Arbor. Wanda Gruber, who years later returned to Poland and made quite a career as Wanda Rapaczyńska, assisted Mrs. Bottone.

Staff of HIAS, Rome, Early 1969 *(I don't remember everyone's names.)*

In the front row, second from the left, is Vicky, my coffee companion. Next to her are Sergio, my boss, and Mrs. Miller, a caseworker. Standing first on the right are Wanda Gruber and Maja, both from Warsaw, with Mrs. Dresner, a caseworker, in the rear. Next to Mrs. Dresner, also in the rear, is Jenny.

Standing second from the left is Marina; beside her, laughing, is Mrs. Bottone, our family's caseworker, followed by Suzy. The elegant woman with a string of pearls, positioned in the center behind Mrs. Miller, is Mrs. Ellis, the administrative head of the office. I am in the front row, first on the right.

I do not remember who assisted Mrs. Dresner or Suzy. I also forgot the name of our very pretty receptionist from Katowice. And there was Julian, a boy from Warsaw who was a messenger; he delivered documents, mostly to various embassies. Work was piling on, and it was clear that there would be increasingly more. The post-March avalanche gathered in size and momentum; Jews were leaving Poland on every train to Vienna. People said that everyone would leave.

* * *

Despite the fact that we've been exiled for Zionism – "those who regard Israel as their homeland" provoked Gomułka – the facts of where we immigrated prove this accusation false.

Dariusz Stola cites the following data from the Polish Bureau of Passports of the Ministry of Internal Affairs regarding the influx of applications for permission to emigrate to Israel: "This year [1968], 3,437 people left Poland declaring that they are emigrating to Israel. The exodus reached its height in 1969 when 7,674 people emigrated." In summary, 11,111 Polish Jews left the country during those two years alone. Where did they go?

The document entitled "Immigration to Israel 1948-1972," compiled by the Israeli Central Bureau of Statistics, states that 1,349 people came to Israel in 1968, reporting Poland as their last country of residence – that's **39%** of those who departed with Israeli visas. The majority, 61%, went to Western Europe or to North America. In 1969, the number of people who reached Israel was 1,735, or **23%** of the total. 77% went elsewhere – more than in 1968, likely because eventually, additional options of Sweden and Denmark became available. **Altogether, for those two years, only 28% percent turned out to be "Zionists" while seventy-two percent of emigrants, 8,027 people, emigrated elsewhere.**

Distribution of destinations to which the exiled Polish "Zionists" resettled in 1968-69

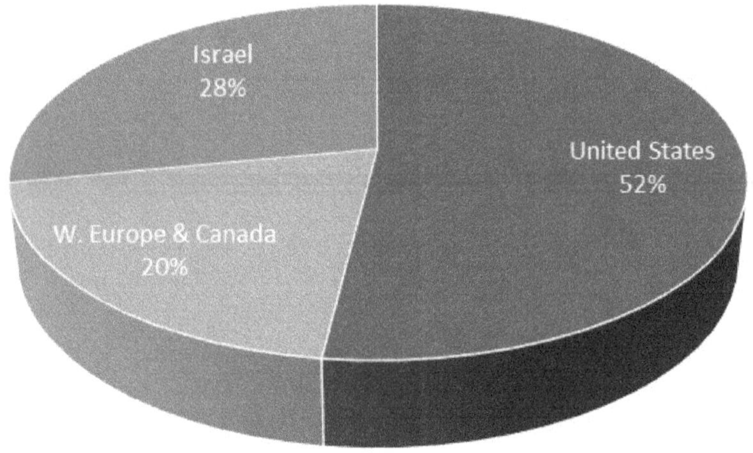

Roberta Elliott, then Vice President at the central HIAS bureau in New York, shared the following data on Polish Jews who arrived in the U.S. as refugees: in 1968—491 people; in 1969—1,193 people; and in 1970—4,128 people. I include 1970 since most of those who left Poland in 1969, like us, had to wait in Rome for a visa and likely reached the U.S. the following year.

In total, over those first two years, 5,812 people immigrated to the U.S., while 2,215 resettled in Scandinavia, Western Europe, and Canada, and 3,084 "Zionists" went to Israel. The pattern continued—HIAS reported that in 1971 alone, they helped another 1,152 people resettle in the US.

* * *

I reflected upon those events in later years, with added knowledge and decades of distance. HIAS ensured that thousands of stateless Jewish exiles of all ages and circumstances were accepted in various "good" countries. They raised money, reached the legislators and immigration power brokers, and created effective behind-the-scenes pressures. Banished without citizenship and right of return, we were accepted by our adoptive homelands **unconditionally**. No one was left to fend for themselves; everyone settled somewhere. I did not understand this in Rome; that's not what a 20-year-old thinks about, but the enormity, nobility, and effectiveness of the HIAS undertaking is really **impressive**. My deepest gratitude and respect. CHAPEAU BAS.

* * *

While in Rome, every family received a modest monthly allowance to cover expenses. This money was provided, administered, and distributed by Joint, the American Jewish Joint Distribution Committee. Founded in 1914, Joint has a lofty and beautiful mission: it "… lifts lives and strengthens communities" in 70 countries. "We rescue Jews in danger, provide aid to vulnerable Jews, develop innovative solutions to Israel's most complex social challenges, cultivate a Jewish future, and lead the Jewish community's response to crisis." Formidable.

In contrast to the punitive costs and multifaceted attacks on our dignity in Poland, we were treated with empathy and care in Vienna and in Rome. Our stay was fully subsidized and well-orchestrated. Someone worked out the method and seamlessly organized our new Italian travel documents and visas, made travel reservations, and bought tickets, including the journey to the final destination. If needed, one could even get suitcases for the journey. We didn't pay a dime. Our only cost was time and accumulating trauma.

None of it was a gift or a handout; HIAS is not a charity. After some time in America, each family received a polite letter from HIAS with a detailed account of accumulated expenses. The letter explained that this is an invoice that represents an interest-free loan **to be repaid, however and whenever possible**. There was no pressure, no demands, no dunning phone calls. Pay as you can. I told my parents and HIAS that I would repay this loan for our family, but it would take me a while to get started. They agreed. I paid nothing until I finished my studies. Afterward, I paid everything back with pleasure, gratitude, and with generous interest in hope that this money would help another family start a new life. After all, there are still many people who, by accident of birth, live among evil and are blamed for being born the way they were born.

Esther and Zygmunt Binder, Detroit, Michigan (1975)

EXTRAORDINARY WORK

*You pay for freedom with your entire self –
so call it freedom that you can, paying always anew,
possess yourself.*

Pope John Paul II

Sergio, my boss, was responsible for the routine common to all families – he knew all the steps, anticipated what was next, and kept track of progress. Fine-tuned over years of experience and thousands of families, the procedure incorporated the specific requirements of each embassy, so each submittal was complete and processed smoothly. Common to all was a detailed autobiography of each person and a lengthy questionnaire specific to the chosen country. After a thorough check by the caseworkers, the paperwork was submitted to the embassy, and if complete, an appointment was set for the initial interview. Soon thereafter, the required medical exams were scheduled. Weeks went by in-between while the embassy examined the application, completed all the background checks, and secured sponsors for each family. Sometimes, the process ended in denial because something was objectionable in the life story or with health, and the process started anew with another country and another embassy. Sergio was good at what he did; he anticipated all the developments, knew people in various embassies – everywhere, actually – and called them frequently, explaining and pressuring that family X filed papers three weeks ago, and no one had contacted them thus far; he called various depots and warehouses to find space for the lifts which started arriving from Vienna in bulky numbers… he lived on the phone.

On my first day on the job, Sergio described my role as "hovering over each process, person, and piece of paper so nothing gets hung up or forgotten." I expected mainly administrative work, but nothing could be further from the truth. The most challenging and time-consuming were matters beyond routine – the stuff that just happens to traumatized people without language skills in a foreign city. Someone broke a tooth, a leg, or the only pair of reading glasses; lost a suitcase or a document; took the wrong bus or the right bus in the wrong direction; went all the way to the suburbs and is now terrifying the local police station with a panic attack in Polish. Mrs. R. had just arrived from Vienna; her elderly parents, still in Poland, were to follow within weeks, but the father suddenly suffered a heart attack and died, and she hopes to be allowed back into Poland for a few days to attend the funeral and help organize the mother's departure (the answer was NO!). A girl who discovered she was pregnant and pleaded for help in arranging an abortion (Really? In Catholic Rome?); we were able to help her. A Jewish doctor in Rome agreed to perform the abortion. Altogether, a plethora of human needs landed daily in our laps, and I simply had to juggle, improvise, prioritize, and deal with them.

Unexpectedly, among my daily tasks, a lot of time was spent contacting individual families. HIAS and the embassies expected the petitioners to be available as soon as needed at the drop of a hat. After all, this is now their only priority. True, but not completely practical. People were eager, but they didn't sit at home waiting for the phone to ring. And, of course, there were no cell phones. To get in touch with our families, I called the only available number, the home of their Italian landlord. Sergio helped me compile a list of Italian phrases for every likely eventuality, and, using those, I asked for the *persona polacca* (sic!). I was lucky if they were home. Otherwise, we proceeded to the blind-leading-the-deaf phase of the conversation in which I tried to explain who I was and to leave some instructions. I recited from the cheat sheet that I called from the *ufficio immigrazione,* and would they please convey to Mr. or Mrs. to contact us immediately? Us means HIAS, which I spell in Italian style, **H**otel-**I**mola-**A**ncona-**S**avona. I did it well; I caught the beautiful Italian sing-song quickly, the few initial sentences rolled off my tongue fluently and without any accent, and my Italian interlocutors usually didn't understand that this was IT, my entire repertoire, that I really don't speak the language. I even tried an honest admission "*Mi scusi, Signora, ma io veramente non parlo l'Italiano*" ("I am sorry, Madam, but I really don't speak Italian"), but that usually got a laugh.

Still, my monologue was the easy part. I tried politely to end the call, but no, it was now their turn, and they weren't about to miss this opportunity. After all, this was a chance to discuss life in general and theirs in particular, with an official person from the *ufficio immigrazione.* They usually started by telling me their tale of woe: how difficult it is to have Polish Jews as tenants. I hung onto every word, desperately trying to grasp the meaning and, simultaneously, as they poured their hearts out, I feverishly flipped through the pages of my Italian-English dictionary. Someone hadn't paid rent on time; came home late at night without a key, rang the doorbell, and woke the entire household; the shared bathroom hadn't been cleaned—who was supposed to clean up after them?! Someone left the refrigerator door open, spoiling half the food; Biscotti, the family dog, had been let out onto the staircase — *grazie a Dio,* he didn't run into traffic(!); the family argued constantly, and loudly — *let them find another place to live!* Someone even asked, quite reasonably, if a translator couldn't visit every so often and help resolve the accumulated grievances and misunderstandings. Life itself; endless variants of the collision between my linguistic ignorance, ordinary Italian talkativeness, and genuine need. In complicated cases, I had to ask Sergio for help. He would have loved to assist, but he was usually too busy, glued to the phone — sometimes on two lines, a black receiver in each ear. He, too, waited, more or less patiently, for me to become self-sufficient — meaning, to reach some proficiency in Italian.

In a few weeks I managed, limping. And a few months later I spoke Italian fluently.

In more urgent matters, or when all else failed, I sent telegrams, which was easier because the communication was one-way, without conversation. I called the post office (*telegrammi, per gentilezza*), and spelled out my several telegrams each day because they were, of course, in Polish. Within a few weeks, I recognized the ladies who worked in the *telegrammi* office, and they recognized me. I probably was the only one who sent daily batches of telegrams in Polish. We greeted each other by name and exchanged pleasantries before getting to the task. The Italian alphabet has only twenty-four letters, and its spelling code words are mostly names of Italian cities — that was easy to learn. So the word *proszę* ("please" in Polish) becomes *Palermo-Roma-Otrento-Savona-Zara-Empoli,* while *natychmiast* ("immediately") spells out as *Napoli-Ancona-Torino-York-Como-Hotel-Milano-Imola-Ancona-Savona-Torino.*

The ladies at *telegrammi* were incredulous at the strange

words my spelled dictation produced and sympathized with me: *La vostra lingua è molto difficile*—"Your language is very difficult." Yes.

It was much easier to communicate with the embassies because everything happened in English. Most often, I dealt with the American embassy on Via Veneto, but I also called, visited, and spent countless hours in several others, usually to explain some oversight, to fix something, or to deliver a necessary document. The papers could go by messenger, but Sergio often sent me to deliver them, hoping that I would get to talk with the recipient and somehow move matters along. At the onset, I was getting lost in the city, struggling with security guards who didn't recognize the new face, and wandering from floor to floor looking for the right office or window. All that I learned rather quickly. I knew which entrance to use. The guards waved at me – routine. More and more often, I was asked to translate a document or a conversation. It was not my job; it would be appropriate to send the matter to the caseworker, but the embassy staff also learned that I somehow managed, and the caseworker's packed-to-the-gills calendar simply meant that the matter would move more efficiently if I participated.

My salary at HIAS was forty thousand lira per week, or about sixty-five US dollars at the then-current exchange rate. Per week! But to me, it was a fortune. Together with our allowance from Joint, it enabled Mama to shop at the stinking market nearby and allowed me a small treat such as my daily espresso with Vicky or even an occasional, luxurious *gelato*.

The work was not easy. I dealt with matters which, until recently, I couldn't even imagine. I explained to people what would happen next and what is reasonable to expect, I helped translate their biographies into English, and I consoled the ones for whom matters didn't go smoothly – perhaps someone told them that Canada does not accept older people or that someone with a health history similar to theirs just got turned down. "What now?" they lamented. "There are other countries," I persuade, "they won't leave anyone behind" – all the while aware that I am talking about issues of vital importance to traumatized people with suspended lives, in shock.

There were also those—not many, but there were—who were not in a hurry at all; often young, without families, they enjoyed this all-expenses-paid Roman vacation. They toured, partied, delayed, and then there was a young man who pretended to be sick whenever an appointment was scheduled for him at the embassy. Patiently, they gave him another date and time, and he carelessly traveled out of town when the appointed time came. When confronted that it all costs much money and effort, he replied arrogantly: "So what? Will you send me back to Poland?".

Thankfully, there weren't many like him.

MY ROMAN LESSONS

To call it a setback, is like calling Expulsion from Eden
a minor misunderstanding

Sharon Kay Penman, American novelist

At night, in hushed whispers, my parents confessed their worries and fears about the future to each other. They likely talked during the day as well — there was plenty of free time — but darkness was a blessing. Our beds were just a few feet apart, offering little privacy, so I couldn't help but overhear their concerns: that they were neither young nor healthy, that they had no money and no head for business, and that they didn't speak English.

Tata was sixty-one when we left Poland. Mama was younger, barely fifty, but her health was frail, and her nerves were shattered after the losses of war and years in the Siberian labor camp. They both carried the weight of the enormous tragedy of the Holocaust. No one in Poland thought to create institutions to provide Jewish survivors with therapy, medicine, or even empathy. They were left to their own lonely, meager resources to cope with the unimaginable traumas that had become their lot in life — often surrounded by antisemitism, a constant reminder of who they were.

Were it not for exile, they would have eventually retired, rested, and collected their hard-earned, modest pensions. Mama could have shared stories of aches and pains, wives' tales, and the merits of various herbs and diets with other ladies in the packed, dingy waiting room of the medical clinic on Podwale Street. With its worn paint and fatigued furniture, it was therapeutic in its own right—a fitting companion to the few minutes one got to spend with the rushed and overworked doctor. But Mama would never visit there again. Instead, she would see an American doctor, struggle to explain her symptoms and understand the advice, and leave feeling inadequate and perhaps humiliated. And doctors were expensive in America.

My parents imagined and expected the worst.

Tata is a master brush-maker. Do they need brush-makers in America, or are all brushes imported from elsewhere? And what if Tata falls ill? I am beginning to understand just how difficult this forced emigration is for them—how frightening. This "Roman Holiday" is not much of a holiday for them. They have had enough adventure during the war to last a lifetime, perhaps several. What they crave now is routine and familiarity. "Safe," "calm," and "peaceful" would be the greatest rewards for having survived. When they dared to dream, they dreamed of "security."

But their lives have been upended and suspended, with no clear path forward or certainty about when and where they will begin again. Like everyone else here, they must wait. HIAS provides a measure of safety, but "calm," "peaceful," and "secure" still feel impossibly far away.

For me, it's different. Rome is magical. I drink good coffee and indulge in gelati, their improbable colors gleaming from the glass cases of cafés along my route to work. I already have favorite flavors. And I am busy—too busy from morning to night to wait for anything, too young to worry. Yet even I am anxious for my real life to begin and cannot quite imagine the new "normal" that awaits us in America.

* * *

After each family met with their assigned caseworker, the constructed dossier landed on Sergio's desk. He reviewed it for oversights and inconsistencies and passed it on to me so that I could start making routine appointments with the designated embassy and doctors. I called the families as well to explain the process. Sergio didn't have a language in common with most of them, so, aside from their caseworker, I will be their contact for the critical months ahead while the plan they constructed was put into motion.

LESSON ONE: THE CAT

I remember a brother and sister, roughly my parent's age. They each left a professorship in humanities at the University of Warsaw; it will not be easy for them to rebuild their professional lives in a foreign country. Amazingly, they emigrated with their cat; apparently, this is their only family. The cat was perhaps the first pet of our emigration to arrive in Rome; there is no procedure or budget for pets. Is it ridiculous and fair to claim that the cat is Jewish and has been exiled? Is the cat to be treated as baggage or as family? What about vaccines? The cat turns out to be a time-consuming logistic challenge, likely to require a costly, lengthy quarantine. Sergio was visibly displeased, *"We are not here to take care of cats. People are waiting!"* He muttered under his breath. The cat's family despaired at every turn, fearing that this was the end, that someone would say at any moment that the cat simply could not go to America, and parting with the cat was incomprehensible. In Poland, the cat was a loved member of their household, practically its centerpiece. Would they have to leave it here, in Rome, where cats are born on the street and are destined to die there… scrawny and scabby, they fend for themselves on every cobbled corner. I imagined the brother and sister's sleepless nights fearing for their beloved pet, imagining him scrounging for food around Largo di Torre Argentina, in hopeless competition with hundreds of other, tougher cats and rats adept in the art of survival. A nightmare. Danuta Trautman told me that some departing Warsaw Jews took their beloved four-legged friends to a well-reputed pet hotel in the suburbs and prepaid their room, board, hygiene, and any arising medical needs "for life." She also told me of a persistent rumor that these pets were put to sleep within a year.

I, who until recently sipped mulled wine at the Student Union in Wrocław, and my biggest challenge were differential equations—I suddenly began to understand that it's not just about the love of the cat but also about trust and responsibility. All this dawns on me suddenly, and I start speaking to them about the fate of the cat gently, trying to mitigate Sergio's grumpy rumblings, the tone of which is unmistakable. It is clear to them that Sergio is not an ally in this cat affair, and whenever they walk into our office, they head straight for my desk, avoiding their nemesis. This story has a happy ending: the cat eventually emigrated to America with a separate plane ticket, seated between his two loving caregivers. And a lesson: *responsibility* and *trust*.

LESSON TWO: THE COFFIN

Another elderly couple traveled, unbelievably, with a coffin which contained the remains of their only child. The whispered tale, which the couple confirmed in their written autobiographies, is that their daughter died as a child years ago of scarlet fever. I couldn't even imagine the miracles and layers of bribery that allowed for the coffin to be exhumed and taken out of Poland. How? I wondered. In a separate lift? And a question that weighs on me to this day: **What motivated this family to emigrate**? They likely lost their families in the Holocaust, then they lost the daughter, and now, older, childless, and incredibly burdened, they didn't want to stay in Poland, nor did they want the remains of their only child to stay in Poland. The coffin came to Rome from Vienna labeled as SPECIAL BAGGAGE. I didn't know where it was kept in Vienna, how it got to Rome, and where it was now. The Italian customs authorities demanded, reasonably, I think, that the coffin be opened and inspected. "Who knows what's inside," repeated nervously the clerk with whom I spoke. *Droga, Signorina, droga!__Drugs!* I was out of my league here; the matter was over my pay grade, and someone else blissfully took over.

The coffin had to be placed somewhere for the duration of its stay in Italy, the length of which could not be determined. There was talk of a crypt in the cemetery. In Italy, the dead are usually buried above ground in multi-story structures with numerous openings, where coffins are inserted like drawers in an old-fashioned apothecary cabinet. But a "drawer" for a coffin is forever, isn't it? Could we rent one instead? Or would a garage on the outskirts of the city be a more practical solution?

Jenny researched the matter and discovered that no one would insure the coffin unless it was opened and its contents documented.

Sergio could probably figure this out, but he didn't want to know about the coffin; better that he doesn't know, he said. He yelled at me not to get involved; others would handle this matter. But his instructions were unrealistic; we will eventually have to mention the coffin at the American Embassy – after all, we planned to ask for permission to import this unimaginable cargo. I couldn't just say that we ask to bring into the US a closed-and-shut coffin stored in an unknown location, containing alleged remains, which got here somehow. I was so entangled in the logistics that the tragedy and macabre of the situation almost eluded me. The parents of the coffin were different from the owners of the cat; they neither cried nor despaired – all this was long behind them. They were stoic, calm, and dignified; no demands. But it was clear to everyone that they would not go anywhere without the coffin. After many months, when I was leaving Italy, the complicated formalities were still underway. I worried – will my successor give this matter suitable attention? Will they speak with the parents gently?

I don't know how it all ended.

And a most painful lesson: *some losses are forever.*

LESSON THREE: MY IDENTITY

Leon from Szczecin left Poland alone. Somehow, his father was already in West Germany, and Leon hoped to join him. But his father died suddenly while Leon was still in Rome. We tried, but Leon did not get permission to go to the funeral. There was an open application for immigration to Germany, and Herr Consul feared—perhaps reasonably—that once in Germany, Leon would simply disappear. So the father was buried without his son present, and Leon's chances of going to Germany withered. After all, his stated and only acceptable reason was to reunite with his family, and suddenly, there was no family.

During heated discussions about Leon's case, the German consul took an interest in me. "You studied German in school?" he asked.

"No," I explained. "The foreign language in our school was English. I learned German from my Wrocław neighbors—Frau Kusch, who lived on the same floor as we did, and Frau Liebling, who lived in the next building and wore a winter coat even in the summer. She had circulation problems; her legs swelled, and she was always cold. She often asked me to walk her dog, which I did with pleasure."

"You were born in Breslau?" Herr Consul exclaimed, using the German name for my Polish birthplace. "Then you're German! We should talk soon about you emigrating to Germany."

A dilemma. It was not the proposed issue of emigrating to Germany – I never even gave it a thought – but simple *savoir vivre*: how to politely let him know that I am not German. In fact, "quite the contrary." I also promised myself to reflect later on the subtle issue of whether identity could be "quite the contrary," something opposite of who I really am. Herr Consul and I simply applied different criteria to the matter. His suggestion that I was born in Breslau sounded audacious to me – I was born in Poland, in Wrocław. For him and the people who shaped or dictated his views, the post-war land settlements were irrelevant, and my city was still Breslau. Finally, I promised myself to think about the boundaries of this new issue: is it a matter of linguistics? Of ethics? Of administration? Or – a scary but realistic alternative – of my own prejudices? Whatever it was, I was sure I was not German. The very notion bothered me.

The lesson that I keenly practice until today—and it's amazing how often it comes up—*is that my **identity is a matter of choice. MY CHOICE. Who I am and where I belong**—MY **IDENTITY**—depends on my point of view, mine alone.* Others may see it differently, but I and only I decide about my identity.

Only people and systems that practice ignorance or hatred usurp the right to determine the identity of others and judge them for that identity.

LESSON FOUR: THE PRICE OF OUR EXILE

A shocking development: one of "our" women tried to commit suicide in Rome. Her son, Jerzyk Lajnwand, attended our Jewish school in Wrocław, a couple of grades below me. Not even her family suspected that she struggled with such dark thoughts. She chose to jump in front of a train at Stazione Termini. As trains do at railroad stations, this one also moved very slowly; it didn't kill her but left her unconscious, terribly fractured, and with injured internal organs. Along with her family, I sat beside her hospital bed for several days and nights, in part because of my HIAS duties, in part out of Wrocław loyalty, and simple decency. What if she whispered something and no one understood? And another overwhelming lesson: *this is the price of our exile. **THIS IS THE PRICE OF OUR EXILE.***

Will the burden of these realizations end with our generation, or will our children carry it as well? The imprint of the Holocaust, the fears and tears, the anger and pain, the helplessness, the struggle with forgiveness, the "quite the contrary" – we carry this bundle, somehow, even if so few of our parents ever talked about it. Psychology refers to it as intergenerational transfer of trauma – the study of trauma that gets passed down from those with direct experience to subsequent generations. Will our children carry the struggle of losing a homeland?

THIS IS THE PRICE OF OUR EXILE.

* * *

But for most families, the time in Rome was simply a tightly woven tapestry of waiting and uncertainty. Some feared they would be refused entry to their chosen destination and eagerly, perhaps too eagerly, explained that their communist party membership was the only way to be promoted at work or to get an apartment with running water.

Miss Sabina, what shall I write?

The truth. They know everything anyway.

Some had very specific expectations; scared, confused, and somehow emboldened, they mistook HIAS for a travel bureau.

Miss Sabina, the best for us would be Florida. You know — because of my arthritis.

Truthfully, no, I didn't know. I was just an office girl, and my circumstances were quite similar to theirs — how could I arrange Florida for them? But in a private moment I did ask Mrs. Dresner if Florida is indeed a good place for people with arthritis. "Absolutely not; it's very humid – the worst for arthritis," said Mrs. Dresner. "A dry place like Arizona would be much better." So, next time I saw the couple, I asked cautiously: "Have you thought about Arizona? I hear that the dry climate…." But the suggestion irritated them; they didn't even let me finish. "Arizona?! What would we ever do in Arizona?!" I quickly agreed that it was a bad idea.

In the obligatory autobiographies required by all embassies, the authors sometimes invented a profession or enhanced their education, omitted a fact, embellished, understated or emphasized the importance of this or that life decision, or maintained that they are Jews, which apparently was not always the case. Many families with Polish-sounding surnames addressed the issue by explaining that the name was changed, yielding to external pressures. They claimed that their father or grandfather really was Goldberg, not Złotogórski ("Goldberg," in Yiddish, and "Zlotogorski" in Polish, both mean "Golden Mountain") and that they were forced to have a Polish-sounding name in the time of war, at the directive of the communist party, in the army, at work, to avoid having their child bullied in school... I knew many families for whom that was true. There were even anecdotes about it. *Mr. Kowalski applies for a name change; he wants to be Nowak. "The clerk fumes: "Didn't you just change your name from Rosenberg to Kowalski a few months ago?" "Yes, I did," explains Mr. Kowalski. "But there is a new problem now: people ask what my name was before it was Kowalski..."*

Later, in our new adoptive homelands, some of my friends indeed returned to the real Jewish surnames abandoned in Poland by their parents.

"WE DON'T WANT YOU HERE!"

Our departure in December 1968 was relatively early in the wave of the post-March exodus. The pace accelerated since then and now, proverbially, all roads led to Rome. New trains arrived from Vienna almost daily, each carrying more shaken-to-the-core Jewish families from all over Poland. The folders with their stories would be on my desk a few days later, and I would be learning new lessons.

For the rest of my life, I'll be keenly aware that these Roman lessons were merely the first step in comprehending the enormity of our losses. *WHAT DOES IT MEAN IN THE DEEPEST SENSE TO BE EXPELLED FROM YOUR HOMELAND?* Homeland is usually an eternal birthright, isn't it? Unless your homeland no longer wants you, like a parent who orders a child to leave home. Go, and never come back!

Emigration is very different – you leave one place and go to another *BY CHOICE*. You thought it through, you decided, you will give it your best shot and hope it works out. And, if it doesn't, you can always go back. We had no such option. The fate of an exile is to search for a new home, to wait until it reveals itself, to change, to molt, to adapt. But what if you can't adapt? What if the new place never becomes HOME?

A girl from Warsaw, about my age, told me she didn't know they were Jewish until the day of their departure; the accusations and insults ubiquitously hurled at the Jews had nothing to do with her. She even confessed to having been a bit of an antisemite. Only on the train did her parents tell her that this was not a vacation; that they were Jewish and would not return from this journey. Her father worked in some ministry; they were an assimilated family with a Polish surname and deeply hidden ancestral roots. When someone discovered their shameful Jewish secret, the ministry fired the offender on the spot, staining him with some crime of disloyalty to Poland and to its people. There was no hope for another job. Quietly, the parents made their plans to leave. The girl did not even sign the paper, forfeiting her Polish citizenship. Somehow, her parents managed to pick up her travel Documents; the door to their apartment was locked, and all their belongings were intact. The personal history of this family will not be easy to translate or to explain.

A couple in Wałbrzych, the Zweigs, owners of a spice-and-colonial-goods store, were unceremoniously walked out of their apartment on Aleja Wyzwolenia 54, each carrying two suitcases. Their spacious apartment was then sealed by the authorities, plundered subsequently of the more expensive content, and finally turned over to new tenants, members of the party. These events were recounted to me by Lea Chaya Rozwadowska, who lived with her family in the same building. Lea, a little girl then, scared and curious, tried to get a closer look at the proceedings, but her family did not allow it for fear of "being found out." It took years for Lea to understand the hushed concern: they, too, were Jewish, but it was a secret.

Sometimes, there was great joy when part of the family that stayed behind in Poland arrived in Rome—now the family was reunited. Sometimes, there was great sadness and paralyzing fear because the family needed to separate. "Our son will go first," they told me in trembling voices, trying to convince themselves that this is for the best. "He has a good profession... he will get settled and prepare everything." But, in reality, they swallowed tears and choked with fear, unsure of the length of this upcoming separation. Will they ever see each other again? The older generation probably remembered similar goodbyes in times of war.

Our world collapsed within months. The March Events, strikes at universities, being labeled "the fifth column," arrests, "suspended in rights of a student," posters full of anti-Jewish and anti-Israeli slogans, loss of employment, public slander, the ridiculous "Zionists to Siam," closure of our modest Jewish institutions – congregations, schools, clubs, and cooperatives where many of our parents worked, especially in Lower Silesia.

My Jewish school, the only school I ever went to from 1st grade to matriculation, was now no longer Jewish. They closed the Jewish youth club on Świdnicka Street, where I often went for Saturday evening dances. That's also where, in the Poetry Club, I learned to love Tuwim and Pawlikowska–Jasnorzewska. The Jewish Theater stopped touring; people said that its director, star, and good angel, Ida Kaminska, also plans to leave. Hushed conversations at night. Mama's tears because she has two brothers in Poland, her only family after Shoah... And a decision – in truth, I was the one who forced it- let's leave right away; there is nothing to wait for, and it will only get worse. In bottomless sadness and disappointment, outraged and offended, I didn't want to live with my head bowed and to atone for the implied guilt of my Jewish birth.

Ewa Herbst describes the moment of her decision to leave in the preface of her moving book of poetry, *"Document Podróży"*: ("Travel Document," Wydawnictwo Austeria, 2017, 23-24.) "I would like to decide only for myself, but I know that my decision will affect all members of my family [...] Dad had already declared that he is staying. My 19-year-old brother decided to leave after a very unpleasant incident he experienced. Mom's only sister is leaving with her whole family; both she and her husband lost their jobs; they also fear for the future of their children. Mom herself would like to leave, but I know she won't if I decide to stay.

It is late evening; I lie on the couch in my room. Mom is sitting on the legs of the couch, Dad in the chair next to me, or perhaps the other way around. No one says anything.; they await my verdict. [...] Finally, I say with a clenched heart, "I'm leaving." [...]

Dad walks out. He falls on the couch in the next room and sobs deeply, like a child.

Our family ceases to exist."

Afterward, everything accelerated as if in an old Chaplinesque film – the promise of Israeli visas, application for permission to leave Poland, permission granted – and a tough deadline of three weeks to liquidate our lives and to depart. Selling whatever we could and giving away the rest, buying the pathetic merchandise available in Polish stores with hopes that there would be some use for it in our new, yet-to-be-defined lives. Neighbors, like vultures, circle around, waiting for the scraps of our belongings we may leave behind. Paying fees and collecting stamps in endless lines. Packing, customs clearance,

Four classmates at the Reunion of our "excursion" in Israel, 1993. From left: Sara Levison (Chicago), Lutek Fiszbin (Haifa), Staszek Szpetner (Tel Aviv), Sabina Baral (then Binder Way, San Francisco).

In 2009-10, Staszek and Lutek helped organize our class reunion in Wrocław on the 45th anniversary of our baccalaureate. Sara didn't go to that reunion; she didn't want to go to Poland ever again.

faster, faster… Saying goodbye to those who had the courage to come and say goodbye. The train, the border… And now, barely months later, we are in Rome. Everything in our lives has changed, and the only sure thing is that more changes will come; we will be searching for HOME for some time to come.

Looking with a bit of perspective, it was clear that our decision to leave Poland was not made by weighing options, with awareness of consequences; it was not the chosen best alternative; it was THE ONLY alternative. But now, in Rome, my parents had time to think, and I struggled to integrate the in-your-face lessons of my job. Separated from the life we knew and no other vision available in its place, we could begin to comprehend the consequences. It will take years before we will know the full price. I think that everyone was stunned – even the boy who pretended to be sick to avoid embassy appointments. Or, perhaps, especially him.

* * *

Edward, my future husband, left Poland in June of 1969 by ferry from the Polish port of Świnoujscie directly to Ystad in Sweden, days after receiving his Medical School diploma. Five Jewish boys from the city of Bytom, each alone, were on that ferry: Misio Edelman, Adam Letzter, Wiktor Fried, Benek Bernholz, and Edward. In the port, left behind, five families waved goodbye. Girlfriends, friends, FIVE MOTHERS, Holocaust survivors. I cannot imagine their despair when the ferry pulled away. Edward's Mother Hela, pregnant and widowed in 1944, two months before her only son was born, now bought for 100,000 zlotys his right to life in dignity, waved goodbye, and remained alone.

They met once for a few days in Bulgaria… In 1973, Martin (Mietek) Penner, Hela's friend from student days, came for her from Australia. This was the first time he told her that he had always been in love with her. After surviving the slave labor camp in Płaszów, after Schindler's factory, he left Poland when WWII was over, as soon as he could, as far as he could, to Australia. He never married and returned years later to propose to the love of his life, the then fifty-year-old Hela. She followed him to Melbourne, where Edward visited them often. We now go together every year to lay stones on their graves.

My youth, grounded in trust in my own abilities and a well-thought-out vision of the future, ended in Rome. I thought then that I would never again be young or carefree.

Yet, somehow, I still knew how to laugh. In rare moments of blessed levity, I set aside what happened and let myself believe that this, here, in Rome, is my life. Normal. I discovered the city and the language. I ran around museums when admission was free – the first Sunday of the month, I think. We played bridge. On Saturday evenings, some of us went dancing to the trendy "Piper Club." And, from time to time, we hitchhiked for a day or a weekend to places with magical names. Firenze. Pisa. Napoli. I slipped into this life *al'italiana* easily; ordinary things made me happy or sad. I wandered around the city with my nose glued to store windows admiring clothes, such clothes, and one could only dream of clothes like this in Poland. Perhaps such a dress or sweater showed up from time to time in the fancy consignment stores, but, for me, they were unattainable. And shoes… the colorful pairs creatively displayed in store windows were in huge contrast with the two bins in some of the Wrocław stores – one bin for the left foot and the other one for the right.

I met Zoriza's friends, many of whom worked, just like she did, at the *Opera di Roma*. From time to time, someone slipped me an extra pass or ticket and, dressed in my finest, I went to the opera as if everything was normal. Or to the symphony with

Mrs. Dresner whenever her husband couldn't or wouldn't. Tony, the owner of the bar on the ground floor and purveyor of Zoriza's cognac, saw me rushing home after work and sometimes motioned an invitation for a glass of *prosecco*. This invitation, in Italian, also became gradually normal. But nights were increasingly more difficult. Thoughts about my parents' future choked and overwhelmed me. How will they manage? Sometimes, the three of us went somewhere in Rome, and it was I who guided them and navigated the city and the language. I took care of them. They found comfort in my knowing which way to turn, which bus to take, and how to ask for directions. It dawned on me that our roles have reversed. Unexpectedly, unfairly, too soon, and without warning, it was I who was now responsible for them. I became the parent, not the other way around as it has always been. And this was just the beginning.

I turned twenty-one in Rome, and lost now the second year of studies. It worried me. I always thought that my life would begin in earnest after I graduated with my master's degree, and I knew exactly when that would be. Jacek and I spoke of getting married after I graduate. Since we left Poland, the timeline has blurred. And, without a degree, how can I support the three of us if my parents would not be able to?

I was too young to understand that life is the stuff happening to me and around me NOW. That our exile and emigration – that's life. My HIAS job, Jerzyk's mother under the train, Zoriza's two cognacs each morning, the couple with the cat, the coffin in the garage, the growing disorientation of my parents, carefree dancing... that's life. Many years went by before I understood that life does not start when this or that is achieved – it's the stuff that happens along the way.

* * *

After months of waiting, our emigration formalities were

completed, and the date for our departure was set. To Detroit. The press coverage of recent riots left no doubts about the massive racial and economic tensions in the city. Detroit was tough, conflicted, and maybe even dangerous – the modern Wild West. Not ideal. But that's where Tata's family lives. Never having met Tata, they still honorably stepped forward as our guarantor. Karol Żmijewski and his mother will also go to Detroit, thanks to a guarantee from some aunt. For the first time since we left home, I was scared.

* * *

Our stateless status meant that our new countries had to accept us unconditionally since extradition was not possible – we had no nationality and belonged nowhere, so where could they extradite us to? Therefore, a necessary proviso of our immigration to the United States was to locate a guarantor willing and able to deal with any arising issues and costs, for example medical care, since we had no insurance.

Helping others is a good deed, a *mitzvah*. For those who did not have family in the US, a strong Jewish organization usually stepped forward as a guarantor, such as the local chapter of Jewish Family Service. For millennia, *Tikkun Olam* has instructed Jews to heal, repair, and upgrade the world. Helping other Jews is a priority, of course, but the scope of *tikkun olam* covers "olam" — everybody. Jewish organizations worldwide strive to maintain a fund for *tikkun olam* causes. Such funds have gone, for example, toward starting the "Let My People Go" campaign on behalf of the one million Russian Jews, or Operation Moses, to covertly airlift over 8,000 Ethiopian Jews from Sudan to Israel during the 1984 famine. It is also the core emergency funding used to set up field hospitals in areas stricken by floods, earthquakes, or war, and staff them with volunteer doctors, many of whom are Jewish and, often, Israeli.

In 1968-1972, such funds were used to lobby for and to guarantee to the US government the care of the exiled Polish Jews.

But our guarantors were private: Rose Binder with her husband Morris Neuman and her brother Ruby Binder with his wife Ruth. Ruby's and Rose's father, Tata's uncle, whom Tata never met, left Yavoriv before WWI as a young man and went to America. He wasn't alone; between 1880 and the start of WWI in 1914, about 2,000,000 Yiddish-speaking Ashkenazi Jews immigrated from Eastern Europe, escaping pogroms and looking for work. The uncle landed in Detroit, got married, and Rose and Ruby were born. Tata had no idea of their existence; he found them by coincidence when, after WWII, like so many others, he searched for surviving family via the International Red Cross. The people he looked for all perished: his Mother Sara, his sisters Małka and Rachel, his brother Isaac, and their families. But serendipitously, he discovered Rose and Ruby — cousins in Detroit. They corresponded for years, getting to know each other and sharing family photos and stories.

Rose and Ruby were typical of the second generation of Jewish immigrants of that era: hard-working, honest, simple people. Rose married Morris, a plumber, and they lived a good, modest life, saving and pinching pennies long after they no longer had to. Also typical: they invested their life's earnings into educating their two children. Adele became a doctor, and her brother Harvey a lawyer.

Ruby and his wife, Ruth, had no trade or professional skills and, after they got married, they started a modest neighborhood dry cleaning business. It fed them, but the bonanza came when they won the contract for cleaning uniforms for a division of General Motors, one of the then-thriving Detroit car manufacturers. They expanded and opened additional locations and plants.   The American dream was earned by hard work and opportunity, and they did very well.

If not for their honorable and generous gesture, our guarantors would likely have been a Jewish organization in one of the cities with a large Jewish population and commensurate resources: New York, Los Angeles, Chicago, or Miami. We would have been part of a large group of recent exiles from Poland, and everything would have been different. But thanks to family generosity, we were headed to Detroit.

I quit work a few weeks before our scheduled departure and went on a hitchhiking exploration with two brothers from Warsaw whom I knew from Jewish summer camps in Poland, Edward and Marek Odoner. We reconnected in Rome and sometimes played bridge together. They, too, were leaving soon, to Milwaukee. In each of our pockets was now the Italian *Titolo di Viaggio per Stranieri*—another travel document for foreigners, with no rights for the bearer. I was not bothered by that; actually, quite proud. What more could we expect from the Italians in addition to the safe harbor they gave us and time to sort out our affairs? I didn't know it yet, but for years to come, we will also be labeled as "stateless" in the US.

Not much planning went into this hitchhiking trip. With sleeping bags and toothpaste in our backpacks, we parked ourselves on the northbound side of the *Autostrada di Sole* and got into the first car, which stopped. I spoke Italian by then as if I'd always done it. Over the next three weeks, we traveled the length of Italy along the Mediterranean from Rome to the Swiss border in the north and, from there, southbound along the Adriatic coast to the depths of Sicily. Before we departed, Zoriza pleaded with us to stay away from Sicily; it could be dangerous, she argued. So, we went there, of course, not out of spite but out of curiosity. And it was Sicily that left the warmest imprint on our hearts. We admired the Greek temples in Agrigento, the magical, glowing Etna in the island's center, and the obligatory mounds of marzipan in only-in-Sicily colors and shapes that adorned bakery windows in each village. And the plump, sexy girls in blouses so tight that the buttons popped around their ample bosoms; they maneuvered the cobblestoned streets in high heels and swayed their broad hips with a promise of things to come. And the stocky, sweaty, handsome young men with curly, brilliant black hair and rolled-up shirt sleeves. And the elderly villagers who, with toothless smiles, supervised village life each evening as the sun went down, sipping lemonade on the amphitheater of their elevated porches. We stopped in random villages, looking for opportunities to trade a place to sleep for some work around the house or farm. Once, we even slept in a baker's own bed; it was available during certain hours of the night when the baker and his wife baked bread. Our *quid pro quo* was to help distribute the bread in the morning to the surrounding villages.

One balmy night, we simply laid out our sleeping bags on a patch of grass under the starry sky. A nice lady woke us in the morning and pointed out that the beautiful grass was in her front yard. It wasn't clear in the dark, but, indeed, we parked ourselves on her lovely, well-kept front lawn. Embarrassed, still half asleep, we apologized and gathered quickly, ready to leave, but the lady stopped us:

– No, no, that's not what I meant. Don't go. You are welcome inside. We have spare beds.

We stayed with the woman and her husband for a few days. It's as if we visited family. We explored the area, cooked and ate dinner together, talked about life in general and ours in particular… On the morning of our departure, our hosts drove us to the *stazione di pedaggio* (toll station) at the *autostrada* and interviewed every driver who offered to give us a ride. They took over completely, and we had nothing to say about it. How far is he going? Does he have a family? Their choice was a fisherman from the island of Lampedusa with a romantic name, Damore, which means "of love." Damore traveled north to contract his catch at the many fish markets along the way. For three days and nights, we explored various towns and villages while Damore struck fish gold at the markets. He didn't sleep much, and our job was to keep him awake with conversation as he drove to the next stop. He found our tales surprisingly fascinating, moved by the stories of student strikes; he probably imagined us waving flags atop barricades, bloody and courageous in battle... a scene from *"Les Miserables."* We regretfully parted company in Naples; he headed for the Adriatic Coast, and we continued north to Rome. End of adventure.

On our last evening in Rome, Zoriza surprised us with a festive farewell dinner; she invited a number of her friends whom we had befriended during our stay. One of them was Tony from the downstairs bar; he and I have gotten to know each other a bit closer. He was paternally troubled; the whole Detroit thing didn't appeal to him at all. Detroit is the worst of all American cities, he bemoaned. And, actually, what do we know altogether about this America? Not wanting to get into a discussion, I explained that we had no choice. We are not Italian and can't stay in Italy.

"Zoriza is also not Italian," – replied Tony soberly.

"Yes, but Zoriza's husband is Italian," I argued. *"That gives her the right to stay."*

Tony was ready for a sacrifice:

"Then I will marry you, and you can stay here as well, just like

Zoriza."

He was convinced that America is dangerous, and Detroit in particular. They shoot people on the streets and burn houses, and it is altogether unclear why we would go there since all is well in Italy and we are here already. Dear Tony, he probably watched too much TV, and the coverage of the 1967 Detroit riots projected drama and danger of the Wild West. There was, of course, an element of truth in his concern.

I turned down his marriage offer with sincere gratitude, noting quietly that this was the second marriage proposal in a few months, and I turned them both down: first Jacek, now Tony… will I end up an old maid?

I said farewell to my Roman friends on the broad, gentle steps of the church of Santa Maria Maggiore. Someone brought a transistor radio, the technological craze of those days (I checked; it wasn't the Polish "Edelweiss"), and we danced on the steps to the already familiar Italian hits: Mina, Nada, Adriano Celentano, Johnny Hallyday, Gianni Morandi… A delivery came from Tony's bar – a gift of several bottles of *prosecco*. And this is how I bid goodbye to Rome. In the morning, we boarded a plane – oddly, a Belgian Sabena – and left for America. End of waiting and the beginning of immigration.

Zoriza rented our room to another Jewish family from Poland.

Business was brisk.

* * *

Many years later, I visited Zoriza during one of my stays in Rome. Amazingly, she recognized me right away and was overjoyed. However, I was terrified. The spacious, bustling with energy apartment of my memories lost color and luster.

The room we once rented was filled with dusty junk. And Zoriza, the full of zest Zoriza, the lively, vulgar Sophia Loren of Belgrade clad in high heels and low-cut dresses, barely ten years older than I, looked like an old village woman with thinning hair somehow yellow rather than grey, yellow-black teeth, and sunken cheeks. In the intervening years, Italy passed a law permitting divorce, which proved to be the final blow to her relationship with Mario. Papa died, and Zoriza was an eligible widow, but Mario chose not to divorce his wife. Zoriza was heartbroken and aged as a signal that life was over.

Later yet, during another stay, I wanted to show my Roman home to Ed. We took a cab to Via Principe Amedeo 231 one evening. The area was rejuvenated, lively, and festive: people, bars, restaurants, garlands of lights… I peeked into the bar, which used to be Tony's, but I recognized no one. The door to the building was locked. There was a list of tenants by the doorbell, but Zoriza's name was not there.

Sabina Baral

אין דער ערשטער רײ פון אויבן (פון רעכטס אויף לינקס) סאבינע בינער,
אידעס סטשענבאום, בעלע ליבענבערג, פעליציע רוטשטײקאיאס, מאלגאָרזשאטע
הײסמאַן, בראַניסלאַוע קענינג   2־טע רײ: שמעון זײדעל, יוליע פראַנק, מלכה
רוטשימיעוס גאָלדשטײן, מאריע גילדען, סטאַניסלאַו שמעטנק, פאַליע לענקין;
3־טע רײ: עוגעניע קובערניק, כיל ווײסמאַן, עדואַרדע ליבסטער, יצחק מיינ־
מראוב, לודמילע קורצער, נאַרבערט וואַמילעהיובש; 4־טע רײ: יוסף פּערעקאַל־
סקי, רואזאליע גרינבורראַנב, מאַתעוס ליובשעוווסקי, ראוזע אלבסאַן, הלל בעקלס,
בעלע ראָשגערבערגער;   5־טע רײ: וינע פרײדלין, בעריס פרײדלין, באַרבאַרע
גריין, גוטשעגאַוטש לאַנקים, עוגעניע ספעטעמעל, לעאן זײדעל;   6־טע רײ: נאטאן
אָטאַטשטאָם, רווטע ניסקובאַום, לודויק פישבין, זאָשיע לעהוינטער, לעם נײ־
בורגער, מאיינע טעכטער.

Our class tableau published in "Folks-Sztyme" on the occasion of the graduation of the largest class in the history of the school (1965), miraculously preserved by a classmate in Copenhagen

AMERICA, HERE WE COME! DETROIT

If America is a nation of immigrants, Jews are a nation of refugees

Mark Hetfield, President and CEO of HIAS

We are now in Detroit.

Our next stop is a tidy, two-story red brick house on Curtis – a long, straight street lined with beautiful, mature trees, broad sidewalks, and brick houses similar to ours on both sides. We are led to the second floor. It looks modest but is fully equipped: brooms and a vacuum cleaner in the closet, cutlery in the kitchen drawers, towels, sheets, and bedding. Two bathrooms! There was no bathroom at all in our apartment on 25 Włodkowica Street in Wrocław, not even running water. The rusty toilet in the hallway shared by five families had neither a seat nor a cover, and the torn newspaper stuck on a nail in lieu of toilet paper rounded off the experience; toilet paper was a hard-to-get luxury item in Poland. Every week, like a pilgrimage, I went to the communal baths on Teatralna Street with a towel and soap in my backpack, and after buying a ticket for twelve zlotys and waiting in a long line, I took a luxurious bath. The ticket allowed me to stay for an hour, and I did, until the last minute. Sometimes, I miscalculated and stayed too long, my bliss interrupted by one of the cleaning ladies banging on the door – the next person was waiting! Then one bathroom for several families in the *pensione* in Rome, one in Zoriza's apartment… and here, in Detroit, a bathroom for my parents and another one, just for me! Could it be that our American Dream started at once and without special efforts on our part? I suppose that everything on Curtis will probably need to remain in the apartment when we move, whenever that will be. But it felt good to walk into a well-equipped, functioning place to live.

New Aunt Rose gave us a guided tour of the apartment. She approached this activity with pride and meticulous patience; after all, there was a lot to learn. The iron has buttons, she explained: you push the red one to iron cotton, the purple one for linen, and the light blue one for silk. Very convenient indeed. And a revelation—Rose said that bedding, sheets, and pillowcases need not be ironed at all—the fabric is non-iron, she enunciated. We looked at each other dumbfounded—non-iron?! It does not wrinkle? A miracle! Rose next turned her attention to the telephone, a clunky, old-fashioned dial apparatus in an unexpected pastel color. Rose described what it was and demonstrated its wondrous performance. She dialed the number of her own home; her husband, Morris, picked up, and Rose explained, carefully articulating each word and barely containing excitement, that this really was Morris; it's his voice we magically heard! She motioned with reverence at the cord which, she somehow implied, was the miraculous conduit of Morris's voice, and beamed with pride as if the phone was her own invention. I was somewhat indignant—who did she think we were? Could she possibly think that there were no telephones in Poland? I believe she did; the only Poland she knew was from the stories her father told her, where the goat and the chickens shared the one-room family house. I casually mentioned that I studied electronics, but this made no impression whatsoever; Rose did not associate the miracle of telephony with "electronics" and probably found it impertinent that I changed the subject to mention my field of studies while she explained how to use the telephone.

After Rose left, Mama sighed deeply; I knew she was thinking of the extravagantly expensive damask bedding in our lift. It was custom-sewn for emigration in hopes of being sold to someone more lucky or more deserving, someone who could afford it – not us. It was too good for our modest lives. And now, the prospects of selling the damask paled with the revelation of non-iron. A huge concern: since bedding here is non-iron, who would want to buy, and iron, the damask? I quietly suspected that its fate may be similar to that of my sleeping doll, Małgorzata – a lonely, hidden existence of something too good to be used. We didn't know it yet, but we'll soon have similar concerns about much of our packed-for-exile baggage. But for now, we felt rich: the fully furnished home on Curtis with non-iron bedding and our soon-to-come lift, which was full of newly purchased, hard-won-with-bribes treasures.

And Yiddish is back in our lives, centerstage! That's how my parents communicated with the new Detroit family and with our caseworker at the Jewish Family Service. We somehow slipped into Yiddish at home as well, without planning or prior agreement; it just happened. Our *lingua franca.* Nobody said it aloud – maybe nobody realized it – but we will no longer speak Polish. The world shrunk dramatically for my parents since December 20, 1968. In time, they will master sufficient English to get by in a store, on the street, or at an office. They will sing in a community choir, and some songs will be in English. They will know the words to the Star Spangled Banner. But, from here forward, they will always struggle with newspapers, books, theater, or movies. Their ongoing relationship with culture, current events, and social contacts will primarily be in Yiddish. Jokes will be especially hard: in English, my parents will become humorless. They are multilingual, but English is hard for them; they feel inadequate, handicapped, isolated, and dependent. Yes, they feel, and they are, dependent. But Yiddish helps.

During our first meeting a few days after arrival, our caseworker handed us a check—a modest sum to see us through the first month. They will help us find work, she said, but until then, there will be a monthly allowance. Great relief. Thankfully, each of us started work within the first month, so there was no need for further checks. We also learned that the owner of "our" house on Curtis recently passed away. The house was left in the care of the Jewish Family Service until the heirs decided what to do. The owner's personal belongings were placed temporarily, under lock and key, on the ground floor. It's unclear how long we will be able to live there; it's likely that at some point, the house will be put on the market. But for now, we are not even expected to pay rent until we find work. It felt safer knowing at least that much. And about the check – funny – we didn't know how to deal with it. Rose will surely help.

I asked about continuing my studies. "Good news," said the caseworker: Detroit prides itself in a highly reputed university, Wayne State. Bad news: the school is downtown, about an hour away from where we live by car, two hours each way by bus, with connections. More bad news: there is tuition to pay. When we start working, we will be expected to pay rent in an unspecified amount. So, I WILL resume school, but the question of "when" was simply premature. We couldn't get our arms around the math of our lives, not yet. This equation still had too many unknowns, and we didn't understand the governing parameters.

And a new, incomprehensible problem: everybody warned us not to leave the house. DON'T. What does it mean? For how long? It's okay for now; as it is, we don't know where to go and how to get there. Our only outing thus far had been the trip to Jewish Family Service for the initial interview, and Morris drove us there. The fridge was full of food, which the family thoughtfully stashed there prior to our arrival; it should be enough for a week, maybe longer. But eventually, we will need more food and a mailbox; we will need to go to more meetings at the Jewish Family Service, hopefully to some job interviews as well, and eventually to work. I'll have to go to school. How can we live without leaving the house?

The caseworker marked two points on the local map she gave us: their office and our home on Curtis. If not for the vast distances, finding our way would actually be easy. The city is laid out in mile-long, regular quadrants. The endless streets are straight, with the main ones running at mile intervals. Those running east-west are even numbered: 6 Mile Road, 8 Mile Road. Our Curtis is roughly halfway between 6th and 7th — sort of a 6-1/2 Mile Road.

Streets running north-south have names; our segment of Curtis is located between Wyoming and Livernois. The higher the number, the farther the street is from the high-rises and lowlifes of downtown. We also learn that higher numbers signify safer, newer, and more affluent areas. Rose lives near 13 Mile Road, and Ruby, as befits a truly wealthy man, resides even farther out, close to 18th.

Our stretch of Curtis looked beautiful, but it was not a "good address." It's a "black neighborhood," meaning it is inhabited by black people. That, according to Rose, justifies the categorical warning of not leaving the house. "When you have a car, you will just walk from the house to the car," she explained. Someday, you may even have an attached garage, and you will get into your car without leaving the house. No one walks on the street."

I was speechless.

Should I have married Tony and stayed in Rome?

It will take time before I fully grasp the complicated and unsettling social dynamics of Detroit in those years. Until recently, this beautiful area we live in was expensive, considered "very good," and predominantly Jewish. The shift began when the first Black family bought a house in the neighborhood. As if on cue, those paying attention put their homes up for sale. White buyers were scarce, as the neighborhood had already "turned." The more Black families moved in, the more property values declined.

In less than a year, the neighborhood was transformed: Jewish residents relocated to distant suburbs in the city's northwest, and most homes were now owned by Black families. The only remaining white residents were those who had waited too long — by then, selling wouldn't yield enough to buy in a "good" Jewish area. A troubling, shameful reality in which "white" and "Jewish" implied good and safe, while "Black" translated to don't-leave-home and no-one-walks-the-streets. Sadly, this wasn't unique to Detroit; many American cities experienced the same pattern. Maybe not only "of that era."

* * *

Kroger, the massive supermarket closest to us, sits on 8 Mile Road near Wyoming. It takes us about 45 minutes to walk there; longer on the way back, weighed down with bags of groceries. It was summer; I didn't even want to think what it will look like in a cold, snowy, slushy winter. Some sections had no sidewalks — not that anyone seemed to need them since "no one walks on the street."

We haven't come across any specialty food stores — no greengrocers, no dairy shops — and the bakery didn't sell bread, only incredibly sweet pastries, brightly frosted in ridiculous colors. So, love it or not, Kroger was our food destination for now. And only during the day to avoid tempting the alleged danger.

Finding anything in that Kroger was another challenge. The food was arranged along regularly spaced, numbered aisles, each lined with five or six levels of shelves. There were countless options for every product.

I once wanted to buy tomato sauce for pasta. Actually, I had hoped to make it from scratch, as I had proudly learned in Italy, but Rose laughed good-naturedly, unable to understand why I would spend half a day making pasta sauce when I could buy it ready-made and, in her opinion, just as tasty. That's what modern American cooks did.

So, on my next trip to Kroger, determined to be modern and American, I set out to buy tomato sauce. Despite my fluent English, I could not, for my life, distinguish between the dozens of tomato products. Stewed tomatoes, peeled tomatoes, crushed tomatoes, diced tomatoes, pureed tomatoes, chopped tomatoes, roasted tomatoes, tomato paste. Endless varieties of packaging, multiple brands — cans, jars, and tubes in every size. Which should I buy?

I still wonder why American markets stock so many choices — the inventory costs must be enormous. But at the time, I was simply overwhelmed. I should have found the experience funny, but instead, it saddened and embarrassed me. Now, decades later, in a world where people walk the streets, warmly greet strangers, and live without pressures or impediments—and where every option is available to me—I actually make tomato sauce from scratch. That's what modern American cooks do now, in my world.

Excursions to Krogers were a serious group activity; we spent tedious hours looking for cheese, toothpaste, or laundry detergent. Mama searched the aisles with a pocket dictionary because most packages were identifiable only by their label; you couldn't see what was inside. Some items came in various sizes, and we usually bought the smallest since it was the cheapest and, importantly, we needed to carry it all back. Sometimes, it drizzled, and the heavy paper bags disintegrated en route from oppressive humidity; plastic was not in vogue yet. Some items, commonplace in Poland, like yeast, were hard to find altogether. Other products, such as household cleaners, had a mysteriously large representation. To clean the bathroom, you evidently needed a general-purpose bathroom cleaner, as well as a toilet bowl cleaner, a tile cleaner, a grime remover, a drain de-clogger, and a shower curtain mildew remover. There was even a choice of toilet bowl deodorizers and fragrances, for example, rose or lavender. Really?

We were concerned about the challenge of shopping after we start working – it will have to be on weekends only, since there wouldn't be enough time after work to finish before "dark and dangerous" sets in. We will also learn that, surprisingly, fewer things here are perishable, and most items keep longer, so we will not need to shop as often as we did in Poland or in Italy. Years later, when Edward and I moved to Sweden, my American shopping habits came into question. I bought enough dairy to last for a while and discovered, with great surprise, that milk went bad after a couple of days, even in the refrigerator. Of course, it's MILK, an animal product, and it should go bad. And a scary thought: what have I been drinking in America all these years? A riddle: What is it? It looks like milk and tastes like milk, but it doesn't turn sour for weeks.

* * *

We didn't talk about Poland; the challenges of everyday life absorbed us completely. Until our lift arrived in a few months, we had almost no objects from home around us. There was little to remind us that there was a time, actually not so long ago when we moved around in a familiar world, we were resourceful and fully functioning, we could leave home without fear, we had purposes and destinations, we had shelves lined with books, and we had people in our lives... Here we were completely lonely. We just had each other.

WHAT COMES FIRST: A JOB, A CAR, OR ENGLISH LANGUAGE CLASSES?

I always like walking in the rain, so no one sees me crying.

Charlie Chaplin

Today, our caseworker at the Jewish Family Service asked about qualifications. I heard pride in Tata's voice when he said that he is a brush-maker. He can make the most beautiful shaving brushes from badger hair and fine paintbrushes, too – different for watercolors, different for oil paints, and different for gouache. He is a master of his trade; artists from all over Poland ordered paintbrushes from him, even from abroad. "We are in luck," said the caseworker, "there is a Jewish-owned brush factory in Detroit. Maybe they could use someone."

She then turned to me. "What can I do?" I was perplexed. "Nothing yet. I tutored in math. I am fluent in several languages." No reaction. She doesn't even make a note or ask which languages—maths and languages are apparently not marketable. But she lit up when I mentioned that I had two years of drafting as part of our University of Science and

Technology curriculum. "Oh, you are a draftsman?!" I don't protest. Great (she says "*grrrreat*"), we will find something.

A couple of weeks later, Tata pushes a button on the machine, which makes brushes by the hundreds in the Detroit Quality Brush Factory. He will do so day-in-and-day-out, nine hours per day, six days a week, until he retires; the badger hair he was so proud of is long forgotten. Tata learned his trade by apprenticeship, which started when he was eleven years old; now, his skill was replaced by efficient quantity. Mama got a job in the same place, which was extremely important because she suffered from anxiety attacks, and the hour-and-a-half bus rides each way, with connections, terrified her even when she traveled together with Tata. They started this journey early, in the dark morning, and returned after dark as well, exhausted. I caught a secret look at them as they left the house, holding hands for comfort and encouragement, and it broke my heart. They have always been dignified and carefully dressed; now, they appeared disheveled, wrinkled, and worn out. Sometimes Mama came home devastated, with tears in her eyes because someone spoke to her on the bus, which she didn't understand, and it shamed her. She carried with her, at all times, her pocket-sized English Phrasebook, which was already falling apart. The booklet was organized in practical sections such as "In the Store" or "At the Train Station" and was more useful when Mama tried to address somebody rather than when she herself was being addressed. Both of them wanted to start English classes. I even found a nearby community college in the phone book that offered inexpensive evening courses in English as a Second Language. But there was simply no time for classes now. The jobs were most important, and this absorbed all their time and energy. There was also the matter of getting to that community college in the dark. A sequence of intermediate goals clarified: we must first save enough for their driver's classes, then they must somehow learn enough rudimentary English to pass the driver's test, get a license, and eventually buy a car. This will hopefully ease the routine so they can start proper English classes. It's a pity that we left Poland so suddenly; they could have studied the language prior to our departure.

And I worked as a draftsman in an architect's office in the nearby suburb of Oak Park. University will have to wait for a while, certainly until we save enough to buy a car for my parents. We pooled our first paychecks and paid for a driver's education course for Tata. On Sundays, Tata was free during daylight. The instructor was Jewish and spoke Yiddish, so that's how they communicated, but the written exam was, of course, standard, and Tata will have to take it in English. He struggled, but he didn't give up. He didn't even complain. The car was simply vital, a path to life in Detroit.

Meanwhile, I learned that Jewish Family Service may, just may, grant me a loan for university tuition. I spent nights thinking and calculating. Now, distance will become a factor because Wayne State University is downtown and far from where we live. A scary conclusion: one car will not suffice. My income was needed to make ends meet, so I will need to continue working for the foreseeable future, even after I go back to school. To somehow keep up with work and studies, I will also need a car for myself; otherwise, much of each day will be spent on buses.

And my sweet, kind, strong Jacek didn't give up either. His letters were full of hope, energy, and plans. He graduated with a master's degree in nuclear chemistry, and he got a good job. "Try to come to Bulgaria," he wrote. "We'll get married and plan the rest together." It all seemed so far away; I didn't even know how to explain to him that I must work in order to buy two cars. That I can't leave the US altogether, anywhere, until I have been here for a year and become eligible for the Green Card? That his chances to leave Poland are slim – they will not let a nuclear chemist out of the country. And even if they somehow consented, where would we find the money to pay the government for his studies? Finally, and most importantly, there is no power on Earth for me to abandon my parents here on their own; they are so lost and need me so much, and they are here because of me.

In the end, after many sleepless nights, I stopped writing to the man I loved because I didn't know what to write and what for. I cried at night.

Price of our exile, yet one more.

My Mother's Polish-English Dictionary. A treasure that moves me deeply.

OUR BAGGAGE ARRIVES

*Everybody sooner or later has to drop the luggage
and the baggage of illusions.*

Carlos Santana

We received notice that our lift has arrived. It contained the sum total of our Polish possessions. American kids inherited fully furnished houses, perhaps summer homes as well, art, bank accounts, and jewelry. My inheritance, our total wealth, was everything my parents accumulated in their twenty-three postwar years contained in that lift. I can't say that it was eagerly awaited. Busy with the day-to-day of our new lives, I actually forgot what we packed there; I certainly haven't missed any of that stuff. Other than books and clothes, these weren't things from our former lives, but stuff we purchased for emigration. I did remember the Edelweiss transistor radio; the stupid prodiż-the-cake-baker, our "samovar," soldered pots and pans, dishes, our pillows, which were, apparently, too large for America; threadbare towels which were rougher than the ones we used now, and the famous damask bedding which needed ironing. The ugly crystal and the Ćmielów china. What else was there, I wondered?

The day came. The lift was delivered and placed in front of

the house, and we all took a day off from work to unpack it as quickly as possible before its contents were stolen (a practical directive from Rose). When we packed the lift for the final time after the customs inspection in Wrocław, everything therein was important to us, precious and valuable. We paid humiliating bribes to be able to take it all with us, to make our new start easier. Now, in Detroit, all those things seemed foreign, and unpacking them was a laughter-and-tears trip down recent but oh-so-distant memory lane rather than a joyous reunion with old friends.

The four down comforters came to good use. I wonder how we were allowed to bring four comforters for three people; surely another bribe. Two of them were expensive and fancy. Mama ordered them from some woman on Nowowiejska Street, covered in embossed Chinese (of course) silk, a different color on each side, stitched in large squares. We used them. They were pretty but delivered only fleeting pleasure; the Chinese silk and fancy Polish stitching fell apart within a few years. Two others were bought in some government store, probably with the help of a bribe. Also stitched in squares, in ugly pink patterned fabric which had the feel and look of stiff oilcloth – they turned out to be indestructible. My daughters somehow loved them as well, and each asked for a *kołdra* (comforter in Polish) when moving away to college. The ugly, pink *kołdras*. That word was then, and still is, part of their meager repertoire in Polish.

Part of the bedding were also three huge pillows – correctly, one for each of us – much larger than the ones used in America. And the famous, over-our-heads-expensive damask sheets, duvets, and pillowcases that had to be ironed. They were never sold – not even an attempt was made; they didn't fit American beds and bedding and, as best I remember, never used.

There was a newly purchased china set of the best-of-the-best Polish brand, Ćmielów porcelain. Since my childhood, I've associated romantic visions with that name. *Ćmielów* of my imagination exuded an air of wealth, elegance, exquisite taste, and the long-abandoned art of table setting. I imagined (or, perhaps, remembered) a scene from a film, maybe from *War and Peace:* heavy, engraved silver laid out in perfect order on a white floor-length tablecloth (of damask, of course), exquisitely cut crystal glass and, amidst it all the centerpiece of style, Ćmielów. In all my Polish years, I have never actually seen Ćmielów. I think it was mostly for export; it was more of a legend than a product. At home, we used the chipped faience left behind by the former German residents of our first apartment. But preparing for emigration, the Jewish neighborhood ladies fought hard to acquire a set of the coveted Ćmielów; no point emigrating without it. To my great disappointment, Ćmielów turned out to be a prosaic, if not boring, white set skimpily adorned at the rim with a narrow gold band. Mama didn't use it in Detroit; our life simply wasn't good enough for Ćmielów. Safely packaged, it sat idly on the highest shelf of a kitchen cupboard, awaiting better times or more important occasions, but life did not comply. When I inherited the nearly intact set, I started using it every day as if to make up for Mama's dreams. The gold band soon surrendered to the demands of the dishwasher and started disappearing – the darn Ćmielów was meant to be washed by hand. Of course. With time, much of it chipped or broke except for three bullion cups and one dessert plate, which I sometimes use and now truly for special occasions. Survivors. I treat them with love and tender caution. After all, it is now "Mama's Ćmielów."

Out of the lift also came a painted tea set we bought in the recently opened "Woman of China" store near the Main Railroad Station. Made of lacquerware—ridiculously—it couldn't really be used for hot tea, only for decoration. Or maybe not. Chinese imports, new and exotic, were all the rage in Poland at the time; we didn't even notice how ugly and impractical the tea set was. After years of sitting unused, Mama finally gave it to the woman who cleaned their apartment. No one else wanted it. By then, the whole world was flooded with junk from China.

Then there were pots. I don't know what we were thinking bringing our old pots to America, but we did. They represented our practical view of life after immigration – we will need to cook, but we may not have money to buy pots. I was truly disappointed when we unpacked them. There were much nicer pots in the Detroit stores, prettier and more practical: shiny, with see-through lids and handles that remained cool even when the pot was on a hot burner. But, for sentimental reasons, I have, and use to this day, Mama's two-quart pot covered in white enamel. It was old already in Wrocław, its holes along the bottom rim soldered more than once by the tinsmith on the corner of Crooked Circle and Ruska Street. It was punctured with numerous solder patches like war scars. My beloved pot with chipped enamel! My older daughter Monica hints that she would like to have it someday; she will. I also looked with great displeasure at our heavy, scratched cast-iron frying pans from Poland.

"They will never wear out," I despaired. American frying pans were clad in a magical, straight-from-the-moon-via-DuPont substance called Teflon—apparently, nothing stuck to it, and that's what I dreamed of. Funny—it never occurred to me for years that I could simply throw out the Polish pans and buy Teflon ones; we never discarded anything still serviceable.

It took me years to embrace the extravagance of pleasing myself or making my life simpler—it was part of my American

"Mama's Ćmielów." That's what is left of it.

transformation. I do have nice pots and pans now.

The most pathetic content of the lift was a collection of thick, heavy, coarsely cut crystal vases, platters, and table glass, which reigned for years in various display cabinets of my parent's home and was also unused. The day came, however, when Mama, too, realized how ugly they were, moved them to basement storage, and finally distributed them among various helpers, caregivers, and housecleaners – just like the lacquer tea set from "Woman of China." When we first arrived, Aunts Rose and Ruth received as presents the best of these cut crystals – the very expensive, colored ones. Blue and purple were in vogue; my parents paid the highest prices and the biggest bribes for them. They certainly landed with some cleaning ladies as well. Poignant – in Poland, they were valuable treasures, and by the time they confronted America, they had become laughable ballast. When my exiled friends gather and reminisce, the ugly crystal is the butt of many jokes and the invariable question: "What did you do with yours?" Or the incredulous "You still have it?!" The very best Russian photo camera, Zorka, was heavy and clunky. It was also complicated – no one in our family knew how to use it. Tata walked many miles and tried to endear himself to many salesladies before he victoriously brought home the large yellow box rumored to be the rage of all photographers in the West. "No one uses Leica anymore; it's Zorka now," we heard. We moved the darn Zorka from place to place for years – *such* a camera, *so* expensive! In the end, we put it in such a safe place that we never found it again. It disappeared before a single photo was taken.

Among the big treasures was the "Diamant" – a folded bicycle made in East Germany. It was a mistake to have thought that you could get somewhere by bicycle in one of the large American cities, but among emigrating Jews, Diamant was considered a luxury of outstanding quality, de rigueur, don't-leave-home-without-it. The myth of a bicycle as a desirable commodity for emigration stemmed from Israel, where bicycles were indeed in demand, especially – considering the small apartments – the folding kind. So, the poor Diamant traveled in the wrong direction and came to America by mistake. It certainly was useless in Detroit. It would take me many long hours to get by bicycle to work and several days to get to the university. Bicycle lanes were as rare as sidewalks. Due to a lack of a suitable storage place, we put it in the hallway of the house on Curtis. We stumbled over it there and in several other hallways of our American lives until someone took pity on it, and it disappeared.

Our bicycle story was not unique. Agata (Garpenlind) Helfgot came to Sweden with her mother as a three-year-old child. When her adopted grandmother, Babcia Henia, emigrated a year later, she brought for little Agata a precious gift from Poland: a folding bicycle. "I was so ungrateful," reminisces Agata. "She probably searched high and low for this treasure and paid a fortune in bribes – and I hated it because it was so difficult to ride. I wanted a bicycle like other children had."

* * *

The samovar went straight to trash.

* * *

My husband, Edward, left Poland with ten suits, custom-made for him by the best tailor in Bytom, Mr. Sitko, especially for his emigration. It's a sweet, sad story. His mother, Hela, wanted nothing but the very best for her son, the doctor. Wool, cashmere, linen, and cotton, all with silk linings — patterned in stripes, houndstooth, or herringbone. Most were double-breasted for maximum prestige, stiff at the chest, and cuffed at the pants. Hela imagined him going to work in a different suit each day, his career supported and propelled by this stylish wardrobe.

Doctors in Stockholm wore scrubs and, later, dressed casually.

Edward tried to wear the suits to a discotheque a few times. He was such an excellent dancer, but no one wanted to dance with him. He simply looked ridiculous in this mid-century wardrobe in a city where polyester reigned and at the time when everyone tried to imitate the Beatles. He hung the suits in the attic of the building, where he rented a room, and simply did not take them with him when he moved.

TREASURES OF GRANDMA GOLDMAN

It requires more courage to suffer than to die.

Napoleon Bonaparte

The greatest treasures in our luggage were heirlooms inherited from Grandma Goldman: a silver table set for four and brass candle sticks. They mark chapters of our family history.

In keeping with a recent ordinance by the Soviet People's Commissariat for Internal Affairs (NKVD), in 1941, Jews from the terrains bordering the Soviet Union were ordered to report to the nearby train station. These deportations, ahead of the imminent German invasion, were actually a blessing, but that became clear only later, after the war. At the time, people didn't know where they were being taken and what awaited them there.

Summoned to the Sanok station were four members of the Goldman family: my maternal grandfather Samuel and three of his six children—the youngest, Esther, my mother; the oldest, Zacharje; and one of the middle sons, Jankiel, called by his Polish name, Janek. Samuels's wife, my Grandmother Sabina

Haas Goldman, a woman of faith and tradition, considered the situation. It was not clear where her husband and children would be taken or for how long the family would be apart. She feared the worst. In an extraordinary gesture, she chose to pack silver for that journey, the table silver that was Esther's dowry. She instructed her daughter that if things became difficult, she could sell the silver, a piece at a time, to feed herself and others. And if things were good… well, it was her dowry. Grandma also added a pair of brass candlesticks, the ones she herself used for Shabbat, because there may not be any candlesticks where Esther was going. The heavy silver candelabra used for Passover and the High Holy Days were, in time, to be inherited by her elder daughter Chaya, who was already married and had three children of her own.

And so my Mother, Esther, a young girl from a good Jewish home in Galicia, headed for the railway station in Sanok with her father and two brothers, burdened not just by circumstance but also by her valuable, heavy luggage. "Where are they taking us?" she thought, fearing it would be far from anything familiar. The dowry implied she may be gone for a long time. Should she instead have brought food? She worried. This could not end well.

My Grandmother stayed behind. Without Samuel at her side, it will be her at the head of the table. Not called to this train were also Chaya, the oldest daughter, and her family, as well as another son, Froim, the musician. The whole village listened when Froim played his accordion. The fourth of her sons, Hersh, was an officer in the British Army since 1937 and fought in Palestine. Finally, also part of the closest family left behind was Zacharje's wife, Ita Winter Goldman, and their three little children, two of whom were twins. There was a large extended family, all Goldmans, in the nearby villages of Domaradź, Albigowa, Dębica, and Gać. Sabina consoled herself that they would stick together and help each other. The fields and orchards would certainly feed them. Or so thought my Grandmother.

They all perished: Ita and her children in Auschwitz; Chaya, her husband, and their children, along with the over forty members of the extended Goldman family, in Bełżec. A letter from the British War Office advised the family that Captain Hersh Goldman, having fought bravely, died in Palestine. I remember this letter – it was treasured in Wrocław, along with the few remaining family photos. And my Grandmother Sabina and Froim died in Nowosielce. Another story.

It was extraordinary that Grandma sent Mama away with her dowry in these tumultuous times. People buried their valuables under the porch or in the fields, traded what they could for a promise of a hiding place, and bought a loaf of bread for a string of pearls, but Sabina Goldman gave the family silver and brass to her departing youngest daughter.

The train took Mama and the others to a labor camp on the banks of the Ob River in Siberia, near Barnaul, close to Novosibirsk. As Mama and my uncles told the story, Grandpa Samuel went every day to the barren, snowy platform of the Barnaul train station, hoping that someday the rest of his family would step off the train.

Many people arrived, bringing horrific stories of what was happening in Poland — burned villages and plundered homes, rapes and beatings, mass shootings in the forests, and gassings in trucks, ghettos, and camps. Still, Grandpa Samuel trudged several kilometers through the Siberian tundra each day to meet the train. But over time, his hope and strength gradually faded until none remained.

Not so long ago, in Nowosielce, he had been the head of a

beautiful family. They had worked hard but wanted for nothing, and there was always room and food for the poor and hungry at their Shabbat table. Before long, he died—from hunger, from cold, and, most of all, from sorrow.

Starving and chopping trees in the Siberian woods, Mama and her brothers willed themselves to survive for four years, freezing and stubbornly writing letters to their Mother and siblings: "We said Kaddish for Papa, but we are alive and long to hear from you" Maybe the letters got there, who knows… no one survived to tell.

When the war ended, Esther, her brothers, and Grandma's treasures made the six-week-long train journey back to Poland. Mama wasn't much for religious tradition, but she used the brass candlesticks on grand occasions. I sometimes use them as well now, and surely, someday, my daughters will light candles in them from time to time. But the silver, the exquisite set from another life, wrapped in gray felt, spent twenty years in the same oak credenza as my doll Małgorzata, a shelf or two higher. It waited for better times, for an occasion that never came. It belonged in a home full of life and tradition, on a table set for a large family. Perhaps Mama was right that its home was not in Wrocław, that it could not share the space with all the pain that lived with us on Włodkowica?

Maybe she planned for it to be my dowry someday? Or perhaps she simply wrapped in that gray felt her whole lost pre-war life and could not gather the strength to unwrap it?

The richly engraved cutlery, a full set for twelve, was truly exquisite: for fish, soup, meat, and dessert, nine pieces per person. Nothing was missing.

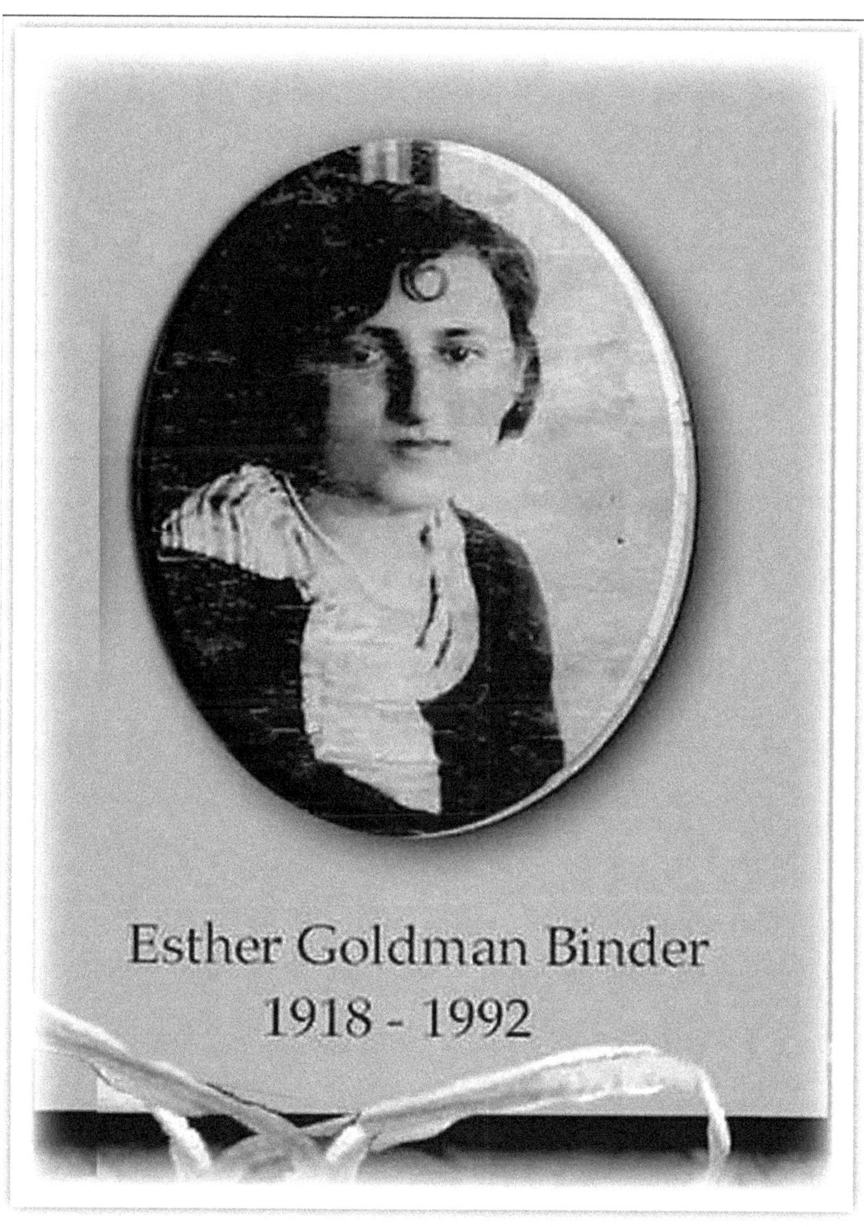

My Mother, Esther Goldman Binder
She left this 1941 photo to her brother Froim on the day of her departure. "Don't
forget your sister," she wrote on the reverse.

My Grandfather, Samuel Goldman, is the husband of Sabina Hass Goldman. Father of Zacharje, Chaya, Hersh, Jankiel, Froim, and my Mother Esther. Neither of Esther's parents survived the War, and neither from German hands.

And then came 1968, and it was time to leave Poland.

We never even considered that Grandma Goldman's silver would not come with us. The very thought was incomprehensible; it was part of the family. But my parents learned via jungle telegraph that there are restrictions on silver. Someone couldn't take their whole set because it was too heavy; someone else had too many pieces. The word was that silver had to weigh no more than two kilos in total and no more than thirty-six pieces. Other rumors claimed that someone had to leave their silver altogether because it was old, pre-war. We were in danger on all three counts.

* * *

ESTHER'S DOWRY

Here you have, Esther, the cutlery
for twelve guests
nine pieces for each
for fish
for soups
for meats
for desserts ...
Grandma Goldman
with shaking hands
squeezed the family silverware
into the depths of a suitcase

For four long years
in bone-chilling Siberian nights
the suitcase at the head of the bed
guarded Esther's sleep

At long last
when there were no more dreams left
and no more trees to fell in Barnaul's forests
the time had come for a long monotonous
slow train ride home home home

The silver train clinked its timid
promise of a family table
set with
fish
soups
meats
desserts

But there was no home
There was no one …
There was nothing

The redundant silverware was put away
on the top shelf of a post-German cupboard
Then March of 1968
jerked the spoons, forks and knives
out of their grey felt slumber
separated them painfully
decimated them
banished them to strangers' tables

Elżbieta Kurowska was moved to write this poem
after reading *Notes from Exile*
Translated from Polish by Janusz Solarz.

In the adjacent building on Włodkowica, across a shared courtyard, lived the family Blusztajn: David, a widower, and two children roughly my age. My Mother and his diseased wife, Genia, were good friends, and I was friends with his daughter, Isabelle. Benek, the son, was a year or two younger. He confessed to me decades later that he spent hours at the window across the courtyard with opera glasses in hand, waiting for me to undress.

David Blusztajn was a tailor. His big treasures were a sewing machine and a mannequin. For emigration, David purchased with a suitable bribe a modest silverware set for six –thirty-six pieces altogether. It seemed to be within the allowed limit, but during the Customs inspection, the officers weighed the silver and declared that it was definitely too much. They removed one soup spoon and one teaspoon, collected a hefty bribe, and everything now tallied with the silver. Strangely, the spoon and teaspoon were still disallowed, even after the bribe, so what was the point? Mr. Blusztajn felt cheated. He was. He refused to give up and surreptitiously threw the two rejected pieces back into the lift when no one was looking.

And then, disaster. When the inspection was seemingly over, and the lift was nailed shut, the officers requested to see the rejected pieces. "This is the end," thought Mr. Blusztajn, but he came up with a plausible explanation. "My son already took them home," he stammered. But the officers didn't give up either; they couldn't allow two offending pieces of silver to be lawlessly taken out of Poland! They have been, after all, disallowed! And Mr. Blusztajn looked like he was good for another hefty bribe. "Then let him bring the two pieces back for inspection; we'll wait." Mr. Blusztajn choked with fear at the vision of the predictable worst, imagining himself behind bars in a Polish prison for years to come. It was late. He sent his daughter, my friend Isabelle, with instructions – let Benek bring back the two spoons! Isabelle knew what happened. She understood the situation and left, thinking she may never see her father again. And then, amazingly, a few hours later, and to everyone's great surprise, Benek triumphantly returned with both spoons. How did this miracle happen? The Kupers, another Jewish family in the building where the Blusztajns lived, bought the same silverware set for emigration. Benek borrowed the two spoons from them. Quick thinking, but not really a coincidence: only one brand of table silver was available in stores, and that's what everyone bought! Róża Goldfarb Holmgren remembered the proud name the set bore: "Duchy of Warsaw." And the darn Duchy weighed two pieces more than Jews were allowed to take!

* * *

But our set was no Polish "Duchy." It was a family treasure, and losing it was unimaginable. Every time we heard a story like the Blusztajn's, Mama's spirits sunk lower, and her resolve grew stronger – we will fight. We simply have to find a way. It was her dowry; she carried it to Siberia and back. It's all we have left of Grandma, of the life in Nowosielce; therefore, it must come with us. She stood in a kilometer-long line with other Jews at the Ministry of Art and Culture to obtain a certificate that Grandma's silver was not of Polish provenance. The procedure was different and unfamiliar; my parents had to write an application for their case to be heard (stamps, fees, lines, more fees) and argued, truthfully, that the 19th-century silver is Austrian, from Kaiser's Galicia. It even bore some German engravings. The final ruling in the case was from the curator of the Museum of Lower Silesia. Again lines, fees, and stamps. At first, a denial and then, miraculously, after persuasion in a different form, a certificate that the silver could be taken out of Poland. Ugly post-German paintings and furniture – no. Grandma's silver – yes. Great joy.

However, "could be taken out of Poland" constituted eligibility, not permission. Customs had their own rules: weight and number of pieces. Endless discussions at home: if only thirty-six pieces are allowed, is it better to take a full set but for only four people, or the basic subset of knife, fork, and spoon for twelve? And, will either of these options pass the weight test? All this was painful – a family treasure reduced to weighing and counting in order to conform to just invented, arbitrary, ill-willed rules. In the end, void of strength to continue the battle, my parents packed a full set for four, the permitted thirty-six pieces, and left the rest with Uncle

Zacharje. Mama consoled herself, thinking that Zacharje would someday join us and they, as well as Grandma's silver, would be reunited. How would Zacharje convince the Customs to allow him to take a set for eight was not discussed. Besides, Zacharje was ill. I believed the family legend that he would join us later, as soon as he felt better. No one explained to me that it was merely a code - Zacharje will never go anywhere because he has no one to emigrate for. My parents emigrated for me.

I think back to the couple in Rome who emigrated with the coffin of their daughter. For whom and for what did they emigrate? Perhaps for dignity. Having fathered three beautiful children, Zacharje didn't even get to bury them. He didn't even have a coffin or a grave. He never forgave himself for leaving them behind. Hindsight, he thought – and sometimes said so – he should have gone into hiding and stayed near his family. He didn't because it would endanger everyone's life – those who were going and those who stayed – but he lost the family anyway. "They went up in smoke in Auschwitz," he repeated. I heard this phrase when I was a little child: "They went up in smoke." "They went up in smoke." As a child, I woke up in the middle of the night sweaty, heaving, trembling with fear, unable to stop hearing that phrase and imagining what it meant.

Zacharje, alone after the war, lived out of sheer momentum but without any desire, will, or joy. He never laughed and rarely smiled. Perhaps my Mother, whom he loved dearly, and I, who was a flicker of life rekindled, obliged him to go on, but after we left, there was nothing. He chose to let go and died shortly thereafter.

Most of Grandma Goldman's silver stayed with him, and no one knows what happened to it after his death. It disappeared.

Grandma Goldman's brass candlesticks at our wedding in Carmel, California (1999).

SOCIAL AND CULTURAL LIFE

Emigration is a funeral after which life still goes on.

Tadeusz Kotarbiński

Most of "our" immigrants to America ended up in large cities with substantial Jewish populations. More than 10% of New York City was Jewish, even more in Los Angeles. In contrast, in Michigan, Jews constituted less than 1% of the population, and accordingly, only a few of "our" families came to Detroit. Eva Bober, from Wałbrzych, came with her sister and brother-in-law, Bożena and Chester; their father suffered a recent heart attack, and both parents stayed in Poland. The rest of us were students: Sioma (Simon) Zakalik came from Szczecin; the whole family did. In Poland, in addition to his studies, sweet, handsome Sioma played the drums in a Jewish garage band proudly called "Successors to the Thrones." He had a charming smile, swayed his hips, and every girl in Szczecin had a crush on him. Jerry Brenholz was also from Szczecin; he somehow got to Detroit before us, separated from his sister and parents, who all landed on the East Coast. Karol (Carl) Żmijewski and his Mother, Sophie, hailed from Warsaw; the two of them constituted the whole family except for the relatives in Detroit who sponsored them. Marek (Mark) Cybulski was also from Warsaw; he came alone and found himself in Detroit, thanks to a sponsoring aunt. Eventually, we all learned to appreciate his Aunt Frieda's cooking and baking. There was also the Holsztyński family. Mrs. Holsztyński was a prominent nuclear chemist; she did research at the Polish Nuclear Institute where, among many scientific awards, she also received, more than once, an unwelcome dose of radiation. After March, she was thrown out of work. With the consent of her coworker, a jointly completed scientific paper was published without her name. Perhaps this is what hurt her the most. Mr. Holsztyński was a mathematician. They had two sons: the older Włodek, already with a family of his own, left an Assistant professorship in Mathematics at Warsaw University, where he was the youngest faculty member, a huge talent. The Math Department at the University of Michigan in Ann Arbor snatched him in no time. Witek (Victor Holen), the younger, was a mathematics student. Of course.

There were also three other families from Wrocław: the Gurewiczes, the Morgowiczes, and the Cukiermans. Of those, Mr. Gurewicz was the only one I knew from my childhood: a colorful, imminently likable character. He also survived a labor camp in the depths of Russia. The story had it that, hoping for an extra ration of bread, he raised his hand when they asked if there was a dentist in the crowd. He was not a dentist, had never studied dentistry, and wasn't much of a scholar altogether – he probably barely knew how to read and write. But his skill suited the circumstances, and for several years, he did serve as the camp dentist. Using available workbench tools, most likely pliers, he simply pulled people's aching teeth, which was the ubiquitous dental treatment.

Mr. Gurewicz came to America with his wife, three children, and a solid belief that this land of opportunity would be good to him. He will work hard and spread his wings; the American Dream seems within his reach. He had moxie and boundless energy, he was fearless, and there was no limit to the things he was willing to try. He was not a tailor, but he opened a tailor shop that went belly up. He then tried a sparkling water delivery service, which was sort of a precursor to SodaStream. He was ahead of his times; another flop. The Polish food restaurant with his wife in the kitchen didn't succeed either, nor did the dry cleaner. Undeterred, he tried a few more things; the clothing business succeeded for a while but then folded as well. Nothing worked, a story straight from Sholem Aleichem's *Motl, the Cantor's Son*. After a few years, Mr. Gurewicz was out of money, out of ideas, and, most importantly, he lost faith. Unable to support his family, depressed, he ended up in a psychiatric institution and, finally, tragically, took his own life. He was not the only suicide of our exile.

My Roman lesson rings true again: ***this is the price of our exile.***

But we, the young generation, tried to build a semblance of normal life. We met on weekends, played bridge, and took short out-of-town excursions to explore the area. Eva and Carl became a couple.

On Saturday mornings, she and I did laundry together at a laundromat since neither of us had a washing machine in our apartment. We fed coins into the slots, let the machines do the work, and talked—pleasant, carefree moments. In the laundromat, we were truly carefree.

One day Sophie, Carl's Mom, complimented me on a dress I wore. I thanked her, and she accurately observed that thanking for a compliment is an American custom. Indeed. Good manners in Poland called for diminishing the complimented object in bouts of exaggerated modesty: "What?

Eva Bober and Carl Fromm got married by the Justice of Peace in the Detroit City Hall. Sabina (left) was a witness at their wedding (1971).

This old rag?!" Yet, here, in Detroit, I expressed gratitude. Perhaps we are changing already? I was very interested in the upcoming, unavoidable transformation: what will "becoming an American" look like? Will I be aware of the changes as they occur? Will I be pleased? Carl and his Mother decided to return to their true pre-war surname, Fromm. Mark did as well; he shed the Polish-sounding Cybulski and returned to Beiner.

Within a relatively short time, all of us found work.

Eva sat down with a dictionary and, in the Help Wanted section of the *Detroit News*, found two ads for Dental Technicians. The first call resulted in an interview; the owner asked her to make a tooth out of soap. He liked the tooth and offered her a job. She came back with wonderful news: she had a job, and her wage would be two dollars. She didn't know if the two dollars were per day or per hour. It mattered, of course, but she didn't call to clarify – she would take the job anyway. She worked there for five years until 1974 when they moved to California. At first, she commuted by bus forty-five minutes each way. After a year, she bought a brand-new Chevy Camaro. It was the first new car among my friends.

Carl studied chemistry at the University of Warsaw, but his first job in the US was pumping gas and washing windshields at a gas station owned by his family. After two months, he found a job as a technician at Frankel, a company that processed metal scrap from car factories. Within several months, he was promoted to deputy chief of the chemical laboratory.

My new Aunt Ruth, Ruby's wife, liked me. Our camaraderie started when one of the participants in a friendly bridge tournament at their house cancelled last moment. They were in a quandary. Remembering that I once mumbled something about playing bridge, and with no expectations whatsoever, they asked me to fill the chair. To everyone's surprise, mostly my own, I won the tournament. My stock rose tremendously. A few days later, Ruth invited me to lunch in a restaurant, my first. She ordered for each of us a hot dog. It was typical lunch fare, she explained. The dish took me by surprise: an ordinary-looking sausage in a long, soft, white roll, doused generously with mustard and ketchup. It didn't even look appetizing. Mine came first, and Ruth encouraged me to start. I had no idea how to eat it. In the end, my European upbringing and *kinderstube* prevailed, and I launched an attack with a knife and fork. Not good. The knife was too dull or the roll too soft – it tore under the knife, the sausage kept coming out, the ketchup oozed, and the whole thing slid around on the plate. I regretted having started first; I should have waited to observe and follow Ruth's technique. But her method didn't convince me either. She picked up the whole thing and ate. While holding it in her hand, some ketchup dripped, and her lipstick smeared. We looked at each other in embarrassment; I am sure we each had the same thoughts.

Her older daughter, Laura, roughly my age, invited me to her birthday celebration. A perfect garden party, like from a movie: dozens of young people milled around the big house and manicured garden, a few were in the pool, and someone was playing badminton. An emotional scene was underway in the gazebo: a few boys surrounded by a small crowd were hugging. It looked like they were saying goodbye. Laura sniffled; I had the impression that one of these departing young men was not indifferent to her. She motioned me to come closer and introduced me. They are going to Vietnam, she said. I didn't understand.

"To Vietnam?! But there is a war there!"

"Exactly. One of them was drafted by lottery, and his two friends volunteered – they are going to fight."

"Our country is at war, you know. It's our duty."

Jewish boys will fight in Vietnam for their country? Of course.

* * *

For centuries, Jews fought and died for their homelands in the diaspora. Only 150,000 Jews lived then in the US at the time of the Civil War, but at least 10,000 of them served (7,000 for the Union and 3,000 for the Confederacy), and about 600 were killed in battle. About 1.5 million Jews fought as part of the Allied forces during WWII. The largest number were Jewish Americans – 550,000 out of a total of 16 million Americans who served, an astounding 11.5% of the 4,770,000 American Jews, a ratio about 10 times higher than for the overall population. Some 52,000 of these received U.S. military awards; more than 20 were awarded the Medal of Honor, the US military's highest award. Over 2,000 of the Ritchie Boys, an elite American intelligence and counterintelligence group, were comprised primarily of German and Austrian Jewish refugees living in the US, all volunteers, all fluent in German. There were about 20,000 trained in Camp Ritchie; the Jews comprised 10%.

There were about 500,000 Jewish soldiers in the Red Army during WWII; some 120,000 were killed in combat, and the Germans murdered another 80,000 as prisoners of war. More than 160,000 people at all levels of command earned citations, with over 150 designated as Heroes of the Soviet Union, the highest honor awarded by the Red Army. Some 150,000 Polish Jews fought in the ranks of the Polish Army. Over 32,000 fell or were wounded, and about 61,000 were taken prisoner. About 30,000 Jews served in the British army, some in special units of Jews from Palestine, such as the Jewish Brigade, which helped liberate Italy.

*I took this photo at the Manila American Cemetery and Memorial in the
Philippines. It contains the largest number of graves of American military dead in
World War II, a total of 17,184 fallen in operations in New Guinea and the
Philippines. One hundred seventy-one of the headstones bear a Star of David.*

Foreign Jews were also major contributors in developing military science and technology. Einstein, J.Oppenheimer, Feynman, and Teller were the core of the Manhattan Project, which led to the development of the first nuclear weapons; all Jewish scientists.

* * *

Throughout geography and history, Jews demonstrated their patriotism with courage and blood. But THIS war? My head was exploding. In Poland, we were smothered with official sympathy for the North Vietnamese. There were blood drives in all institutions of work and higher learning. More than once, I gave blood for the bleeding Viet Cong at my Wrocław University of Science and Technology.

I realized once again that the changes in my life were bigger than I ever imagined.

After the shootings at Kent State, the anti-war movement gained in scope and intensity. The Chicago 7 trial was in full, ugly swing – an important moment in American history (by the way, several of its defendants were Jewish). At many universities, including mine (I was already a student at Wayne State), a student strike was declared; the organizers called for coming to the campus but not attending lectures. I was in turmoil, remembering all too well the events in Poland which led to our exile.

Again? I thought. *Again?!!!!*

Lectures took place, and some people attended while others did not. The courtyards were full; the whole campus was abuzz with intense political debate. Views about the war were divided. The essence of the differences was evident on posters plastered throughout the campus. Some declared: "AMERICA – love it or leave it"; others, "AMERICA – change it or lose it."

They were all patriots, and all passionately loved their country. They differed in the vision of how to best act upon this patriotism. I struggled. The school was precious to me. Each lecture was a triumph – I was reconstructing my life. After a painful while, our family had two cars now, I still held a full-time job, I took loans at the Jewish Family Service to pay for tuition, and I still had to repay the loan from HIAS, which was a point of honor… And here, I found myself in the middle of a huge moral conflict I didn't understand. My last student protest didn't end well for me.

I watched on television pictures of the victims of shootings at Kent State, among them a visibly pregnant girl. I read the accounts of the Chicago 7 trial. The world was abuzz with news of American planes dropping bombs on Cambodia. I've learned about the secret war in Laos going on since 1964. *"I'm already an American,"* I thought. *"I need to take a stand."*

On the second day of the strike, I did not attend lectures.

All three of Laura's friends returned from Vietnam, but there were only five legs between them. The sixth one stayed behind, scattered in the Vietnamese countryside after an encounter with a Viet Cong landmine.

TRIP TO AUSCHWITZ

We Polish Jews...

We, the truth of the graves, and we, the illusion of living, we, millions of corpses and we, a few, perhaps a score of thousands of quasi non-corpses: we, that boundless brotherly tomb, we, a Jewish burial ground such as was never seen before and will never be seen again.

We, suffocated in gas chambers and turned into soap – a soap that will not wash clean the stains of our blood nor the stigma of the sin the world has perpetrated upon us.

We, whose brains spattered upon the walls of our miserable dwellings and the walls under which we were stood for mass execution solely because we were Jews.

We, the Golgotha upon which an endless forest of crosses could be raised. We, who two thousand years ago gave humanity a Son of Man slaughtered by the Roman Empire, and this one innocent death was enough to make him God.

What religion will arise from millions of deaths, tortures, degradations, and arms stretched wide in the last agony of despair?

Julian Tuwim, *We, Polish Jews*, Fragments
first published in Free World, New York, July 1944,

English Translation by R. Langer

An impersonal letter from strangers in Poland informed us that Zacharje passed away. We couldn't go to the funeral anyway – we couldn't leave the US without Green Cards – but the letter arrived weeks after, underscoring the irreversible finality. It hit us hard. Mama was devastated; she somehow hung on to hope that she would see him again; that they would once again be near each other, just as they have been all their lives. In our tiny postwar families, each person was extremely important, and Zacharje. He was seventeen years Mama's senior, the oldest of six siblings. Mama was the youngest. He looked after her, taught her how to work on the family farm, and admonished her when she did something wrong. He took care of her in Siberia and sometimes chopped her trees so she wouldn't fall behind when she was exhausted and couldn't anymore. And, when they remained orphans after the war, she looked to him with trust and devotion as if he were her father. For me, he was the gestalt of a beloved grandfather I never had. Even as a little child, I understood that he carried unimaginable weight and trauma. I so much wanted to make him happy, to ease his pain even for a minute. I used to tell him that when I grew up, I would darn his socks. I felt victorious when he sometimes smiled. He never laughed.

* * *

I was fourteen or fifteen when Wrocław was hit by a bizarre epidemic of smallpox brought from India by a merchant marine or a government employee. The city and the country were completely unprepared – there were no procedures, no medicines, and only symbolic quantities of vaccine. Before the city was sealed in quarantine, my parents worried about me, always worried about me, and sent me away to safety. I was to stay with Zacharje in Mysłowice, one of the dirty mining towns in Upper Silesia. I spent several weeks there.

I was taken aback when, during my stay, unexpectedly, Zacharje declared that we would visit Auschwitz. I didn't want to go and pleaded that I was not ready... But there was no discussion: "You must see it, you must know."

It wasn't far. The two of us took a slow suburban train—buried in thought, separated by a heavy silence.

I was thinking about his dearest ones, whom I had never met—they "went up in smoke." A family story. A recurring nightmare. He knew their faces,   heard their voices… at night, in tortured memories of better times, he probably dreamed of hugging his children goodnight and then making love to his wife. And he likely imagined their final fear and suffering, blaming himself for being alive.

There were only a few visitors that day, and we were often alone. I was paralyzed by the display cases full of shoes and hair, by the mountains of dolls, eyeglasses, prostheses, and suitcases. I pleaded several times to turn back, but Zacharje's resolve prevailed: "You must know."

The harsh sounds of conversation among a German tour nearby were unbearable; we let them pass. More sticky silence. Still, we managed somehow until we came to the gas chambers and, beyond, the crematoria. No one was there except for the two of us.

Neatly stacked clothes lay on benches and hung on numbered hooks of the antechamber.

We paused. I understood by his demeanor that this was our destination; everything up to this point was a preamble. Zacharje pulled out his tallit, the traditional prayer shawl, and wrapped himself in it. Not the way I remembered seeing him in the synagogue in Wrocław on High Holy Days, with the tallit draped on his shoulders. He wrapped himself completely, covering his face and head. He looked like an Egyptian mummy. And he stood there for a long time, repeating the mantra of Kaddish, the prayer for the dead, swaying and sobbing quietly.

Yit'gadal v'yit'kadash sh'mei raba

b'al'ma di v'ra khir'utei

v'yam'likh mal'khutei b'chayeikhon uv'yomeikhon…

I couldn't breathe. It's as if I unlearned that most natural of body functions. I wasn't choking or gasping for air; I just couldn't, didn't know how to breathe. It wasn't even THEM; it was my Uncle. The unbearable enormity of his pain.

Suffering is locked in the DNA of survivors.

Pain, like eye color, is inherited. Will I pass it on to my children?

Are these thoughts uniquely Jewish?

We didn't talk at all on the way out, or at the train station, or inside the dingy train going back. And then, already in his apartment, I broke out with a high fever. A friendly doctor whom Zacharje summoned – doctors made house calls then – declared with concern: "The girl came from Wrocław; there is suspicion of smallpox."

There were no free beds in the local hospital where the ambulance took me, so I spent the night on a gurney in the corridor. A makeshift screen made of sheets was installed around me, maybe for privacy and maybe in a feeble attempt at isolation. Zacharje sat by my side, undeterred by the possible diagnosis. Everyone except for him wore facemasks. I am sure the phones rang all over the region trying to decide what to do with this "case"; they waited for other symptoms. But none developed, and in the morning, the fever broke.

Zacharje Goldman, Mysłowice (1968)

I saw Zacharje cry when he and Uncle Janek stood motionless at the train station in Zebrzydowice. Janek and his family followed us into exile a few months later, and Zacharje understood that he would never see us again and saw no point in living with pain, which was his only constant companion, so he died.

He was buried in Wrocław at the old Jewish cemetery on Lotnicza Street. We paid some strangers to put a headstone on the first anniversary of his death and someone else – a man someone recommended – to maintain the grave "forever." I hope the "forever" man lives a long life.

I wanted to visit Zacharje's grave on my first trip back to Wrocław. A middle-aged man from the Jewish Community Services accompanied us. He opened the iron gate with a skeleton key; the gate is usually chained and padlocked in a feeble attempt to keep away vandals, drunks, and homeless lovers. It was summer, and the cemetery was all overgrown with thicket, and it actually looked beautiful. We found Zacharje's grave following the map our guide brought, cleaned the overgrowth and the moss, and fashioned a small path to facilitate future access.

Nearby, we also found the grave of Mama's friend, Genia Blusztajn, my friend Isabelle's Mother; it was her widower who struggled at Polish customs with two silver spoons. Genia's weak heart didn't handle well the stresses of "March Events"; she died shortly before our departure. Cleaning the thicket further, we came to the grave of Rachela Cyngiser, the directress of our Jewish school; she died when I was in fifth or sixth grade. The whole school walked behind her casket. Mama wasn't pleased; she was sure that our Jewish tradition prohibits children of living parents from visiting cemeteries; the solemn duty of visiting graves starts for each person upon the death of

Two of the three children of Zacharje Goldman and Ita Winter Goldman. The third was a twin, though I am unsure of which one. All three were murdered in Auschwitz alongside their mother. I don't even know their names

a parent. But these traditions were developed centuries before the Holocaust, when dead people usually had graves, and children usually outlived their parents.

The graves of the Rotbaum siblings, Jacob and Leah, moved me. They were both outstanding theatrical directors; he also painted, and she was also a choreographer. Buried with them was Jacob's wife, Sylvia Swen (Sara Szejnwald), a famous choreographer and ballet dancer who later started a dance school for Jewish children. I danced in her ballet for many years.

In the rear of the cemetery is an imposing, well-kept military section with graves of Jewish officers who wore German uniforms in Breslau. They died in the First World War or even earlier. I wondered who maintains this part. And who will look after all "our" graves in years to come? A cemetery without a community.

In 2010, during my visit to Wrocław on the occasion of my class reunion, the cemetery was closed, and I could not get to Zacharje. I stood by the iron gate with a heavy heart.

For millennia, however poor or small the Jewish community was, there was always a school, a

prayer house, a hospital, and a cemetery. When the Jews left – and they always left escaping persecution – the cemeteries stayed behind. There were over 1,200 of them in Poland before WWII. The Germans were more interested in killing than in those already dead, but they often sold the *matzevas* pillaged from the cemeteries to the local population to be used as pavement, building material, millstones, or to sharpen farm tools. Massive destruction also came after the war and to this day, with continued theft of the *matzevas* and desecration of the buried bodies in search of gold teeth or jewelry. Many cemetery sites were consigned to oblivion by communist authorities, razzed, and planted with trees for a forest. In the village of Wizna, where a fish pond was dug on a cemetery site, the morbid joke is that it breeds gefilte fish.

Now, post-communism, sometimes a keeper steps forward, but often the cemeteries die as well.

Starowola near Parysów. Avrohom Berkowitz from New York inspects the writings on metzevas used to build this cowshed. The metzevas came from the nearby cemetery; they were probably stolen around 1943. The owner of the cowshed recently tried to sell the structure, but his changing price (20,000 PLN, then 200,000 PLN, now 30,000 PLN) made progress difficult. Meanwhile, he charges visitors 10 PLN per person and more for a permit to take photos. He also negotiates discounts for larger groups. A businessman.

There are two other cowsheds built from metzevas in Starowola, as well as some roads and a stoop in front of a wooden outhouse.

Photo and commentary by Krzysztof Bielawski.

MY JOB: GOOD AND BAD NEWS

*Everything will be okay in the end. If it's
not okay, it's not the end.*

John Lennon

My job is going well.

I work in Oak Park, a suburb of Detroit. To get there I only take one bus, barely a half-hour ride, then walk fifteen minutes along a pleasant, tree-lined street. My boss, the owner of the office, likes my work; he often stops by my drafting table and looks approvingly over my shoulder at my accurate, well-laid-out drawings and tidy lettering. We draft in pencil here, which is a blessing. At the University of Science and Technology in Poland, we drafted in ink, and errors were almost irreversible. Sometimes, I was able to fix a mistake by carefully scraping off a faulty line or letter with a razor blade, but more often than not, this crude surgery left a hole in the parchment, and I had to start anew no matter how far along I was. But here, every station was equipped with a wonderful electric eraser, and errors were eliminated in seconds and without a trace. The owner was pleasant and bright; sometimes, we talked for a few minutes about things other than work. He found it interesting and exotic that I was an eyewitness to life behind the Iron Curtain and a victim of government-sanctioned antisemitic persecution. But I noticed a concerning pattern: passing behind my stool, he sometimes rubbed himself against me. The space was tight, I thought. He surely didn't mean to – but I felt uncomfortable whenever he approached.

The good news was that I already earned over $4 an hour. I started at $3.20, and after a few weeks, I got a raise and then another one. I was thrilled even before the raises and did not ask for anything. A colleague explained to me that they started me lower than it was customary, and now, seeing how well I work, they are honorably "catching up." Who would have thought that drafting is such a marketable skill?! What luck!

A couple weeks before I started work, Rose took me to the Social Security Administration, where I was assigned the all-important Social Security Number and issued a card I still have. They asked for that card when I went to the bank to open an account, and I felt victorious. The next request, however, stopped me: "And your driver's license, please." I didn't have a driver's license. I explained that I was about to start working and planned to save for a driver's education. The lady behind the desk looked at me with kind disbelief, complimented my English ("You speak like an American"), and just asked for my address. I then had to select the color of my to-be-printed checks and an emblem: a teddy bear, a flower, or a fish. I chose the American flag. I then deposited ten dollars, which was the required minimum to open an account, and walked out of the bank feeling as if I'd just taken a huge step. "Next time, I'll deposit my first check," I thought.

Payday was every other Friday. The first check was a disappointment. I expected the amount to be my hourly wage multiplied by eighty hours, but it was for less; they deducted various taxes, insurances, and other items marked with acronyms and abbreviations I didn't understand. These deductions and the resulting check amount changed as my wages rose. I multiplied the net amount by months of work, and the hazy dream of a car for my parents began to take shape. It was still far away but visible – a goal rather than a dream. It will be a used car, of course – the longer we wait, the better the car – newer, with extra features – maybe a radio or even air conditioning. Hopefully, it will be in good enough condition to minimize future breakdowns and repairs. And maybe I'll get another raise?

Carl Fromm bought a car after working for six months, a 1958 Chevrolet Bel Air. It had large holes in the floor so you could almost walk on the road, but Carl didn't care; he chose the car because of its tailfins. Eva took out a large loan and courageously bought a new Chevy Camaro. Marek Beiner drove a beat-up yellow Corvair with its engine in the rear and the trunk in the front. We were adapting.

The car dream for my parents materialized in the form of a two-year-old, burgundy-colored Ford Cougar. It was in good shape, and we were ecstatic thinking about how many years of good service it would give my parents. But the Cougar could not deliver on its promise. After a year or so, Tata wrapped the coveted Cougar around a telephone pole, and that was the end of it. Luckily, miraculously, both Mama and Tata walked away from the crash unscathed. Under different circumstances, I would have begged Tata to never drive again, but in Detroit, there was no other option; he needed to drive to work. I gave them the car I just bought for myself, my pride, a brand-new Oldsmobile Cutlass. It was a sad and happy moment for me; I did it because I could, and it made them happy, and me as well. I will buy another one. But this was my first, hard-won treasure.

Tata drove it and other cars to follow for another twenty years or so and, from time to time, got acquainted with various poles, walls, and other sundry obstacles.

CAN ANYONE HELP?

In an instant the most important matters take a different turn

Publius Cornelius Tacitus, *The Annals*

My employer's rubbing advances became a habit. I could no longer pretend that they were accidental, but I didn't know how to deal with it. I tried to arrange my stool so that it would be awkward for him to get behind me. I moved it as far back as possible, but he was undeterred – he simply asked me to move forward, closer to my drafting table, and leaned over my shoulder as if to review my work, all the while rubbing himself against me ever more boldly. What should I do? The situation could be neither ignored nor endured. I was afraid that if I confronted him, he might fire me. There was no one I felt comfortable asking for advice. Finally, I made an appointment with our caseworker at the Jewish Family Service, took the afternoon off, and went by dirty bus to her office.

She was horrified.

"But this is a great job. They weren't sure it would work out, but now they are very pleased, and you're paid so well ..."

Of course. "I know, that's why I'm here."

It didn't go well. She started by questioning my facts – am I sure? It would be terrible if we accused an innocent man of such a thing, an upstanding member of the Jewish community, a family man ... "Perhaps you are too sensitive," she suggested, veiling her thoughts not too subtly. "Aren't you overreacting?" I felt offended by the question. "No, I am not," I thought, but I kept quiet and listened, hoping that some offer of help, or at least some advice, would come at the end. But she went on with psycho-babble about cultural differences, spoke of "Eastern Europe" with barely concealed distaste as if it were a dirty word, and lectured me that "things are different here." Meaning what? It appeared that, in her opinion, I should just return to work and live with the situation. No empathy, no intent to resolve anything. She spoke in guarded terms, but it really was a monologue about the contrast between my provincial "Eastern European" values and this grand, progressive world I now inhabit. And ingratitude. She implied ingratitude. Her final argument was outright demeaning: the cold reality of our status. Surely, she didn't mean to offend me, but she did – she reminded me of my situation and pointed out how hard things are for my parents as well, yet they don't complain. A dirty move. And when I heard her say something like "beggars can't be choosers," I lost it. It was a poorly chosen phrase – she really didn't know how to deal with the situation – but all I heard was "beggars," and I lost control. I was overcome by a swell of bitter-tasting, accumulated helplessness. Our situation was not her fault, but she will not help – and I have no other place to turn. And I exploded at her, for there was no one else to explode at:

"Your caseload just got lighter!!!"

And I ran out, slamming the door. End of chapter. *End of chapter!*

And then came THAT moment. The moment when I

liberated myself from dependency, from humility and humiliation, from accepting help, from feeling and expressing gratitude, from politeness, from favors... **I miss feeling like a person. I miss knowing the right thing to do. I miss belonging somewhere. I miss someone, anyone, seeing ME... I ALREADY LOST EVERYTHING AND GAVE AWAY THE REST. THERE IS NOTHING LEFT TO GIVE. NOTHING LEFT TO GIVE...**

I cried. *I don't want to be an immigrant! I DON'T WANT TO BE AN IMMIGRANT!*

Our caseworker didn't expect an explosion, and in truth, neither did I. I was already in the corridor when she ran after me. I still heard her calling me, pleading that she only wanted what was best for me. But **she didn't know what "best" was;** SHE THOUGHT "BEST" WAS A WELL-PAID JOB BUT REALLY, TRULY, "BEST" WAS REGAINING **DIGNITY**. I was running away from the only person here charged with helping us; I was not there anymore. I was gone, outside, on the street, terrified, crying, all alone on a deserted Detroit street with no people because they were all locked in their cars.

And this is when I stopped being an immigrant and started my life as an American.

* * *

Most American Jews descended from Eastern European immigrants. They landed on Ellis Island poor and hungry, eager for the New World, eager to live without fear of pogroms, to work, and to educate their children. Stories of persecution were aplenty in their families and social circles, and "Eastern Europe" was an ugly provenance filled with ill will, prejudice, and disrespect for "others." Perhaps the lady thought I was taking my American transformation too far and asking for too much, too soon. But this was HER story. Years later, I still think she was wrong.

* * *

A year after we arrived, I received the coveted Green Card, which granted me the same privileges as a US citizen, except for the right to vote. I was still stateless. My big indulgence in the newly gained rights was a half-hour drive across the Detroit River to Windsor, the border town on the Canadian side. I was there for less than an hour – I didn't know what to see or do – but waving the Green Card at the border booth was the whiff of freedom I yearned for.

The final step in reconstructing my national belonging came five years after our arrival. I became a citizen, no longer stateless. I was already married then, the wife of an American. That in itself was sufficient for citizenship, but I didn't want it that way. My citizenship was supposed to be **my own**, earned by myself, not thanks to my husband. We lived in Ann Arbor, Michigan, at the time. The Naturalization Ceremony – this is what Americans call granting of citizenship to someone born outside of the country – took place in the courthouse. Several dozens of us filled the courtroom, a true Tower of Babel. In solemn silence thick with emotion, we listened when the Justice of Peace read our names one by one. Hispanic names, Southeast Asian names, and some Europeans. As if in a kaleidoscope, I saw flashing images of other times, other lists... Wien Südbahnhof, Stazione Termini... That journey was over.

The judge congratulated us on our new status and reminded us of the privileges and duties of a citizen. And then, in this most American gesture, hand on heart, we murmured in unison: **I pledge allegiance to the flag of the United States of America and to the Republic**...

On my way out of the Court building, I threw my Polish Travel Document into the garbage can. In that bad world, the authorities charged 5,000 złotys for the privilege of losing our citizenship earned at birth, born on Polish soil to Polish parents, with Polish as our first language. In exchange, they gave us this disgraceful document that declared to the world that the HOLDER OF THIS DOCUMENT IS NOT A POLISH CITIZEN. This Travel Document seared me – just like the boots with broken heels in Vienna; they, too, landed in the trash. I regretted getting rid of it later; it was, after all, a piece of family history.

Certificate of Naturalization, which granted me the citizenship of the United States.

It classified my prior status as "stateless, last of Poland."

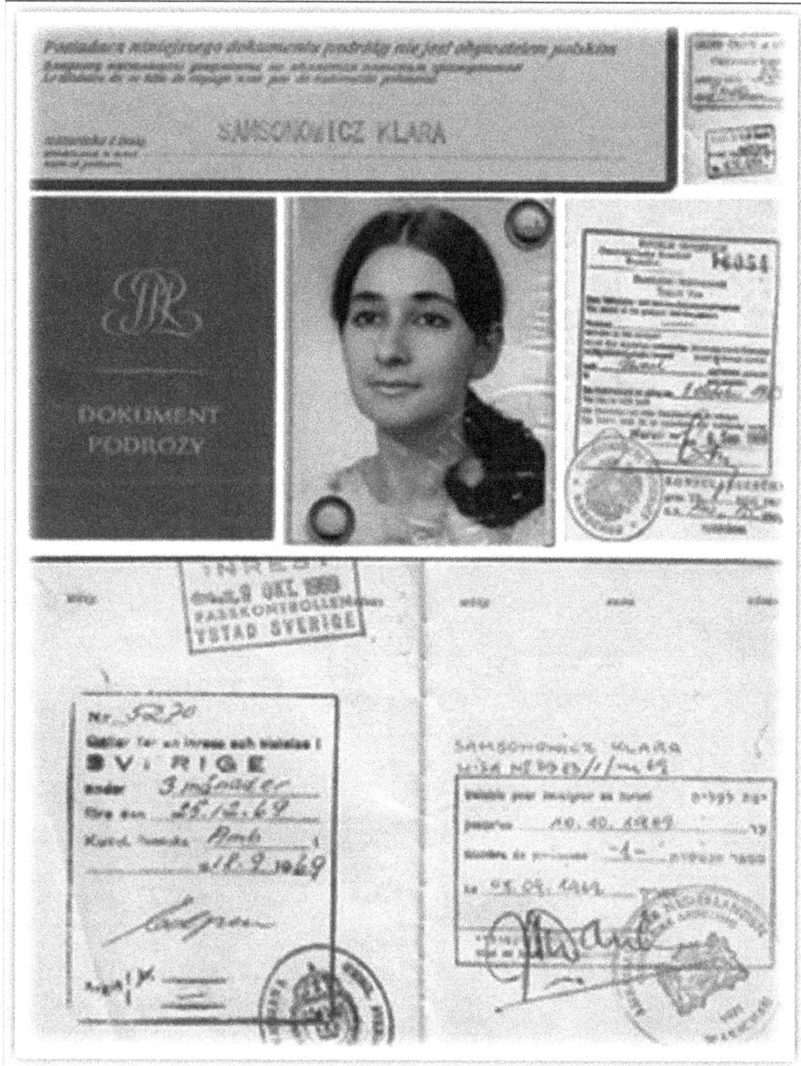

Excerpts from the Travel Document of Klara Samsonowicz (Sigvardsson), who emigrated from Łódź to Sweden.

In the upper left corner, the fateful phrase:

"The bearer of this document is not a citizen of Poland..."

Klara worked for many years in the Swedish healthcare system.

She is the wife of a Swedish Officer and the matriarch of a beautiful, multigenerational family.

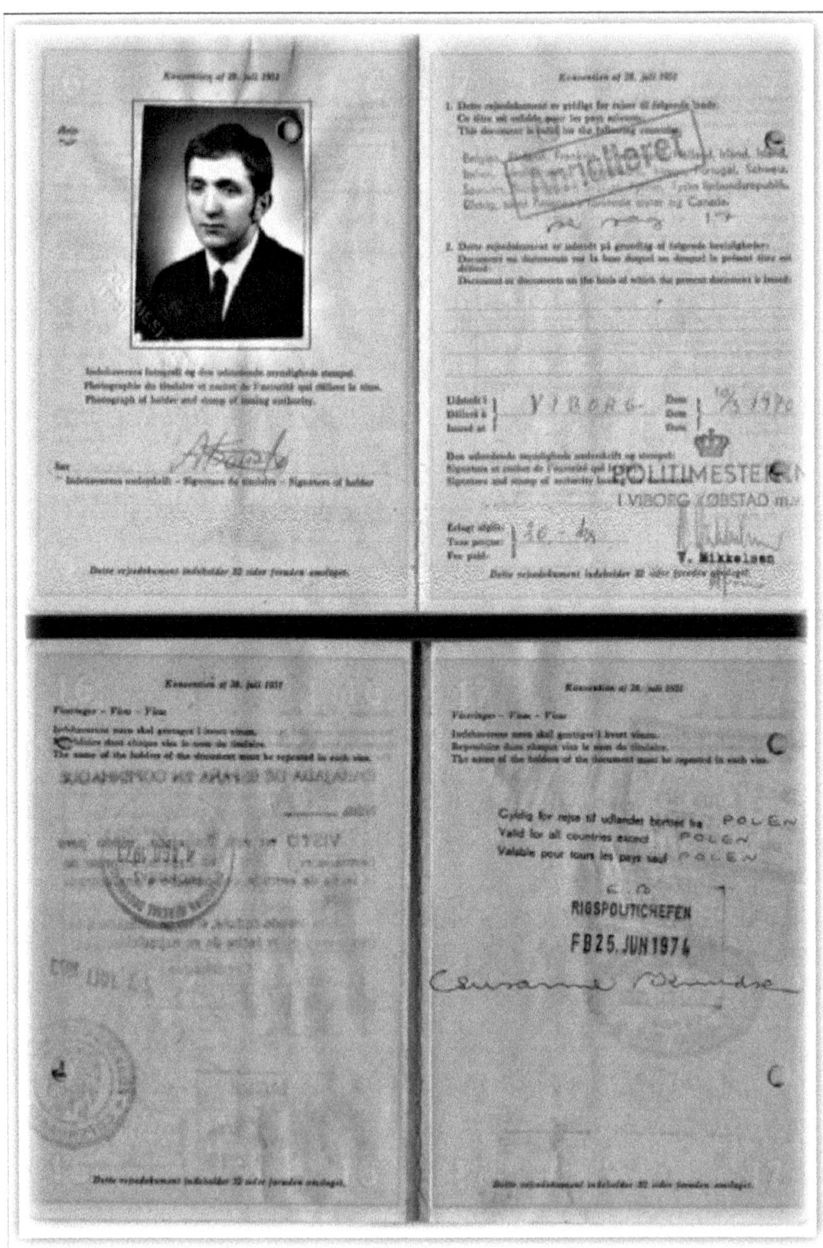

The Danish travel document issued to Adam Koński in Viborg replaced the one received in Poland a year earlier. It also specified that it was "valid for all countries except Poland."

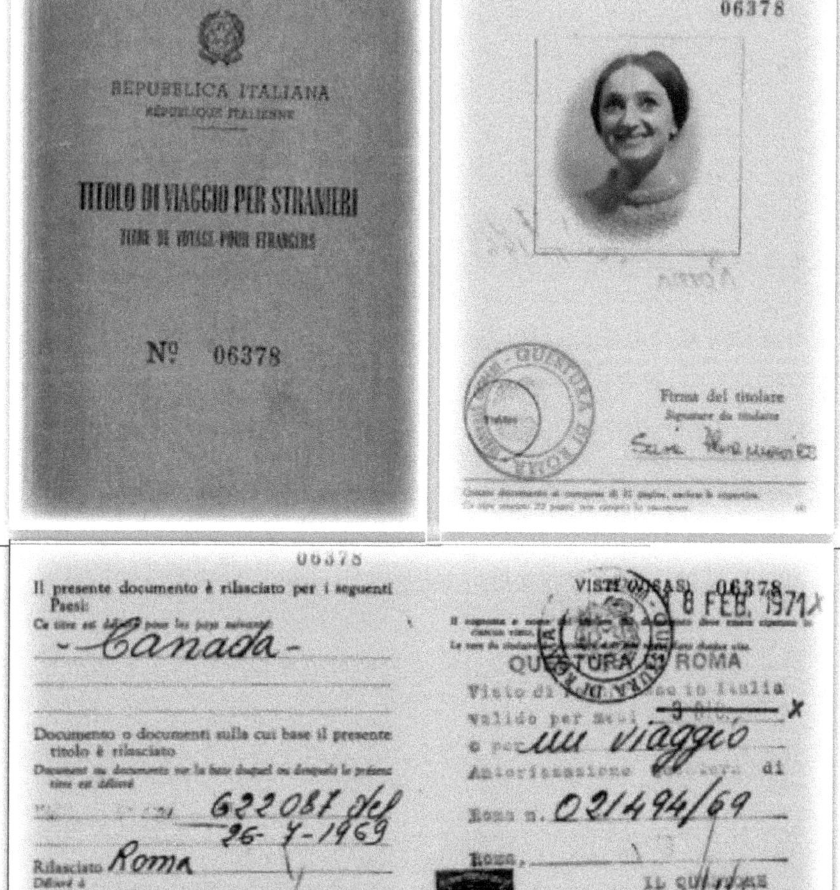

Sara Abramowicz and her family were granted Canadian visas after waiting in Rome for eight months. They traveled to Canada on the Italian TITOLO DI VIAGGIO PER STRANIERI.

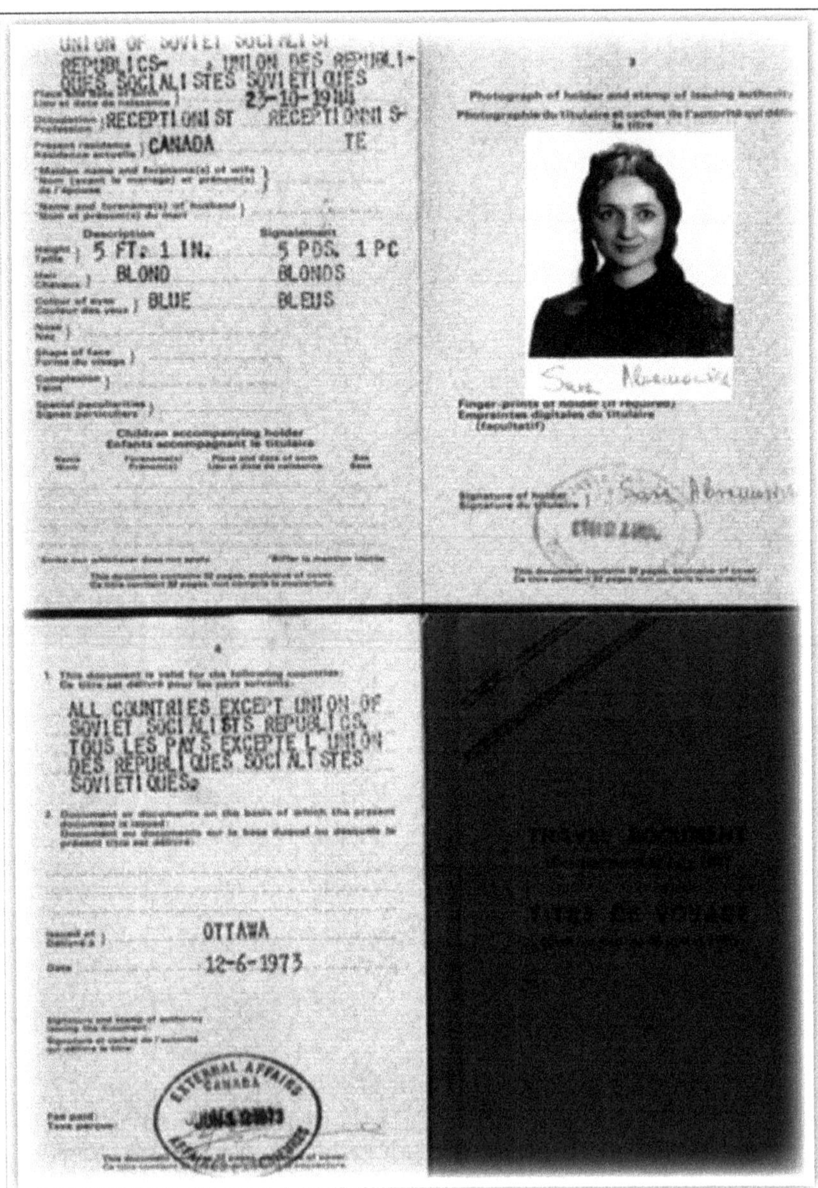

In Canada, the Italian Titolo di Viaggio was subsequently replaced by this Canadian document that is **valid for the whole world except the Soviet Union,** where Sara was born during WWII.

Sara visited Poland for the first time after 38 years and finally put a stone on her Father's grave.

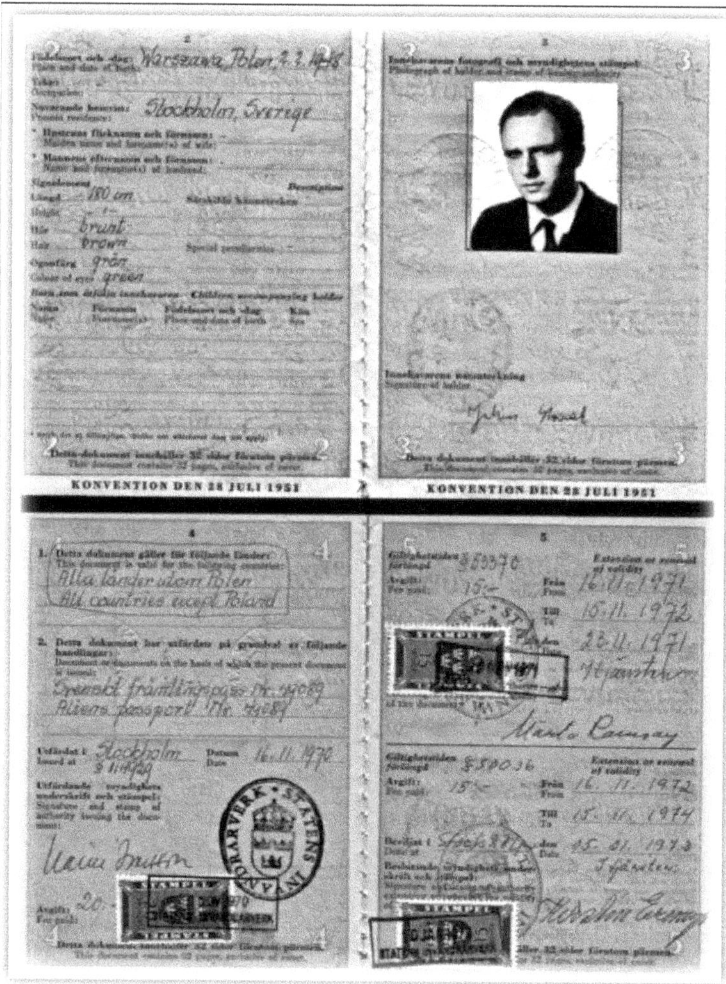

*The Swedish travel document issued in 1971 replaced the one received by Juliusz Głazek upon departure from Poland. It, too, was valid for **all countries on Earth except for Poland**.*

In Sweden, Julius returned to the original family name, Glaser. With a PhD in inorganic chemistry, he was a Professor at KTH, the Swedish Royal Institute of Technology. Now retired, he climbs mountains and dotes on his garden and grandchildren. He also sits on the Board of the Swedish chapter of Keren Hayesod, an organization devoted to raising charity funds for Israel.

Recently, his daughter, Natalie, also defended her doctoral thesis. She is a cardiologist.

THEIR STORIES

Haruki Murakami, *Norwegian Woods*

My generation of March exiles carries heavy weight. Behind our smiles, photos and stories from our travels, scientific titles earned in newly learned languages from the best universities, giggling grandchildren, and flowers in the garden, there is the bitter imprint of personal loss and transferred intergenerational trauma. Tiny, mutilated families and endless stories of murder, hunger, fear, and suffering. Few of us had aunts and uncles; almost no one had grandparents. "How do you recognize a Jew?" "Look for grandparents," was the advice in Poland. "If they have grandparents, they are likely not Jewish."

And then came the March exile, **the only exile of Jews in Europe after WWII**. And our list of losses grew by one more: we lost our homeland.

My story is not unique; it happened in some form to each of us. The nature of specific pressures and humiliations varied because our circumstances varied – and our persecutors creatively covered many grounds. Many families found themselves with no work and no means of support. Some realized that their children would not be allowed to study in Polish universities. Most felt stripped of dignity and excluded from their place in society. All of us lost the blessing of safety and belonging. The March '68 antisemitic campaign was designed to force each Jewish family to conclude that emigration was the best, if not only, option. Most of us did.

Two overwhelming facts weave like a poisonous thread through most of our stories: (1) the Polish government kept a registry of Jews for years prior to March, and (2) for years after our exile, we were not allowed to enter Poland as legal residents and even citizens of other countries.

I include here some of THEIR stories as told and entrusted to me. En toto, they round off the disgrace of the times – a brutal country-wide antisemitic campaign which, historically, signaled an oncoming pogrom. That's what our parents feared.

THE TREJBICZES:

There were four of them: Izydor, his wife Niusia, and two college-age children, Alicja and Marian. Until recently, Izydor was the Budget Director at the Ministry of Higher Education. At the meeting of peers and colleagues, where his already decided Jewish fate was to be publicly affirmed, he was asked if his wife traveled to Israel in 1967 (she did, visiting family). The thinly veiled, absurd allegation was that the Trejbiczes were Israeli spies. Izydor was kicked out of work and the party; he will never again find a job in Poland. Alicja was suspended as a student. The looming fear was that if Marian were to be suspended as well, which was likely, he would immediately be drafted into the Polish army – students were excused from compulsory service, but if he were no longer a student.... Neighbors stopped recognizing them. They had no hopes, no place to go in the morning, no one to meet with in the evening, nothing to wait for. Tainted goods. Their life in Poland has ended. They left, really, without a plan for what will happen next.

They arrived in Vienna in September 1968. Neither the US nor Canada were options since both parents had been members of the Communist Party, which automatically killed their chances for a visa. Scandinavia was not an option yet. Can't stay in Vienna either. No money, all doors closed.

A few difficult months later, the Director of the Swedish National Bureau of Immigration, Kjell Öberg, paid an official visit to Vienna. The Trejbiczes managed to arrange a meeting with him and pleaded for help. He took note. In February 1969, months before Sweden launched a large-scale program of welcoming Jewish exiles from Poland, the Trejbiczes were allowed to enter Sweden and start a new life in a small refugee camp in Lidköping.

* * *

Alicja and her Swedish husband Stefan have lived in Brussels for over 20 years. He represents Sweden in one of the EU commissions. Their children and grandchildren live in Sweden, the country of their birth. Marian, now Meir, moved in 1976 to Israel, where he is the head of a beautiful, thriving family.

THE WAJDAS:

Like so many of our parents, Lusia Wolin and Karol Celler survived the war without any family. Says their son, George Celler: "On October 12, 1941, my Mom and Dad were forced to walk with 20,000 other Jews in Stanisławów (then Poland, now Ivano-Frankivsk, Ukraine) to the local cemetery where the Ukrainians and Germans directed by Hans Krüger shot about half of them. But it took much time to kill so many Jews, and

the job was not finished by nightfall. Those still alive – Lusia and Karol among them – were released and forced into the Stanisławów ghetto. After eleven months, the two of them walked out through the main gate. She was dressed as a nurse, taking out a patient with typhus." Just in time: the ghetto was liquidated within days thereafter.

They arrived in Warsaw with forged documents as Zofia and Marian Wajda, both with impeccable command of the Polish language and "good Aryan looks." They survived. Other than some of Lusia's cousins who also survived and later settled in Sydney, the two of them were alone in the world. They considered moving to Australia as well, but Karol was a lawyer, and his diploma would be useless there.

Instead, they moved to Wałbrzych, a mid-size coal mining town in southwestern Poland. Tenacious and ambitious Marian did well. Opportunistically, he joined the communist party, which opened many doors, and in 1948-50, ascended to serve as the city's Mayor. Zofia meanwhile also studied law. In 1950, they moved to Warsaw, where Marian eventually became Director of Administration for the Ministry of Foreign Affairs, and Zofia, brilliant and beautiful, forged a solid reputation as one of the country's leading trial lawyers in private practice. At the peak of her career, in the '60s, she served on the defense team in the famous Meat Affair trial.

Australia came up again in 1956-57, and, again, they didn't go because, by now, they had two diplomas that were useless abroad.

Their only son, Jurek, studied physics.

And then came 1968.

It was both scary and amazing how some of Marian's colleagues and friends suddenly turned against him. In an all-night meeting at the Ministry, he was accused of visiting a Zionist in London some months earlier. He did visit a pre-war friend in London; it is not clear if he even knew the man was a Zionist – or was he? Marian certainly was not. But in this Jew hunting and hounding atmosphere, a mere whiff of an accusation sufficed. He was fired from the party and retired from his job. He was no longer "one of us"; he was "alien." End of career.

Zofia's job was not affected, so they could financially make ends meet, maybe even comfortably, but ghosts of the past were relentless. If it happened now, they deliberated, and to them – so assimilated, so culturally Polish – could it happen again, in the future, to Jurek? CAN A JEW EVER BELONG AND FEEL SAFE IN POLAND?

"We left, so I should not remain in Poland. And so the three of us could be together," says Jurek (now George Celler).

Their goal was, as before, Australia. While still in Warsaw, thanks to a recommendation letter from the Chair of Solid-State Physics, Jurek received a full scholarship to work on his PhD at Monash University in Melbourne. "We got to Vienna full of hope.

To our dismay, the interview in the Australian embassy didn't go well. It was contentious; the interviewer tried to make my father say that he had to join the party to avoid poverty, but my father didn't want to lie and play the victim. And when the decision came, it was devastating: **I received the permit to settle in Australia, but my parents were rejected.**"

What now? Remaining in Austria was perhaps an option for the parents, who grew up in the Austrian culture of Galicia and were fluent in German. But Jurek? There were hardly any opportunities for a physicist in Austria, and going alone to Australia seemed ridiculously against purpose. He struggled for a year and finally got a visa to the US. At about the same time, his parents received an Austrian residency permit. For a family whose main objective was to be together, this was a major blow. They said goodbye.

"My parents' life in Vienna was very difficult at first. Mom worked for about 10 years as a secretary and typist in a social agency for juveniles in a room filled with cigarette smoke. My Father got an office job at a large insurance company; his work conditions were somewhat better. It took a few years before they got a decent apartment and rights to retirement, which would pay a small pension and offer medical insurance."

Meanwhile, George thrived in the US. He earned a PhD in Physics at Purdue, published over 200 papers, was granted 23 US patents, became a Fellow of the American Physical Society (APS) and of the Electrochemical Society, and received a few awards. He has a beautiful family, kids, grandkids, and a wife from Australia(!) Still, the gnawing pain of separation remained; they had no one in the world except each other. "We traveled to Europe, or they came to us for a few weeks every year. At various times, they considered moving to the States, but they were already older, and the perspective of yet another emigration was overwhelming, and they would have no medical insurance, so we crossed the Atlantic, back and forth, for over 40 years."

And then he shared with me an intimate, poignant detail about identity: "When I decided in the US to change my name back to Celler, I realized that my Father never changed his signature when, during the war in Poland, he changed his name to Wajda. What looked mostly illegible was really Karol Celler."

THE ALTMEJDS:

September 1969. Aleksy Altmejd, a 27-year-old art historian, was in charge of the Bureau of Art Exhibitions in Zielona Góra. When the phone rang, and a stranger asked him to come out onto the street, he went laughing, certain it was a prank by his colleagues. Instead, two men with matching crew cuts grabbed him by the arms, shoved him into an unmarked car, and drove to the Militia Headquarters. There, he was led a long circuitous route into a leather-padded room with bars in the window. No explanation. He waited several hours.

Eventually, a plainclothesman showed up. "We have damning information; the punishment could be up to two years in prison," he declared. What? What?! "We advise you to cooperate. There are many enemies around." Aleksy was shocked. "What are the charges?! Who are the enemies?!" He asked if he could go back to work. "You don't work there anymore." "You can't fire me – you didn't hire me," tried Aleksy, but logic was not in vogue: "True, but we decide."

He eventually learned that there were two charges. First, he is said to have "fueled a hostile atmosphere" during a nationwide outdoor exhibition he organized in Łagów in August of 1968. While the exhibition was in progress, the Soviets and their Warsaw bloc allies, Poland included, invaded Czechoslovakia. Endless trains full of armed troops and tanks on open cars rolled south through Poland day and night. Their task was to oust Dubcek and end the Prague Spring. Crowds who came to the exhibition gathered around the only radio on the grounds, which happened to be in Aleksy's office. This was unpatriotic, they said. He was in charge; he should have dispersed the gathering.

The second accusation was that at another exhibition of the then little-known graphic artist Józef Gielniak, Aleksy "used state funds to promote the work of another Jew." Gielniak's late father was Jewish, they alleged.

Two years in prison. And an instant solution: "...unless you immediately leave for Israel." Around the same time, Aleksy's father lost his job.

They left a month later, and the whole family, Aleksy, his wife, and his parents, along with younger sister Basia, went to Sweden. Basia cried day and night in despair – she did not want to leave.

Brother Victor left as well. After graduating with a degree in Planning and Statistics, Victor, a stellar student, wanted to continue graduate studies in journalism. He came to the admission exam prepared and excited, but moments before it commenced, he was told that he would not be accepted. At the examining professor's desk was his dossier; a Star of David was drawn on the cover. The Altmejds had family in Canada. Victor was fluent in French, and he left for Montreal.

Fast forward. For 36 years, Aleksy managed Galleri Ängeln, a famous art gallery in Lund, Sweden. He is the recipient of the city's highest cultural award, Lunds Komun Kulturpris. Victor still lives in Montreal. His son, David Altmejd, is a world-renowned sculptor; his work is featured, among others, at the Guggenheim in New York, the National Gallery of Canada, and the Louisiana in Copenhagen. His work represented Canada at the Venice Biennale in 2007. The then crest-fallen Basia earned a doctorate in muscle physiology and did research at the Karolinska in Stockholm, where she lives with her family. Their father worked for 12 years in a gasoline pump factory in Malmö.

Józef Gielniak, whom Aleksy indeed discovered for the people of Zielona Góra, died at the age of 40 of tuberculosis. There is no record whatsoever that his Father was Jewish.

There were five Jewish families in Zielona Góra altogether.

This is the only story I know where departure was forced by

overt blackmail.

THE BOBERS:

In 1971, Ewa Bober (Eva Fromm) received a telegram from her mother in Poland: "Come immediately, Father is dying." Her father, Bronisław, suffered a second massive heart attack. Ewa, in the US, already had a Green Card with privileges to travel outside the country – there would be no obstacles from the American side. She phoned the Polish Consulate in Chicago, explained the urgent situation, and asked for advice on the most expeditious procedure. The answer was brief: "You will not be allowed to enter Poland."

A few days later, her father died.

THE GRYNIEWICZES:

Maria Gryniewicz did not leave Poland for reasons of an insolvable dilemma: after the March Events, her daughter Hanka emigrated to Israel, and her son Adam ended up a few years later in Brussels. Adam simply didn't have the money to pay the government for his studies, so he worked the required years and, meanwhile, met and married someone with a Belgian family. There was also a practical reason why Maria remained: she worked for the only Yiddish language newspaper in Poland, the conformist *"Folks-Sztyme"* (Voice of the People). In 1968, for reasons of greatly diminished readership, it became a weekly, but it survived. Maria was the only employee who could use a Yiddish language typewriter. So, even though Jews were losing jobs right and left, and she resigned from the communist party, Maria – perhaps the only Jew in Poland – had job security.

She fell ill during a visit to Hanka in 1984. In a Jerusalem hospital, she was diagnosed with inoperable cancer undetected in Poland. To avoid ruinous medical expenses without insurance, nearing death, she returned to Poland and applied for emigration to Israel, which, under the Israeli Law of Returns, granted her citizenship and all its privileges upon arrival. She wanted to die in Israel.

There were no direct flights from Poland to Tel Aviv. The plan was that Adam would fly to Warsaw, bring his Mother to his home in Brussels, and, after a suitable rest, fly with her to Jerusalem, where a hospital bed awaited. Polish entry visas for Belgian citizens – and Adam has been one for over a decade – were routinely granted within minutes upon arrival at the Warsaw airport. Adam knew the routine well: he frequently managed a stop in Poland to visit his mother during his business travels. He arrived on Monday with prepaid outbound tickets for Thursday for himself and Maria. He figured it would take 2-3 days to pack whatever Maria chose to take with her. The rest would simply stay. Surprise – they wouldn't let him in! They questioned Maria's illness, as it was documented only by an Israeli hospital. It also became quickly evident that on this occasion – a dying Mother – he needed a visa issued in advance in Brussels. "I was taken to a separate room, examined for many hours by twelve different officers, and, at the end of the exhausting ordeal, I received a visa for one day only." Take your mother and go. He did.

This was 1984 – 16 years after the March Events and 10 years since Adam left Poland. They kept track.

Maria died weeks later at Shaare Zedek Hospital in Jerusalem, surrounded by family.

THE SŁOŃSKIS:

The ominous telegram came to Gothenburg, Sweden, in May of 1977: "Come immediately, Father is dying." Roman Słoński suffered a bilateral coronary stroke. They decided to go by ferry, the whole family: Joanna (Słońska) Stahl, her husband Marek, also a March exile, and their two daughters: Anette, 6, and Kattis, 6 months. Marek phoned the Polish Consulate in Malmö; He was advised to submit a written application "and to include 50 SEK in cash in the envelope, to cover FAX costs". Mail took two days; who knows how long it would take to process the application. Pressed for time, they decided to forego the procedure and just go. After all, Swedes did not need visas to enter Poland, and they were all Swedish citizens. The Polish functionary aboard the ferry delivered the bad news quickly: "They will never let you in." They went anyway. It was a 10-hour overnight ride from Ystad, Sweden, to Swinoujście in Poland, with no cell phones. Nerves and tears. Upon arrival, they got off at the Terminal along with all the other passengers and presented four Swedish passports at the control station. All other Swedish passengers ahead of them were waived through. Instead, they were told: "No entry and no appeal," and ordered to wait for the return ferry to Sweden in the international part of the terminal.

Six-month-old Kattis was hungry, but Joanna was so distraught that her breastmilk stopped, just stopped. The supplemental formula required boiling water, but they were not allowed to get it from a food stand on the Polish side, meters away. "There is hot water in the toilet!" barked the official. The tap water in the toilet ran yellow. Poor Kattis turned blue after screaming for eight hours until the ferry started the return journey and services resumed.

Joanna's Father was dead by the time they reached Gothenburg. This time, Joanna did send the consular application with 50 SEK in cash requesting permission to attend the funeral. The reply never came. Again, she went anyway and was allowed to enter, she believes, thanks to a private intervention at the Ministry of Internal Affairs in Warsaw.

Hundreds attended the funeral. Roman Słoński, attorney, was a legal powerhouse, a beloved lecturer and mentor, and a mensch. Speeches by colleagues and the law office brass praised his achievements and character. No one mentioned it because no one knew that Roman was born Roman Wajnbaum. It doesn't even say so on his headstone. His wife, Halina (Szymanowska) Słońska, died three years later. No one knew that she was born Stefania Herzygier. Her headstone is silent about that as well. It bears a cross. They were all afraid. **Being Jewish was a tough secret.**

Joanna and her husband left Poland eight years earlier, and they were still blacklisted.

THE KOŃSKIS:

Adam's parents were a beautiful, if not uncommon, story: his Catholic Mother sheltered his Jewish Father during the war; they married afterward. The Family tried to emigrate to Israel in 1956, but it did not work out; more denials came later. When they were finally allowed to leave after the March Events, his father felt too old and too ill to emigrate; Adam left alone in

December 1969 to Denmark, thinking it would be easy to visit his family from there.

Surprisingly, he found himself in Viborg, in central Jutland, not in Copenhagen, with hundreds of other Polish Jews. There, he met Lene, his Danish girlfriend who became his wife (in the photo, 1971.) His first job was to drive a cab – it was hard without a GPS; he didn't even have a way to contact the dispatcher. Decembers were especially difficult. The streets were decorated, and "hygge" – joy – prevailed. But Adam felt restless and lonely, missed his family, and couldn't wait for the holidays to pass. It was easier during summer vacation: he worked as a domestic, cleaning homes for the elderly or disabled.

"My Father died suddenly in 1977; he was only 63," says Adam. "Mother summoned me to the funeral by telegram. I was denied a Polish visa once before when my entire college class went to Poland to visit the Warsaw School of Economics; I was the only one in class who spoke Polish and the only one not permitted to go. But for a funeral – only for a funeral, and only for Danish citizens, and I have been one for several years – I could apply for a three-day visa at the Polish Embassy in Copenhagen.

It was a daunting trip. On the one hand, it was good to see

my country of birth after seven years, but I missed it. On the other, it hurt that I didn't have a chance to say goodbye to my Father, to talk with him about the trauma of being the only survivor in his family. I was finally ready now, but it was too late. I know that Grandpa Aron and Grandma Zlata died at the liquidation of the Warsaw ghetto. But there also was a sister named Hancia and seven brothers: Moishe, Sevek, Hershek, Yosek, Chaimek, Abramek, and Yankiel. I will never know anything about their lives and where and how they were murdered. And my father will never be comforted by knowing how much it mattered to me."

RIMMA GALLER VOLYŃSKA:

This story starts in 1937 in the Soviet Union, in Taganrog on the Azovsk Sea. Stalin tried to develop uninhabitable lands using slave labor of "undesirables." The police were given quotas on new detainees; most were accused of "шпионаж," spying. Lila

(Leah) Wertman and her husband, Isaac Saltzman, both Polish Jews, were rounded up in the middle of the night. She was pregnant. Trucks arrived, one full of men, the other of women. "Mama was loaded onto the truck, and it was over. She never saw Isaac again. Only after the war did she learn that he died of typhus on the way to the labor camp. The baby she gave birth to died of hunger soon after birth."

For 10 painful years, Lila slaved in the Karaganda (today Kazakhstan) camp system. Soon after her release, she gave birth to Rimma. They managed to return to Poland in 1958 with the wave of repatriation of Polish Jews. Lila looked for any surviving family in her hometown of Warka but found nothing and nobody. They settled in Warsaw.

Lila was a master seamstress. At the Warsaw Opera and at the Jewish Theater, she sewed historical costumes. And privately, for actresses and personalities. And Rimma, beautiful Rimma, a gifted jazz singer, was a star at Babel, the cabaret attached to the Jewish Student Club on Nowogrodzka 5. "Horrible things were happening to members of Babel," recalls Rimma about the weeks following March. "Arrests, interrogations... I feared I would be next. Some of the texts I sang were in Yiddish. Others, by Natan Tenenbaum, were ambiguous, thinly veiled critiques of the government... "

And that day of Gomulka's speech. "Mama and I watched TV holding hands. She lost more, and more tragically than anyone I knew, and now her face was once again contorted with pain and fear: "Rimmochka, what shall we do? What shall we do?" They decided to go to Israel. Together. The sooner, the better. Right away.

Meanwhile, Rimma's boyfriend, an American Fulbright scholar in Warsaw, also Jewish, intervened with a good alternative. "We'll get married and live in the States." He already had a job offer from Brooklyn College; Rimma would continue her studies. They married in City Hall. Paul left first, Rimma would travel in November by the Polish ocean liner, Batory, and Mother would follow as soon as they were settled.

To emigrate and join her American husband, Rimma applied for a Polish passport. But the Polish police clearly kept track of her tainted heritage. American or not, she was a Jew, and for that, she needed to be punished: no Polish passport for her – she was required to forfeit her Polish citizenship in exchange for the one-way Travel Document. The next challenge was when she tried to board the Batory: none of the staff had ever seen a Travel Document, and they didn't want to let her on board! "Wait here!" while the phone to the police whirred... Rimma, the damaged goods, stood for hours with her luggage at the ship's entrance, waiting for someone to decide her fate. As a holder of the Travel Document, she was not allowed in Poland, but they wouldn't let her leave either.

Eventually, they did let her go. And she continued her studies in the US. In 1988, she earned a PhD in Comparative Literature from Brown University and, subsequently, taught at a number of prestigious schools in the US and Canada. She now lives in Toronto.

THE KAULS:

Markus Kaul, a bookkeeper, worked in Szczecin since his return from Novosibirsk in 1946. In 1968, he was, like most Jews, dismissed. In September of 1968, the family left for Israel and settled in Haifa. Assuming that his monthly pension (see pension card # J-75685/5) was below average, only 1,500 zlotys, his 21 years of employment translated to 378,000 zlotys

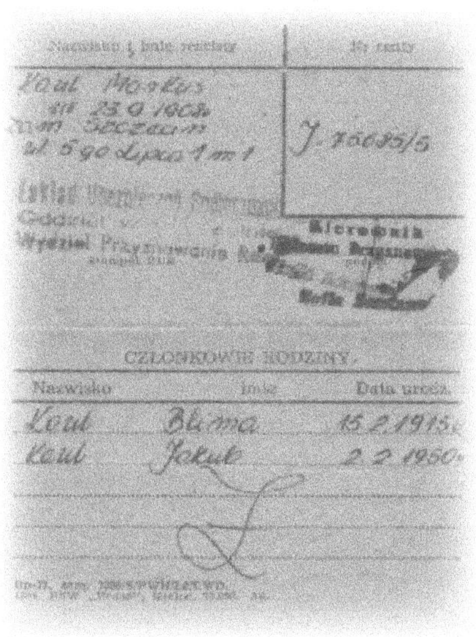

in pensions. Like most, he received nothing.

Jacob Kaul, his son, frequently traveled from Israel to Poland on business as VP of Business Development for AMDOCS and, later, representing his own company. He didn't want to recover any of his father's pension money, but he had an idea for commemoration. In 2008, after lengthy correspondence, he met with functionaries of ZUS – the Polish equivalent of Social Security Administration – with a concrete proposal: to use the unpaid pension monies plus the interest accumulated for over 40 years, for a scholarship in his father's name to be awarded annually to an outstanding University of Science and Technology student in Szczecin. "The person listened to me politely, vacantly, without interest..."

Jacob never heard back from them.

THE HORECKIS:

Juliusz Horecki, an economist, worked in the Government Office of Management for the Use of Nuclear Energy. He was fired from work and expelled from the party a few weeks after the antisemitic campaign started. It was, of course, by an irrevocable decision from above, but the commonly adopted form of additional humiliation was a general employee meeting, where colleagues and subordinates took the floor. Routine at such meetings were accusations of suspected espionage for Israel based on contacts with family who lived there.

In the case of Mr. Horecki, a subordinate stated an additional, extraordinary charge: that Horecki's dog, a Jewish dog, after all, terrorized Polish children. The referenced incident took place during a company holiday. The accused dog, Meatloaf, allegedly barked at the victim's children in a clear act of violent and vicious Jewish aggression.

The gathered crowd of former colleagues and subordinates gasped. Mr. Horecki lost his job.

His wife lost her job in IT as well. Both had impeccable professional credentials but couldn't find employment for months. To put food on the table, Mr. Horecki took a job in a construction company, and his wife got work as an accountant.

On August 30, 1969, stateless, the entire Horecki family left for Sweden. The accused Meatloaf went with them. In the photo, Meatloaf witnesses the Stockholm wedding of Jurek, Mr. Horecki's son.

In Sweden, the Horeckis returned to their prewar family name, Hollenberg.

THE LIBERMANS:

It was heartbreaking for Mania and Michał Liberman to watch their daughter and son leave for Sweden. There were more families like this: older, ailing parents remained in Poland, but they encouraged their children to leave and have a chance for a free and happy life. The Libermans were simple people; they worked in a Jewish cottage industry cooperative called "Rozwój" (in Polish, Progress), which manufactured rag toys, gloves, and felt slippers. After her husband died, Mania was completely alone. One heart attack after another, in-and-out of hospitals. Her daughter, Inka (Liberman) Kantor – a Swedish citizen, a dentist, with a family of her own – tried for two years (1980-81) to go and see her ailing mother presented with medical certificates and letters from the hospital. No. At that time, Swedes didn't even need visas to visit Poland. "You will be allowed to go after Mother dies," offered generously the consular bureaucrat in Stockholm, eating a sausage. It has been over ten years since Inka left Poland, but she was still blacklisted.

"My Mother died in Sweden in February 1982," says Inka. "In October 1981, she closed the door to her Łódź apartment, leaving everything behind, and with a small suitcase in hand, she came to die in Stockholm. My friend took her from Łódz to Warsaw and helped her board the plane." And then she adds: "I am grateful that this is what happened. If she had to die alone, my heart would probably burst."

THE ZAJDELS:

Natka was born in Tashkent, Uzbekistan.

About 250,000 Polish Jews survived the war by deportation or flight to Siberia, the far north, and Central Asia. 21-year-old Mordko Zajdel crossed the border to the USSR days before war broke out, then caught a train to go as far east as he could. It was a long stay; he managed to return to Poland only in 1957, with the family he started in Tashkent.

The plan was to leave for Israel as soon as possible. But, before leaving, Mordko (Natka somehow refers to him in our conversation as "Mr. Zajdel") went to search for any surviving family in Szczebrzeszyn. Nobody was alive, but he learned how they died. Another survivor, Mr. Szwarc, saw it all from his hiding place: the roundups, the mass executions in City Square. He saw Mr. Zajdel's sister trying to escape to the nearby woods; she was caught by helpful Polish peasants and chopped to pieces with shovels."

"Something happened to Mr. Zajdel afterward," says Natka, "He did not talk, and I didn't ask;" such was the unspoken agreement in our family. We didn't leave for Israel as planned. He started working. He was a shoemaker, and in a small room of our apartment, he made shoes to order. Then autumn came, and my brother and I started school. And Mr. Zajdel, together with another Jew, Mr. Lieb, opened a modest storefront with a workshop in the rear. They worked hard, often 12 hours a day, and the little business prospered. Meanwhile, my parents kept applying for permission to emigrate to Israel and were denied time and time again.

One day in 1968, some Very Important Men came carrying black briefcases full of Very Important Papers. And for Very Serious Reasons, the store was closed. Mr. Zajdel didn't work for a full year; savings were depleted, but, finally, a blessing – permission to leave!

Mr. Zajdel's story is not isolated; many Jewish-owned, small private enterprises – usually trade-based – tailors, cobblers, weavers and bakers, and some shopkeepers, were closed by the government as part of the pressures intended to force Jews to leave. Any excuse. A missing receipt, a fly on the wall.

Mr. Zajdel's first job in Israel was at a production line in Tadiran, a TV factory. It did not take long. The accumulated grief, harsh climate, and hard work killed him in three years. He was 52 years old.

THE BRANDYS':

In high school, Marek excelled in maths and science; he loved chemistry. Pursuing Chemical Engineering at the University of Science and Technology was a perfect college choice. The entrance exam lasted two days: the first day in chemistry and the second in math. "I found the questions quite easy," says Marek, "and I finished with time to spare." Yet, a week later, when he eagerly examined the posted scoreboard of those selected for admission, he did not find his name. He failed math. "It's impossible, and I told my Dad." And an immediate option: "I will apply in the second round at the Mathematics Department of the Jagiellonian University." He did and was accepted.

Meanwhile, his father managed to arrange a meeting with Professor Maciej Sarnowski, the then dean of the Chemistry Department at the University of Science and Technology. "We both went. The dean was straightforward and blunt, although not apologetic: "Mr. Brandys, I don't understand. Here is the folio with your son's math exam. He answered all the questions correctly and earned the highest grade, a five, from the examining professor. The five is clearly visible on the cover of his folio. Yet, it has been crossed out and replaced with a two, a failing grade, so your son was denied a spot in our department." Extraordinary. "Given the circumstances, I will accept your son in one of my reserve dean's places. If he is capable, works hard, and passes the first semester with good grades, he will stay – otherwise, we will part company. Good luck." I enrolled.

Incredibly bold, perhaps criminal, to change someone's grade to deny him college admission. But whom would this bold person fear? Were there instructions not to admit Jews, which would render such action not only justifiable but commendable? I wondered if Dean Sarnowski investigated the ugly matter, but there was no indication of any aftermath. "He did not seem surprised," said Marek.

Henryk Brandys, 67, Marek's Father, passed away six months later, in April '69. "As an "old communist," he was entitled to an "official" burial orchestrated by the party. "But this privilege did not allow a Jewish cemetery option, which was our wish. We declined the ceremony. I finished my first year, and in November, Mother and I left for Israel. She wasn't even Jewish."

I asked if the decision to leave for Israel was, perhaps, financially motivated. "No", said Marek. "My Mother had a concession for a RUCH newsstand; we were quite well off." Indeed, these government newsstand concessions brought amazing income: everyone wanted a copy of this or that newspaper or magazine, all published in insufficient numbers. I, too, paid a handsome premium at the nearby kiosk of RUCH to receive my favorite publications. So it wasn't the money. "**We left because staying in Poland was unthinkable**," said Marek.

He finished college at Hebrew University in Jerusalem, then earned a Master's Degree in Applied Chemistry followed by officer training, then 5 years as a chemist in the Israeli Army, PhD in Physical Chemistry, and post-doc at the Catholic University in Washington DC. He lives in Bethesda, MD.

THE ROZENBAUMS:

Chaim Rozenbaum's roots were in the extraordinary all-Jewish village of Iwaniki near Pinsk. His grandfather, Sholem Gloser (left on the 100-year-old photo), father of eighteen children, was a known figure in the village and lived to the ripe age of 108. After WWII, Chaim, now Henryk, landed a job as one of the managers of the Bureau of Control of Correspondence at the

Ministry of Internal Affairs. His wife Michla (Michalina), born in Vilnius, the sole survivor of her six siblings, was for years the head of corrections and editor of the women's section at the Yiddish language newspaper, *"Folks Sztyme."* She also sat on the board of the Social and Cultural Association of Jews in Warsaw. In 1968, both Rozenbaums were retired. Lingua franca in their home was Yiddish. They had two sons: Włodzimierz, a historian, and Leon, a student.

Wlodzimierz's wife, Rita, was fired from her job in technology when, at a public employees meeting, someone pointed out that her maiden name, Lewicka, was the same as one of the strike activists; surely they are related. They weren't. Rita was not an activist and didn't even know this other Lewicka – but none of this mattered. Out.

* * *

"On March 17, 1968, a confidential document was issued by the Chief of General Staff (Central Military Archive 1703/87/35 186-9, 0026/ Sztab). **The instruction demanded a n immediate draft to the army** of those listed by the regional military staff on the basis of information gained from the authorities of academic institutions and the militia. [...] **Those expelled served for two years and were directed to distant garrisons**, maintaining the principle of dispersal. If a student's rights were restored, he could gain a discharge, but "not before completing twelve months of service." Those who had been suspended were organized into special battalions [...] where they completed their **service without arms, with particular emphasis on political-educational work**". *Polin: Studies in Polish Jewry Volume 21, Tadeusz Pióro"*

* * *

Leon was a second-year student of the highly politicized and full of opposition figures Department of Political Economy at Warsaw University. He was friendly with Henryk Szlajfer, one of the leading student protesters; the two were likely seen together on campus. Yet, Leon was not active and certainly was not an organizer of the movement. So it was quite a surprise when a soldier pounded at his door one morning with a document that declared his draft to basic military service. Leon mumbled something about his Category D – a military classification for those medically unfit to serve in times of peace

(Leon was short-sighted). The soldier was prepared; the second document called for an appearance in front of a medical commission, where his condition would be re-evaluated. As it turned out, the Medical Commission did not dispense exams – it dispensed stamps. And so, without an exam, Leon's classification was changed by the swift action of a stamp from Category D to C – suitable for service. His student status did not protect him either since the whole Department of Political Economy was, meanwhile, temporarily dissolved. So it really was not a big surprise – a shock, but no surprise – when the same soldier delivered within days an order to present himself for temporary military exercises in Hrubieszów, the base of one of the "specially organized battalions" where penalized students were to be indoctrinated.

There were about twenty of them in the penal unit in Hrubieszow, and until recently, they were students, none previously known to Leon. Life resembled basic military training: long marches, digging ditches, occasional obstacle courses, and – a specialty of the hour – meetings with political officers. Isolated from the world, even from the rest of the garrison of "real" soldiers, fed newspapers full of holes as a gaping reminder of cut-out articles and, worst of all, uncertain of their future. They were, after all, to be isolated from the centers of student demonstrations. In trying to understand their situation, they once asked for a meeting with a superior officer. "The topic of my lecture will be the harmful influence of Zionism in Poland," he started. One time, surrounded by a group of cadets, Leon felt outright endangered ("the atmosphere was pogrom-like"). At another hearing, he was asked to explain his ties with Polish culture; he replied by reciting fragments of Polish national poetry.

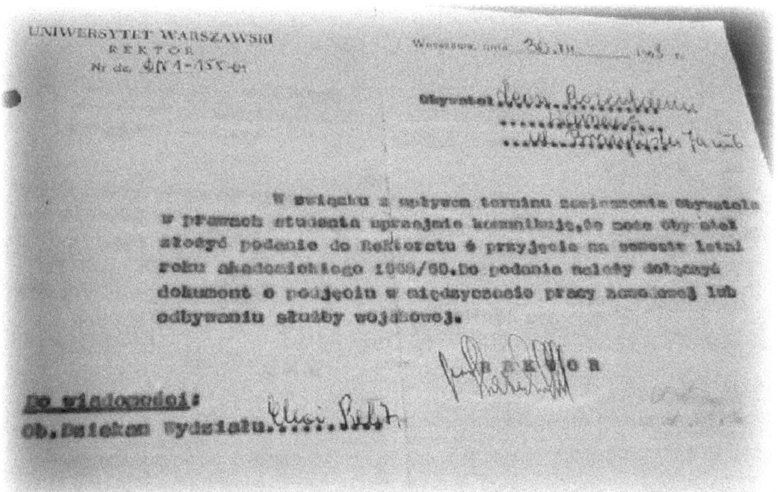

On May 1, thirty days after his induction, he was unexpectedly released. Back in Warsaw, he found his parents distraught and in despair. They remembered other times; they feared that the repressions would continue and escalate. Indeed, it wasn't over yet. Leon was ordered to appear in front of the Disciplinary Commission of the University of Warsaw to learn that his name was on the list of students who "participated in the preparation of, or actively participated in political demonstrations." The list was signed on March 19 by the Commander of the Citizens Militia. And, as the ultimate threat, he received at the end of July a letter (see photo) from the rector's office advising that "due to the expiry of the term of suspension of student rights," he may apply for re-admission to the university for next academic year, provided that he takes up professional work or perform military service in the meantime. Leon perceived **this as a threat of two years of military service**. Time was up, he feared. He applied for permission to leave the country and, in October, left for Israel. So did his parents. Włodzimierz and his now-unemployed wife Rita applied concurrently at the American Embassy.

In Israel, Michla worked in one of the Yiddish newspapers. Chaim was less fortunate – his work, first in a ceramics factory, then in the manufacture of furniture and mattresses, was tough and physically demanding.

In 1980, Leon moved to New York, where he still lives.

Leon and I discussed at length what may have been the reason that he was chosen for this special treatment. Why him? And, for that matter, what was it about? He really had nothing to do with "organizing, planning, or preparing…" We didn't arrive at any reasonable conclusion.

"I left because I did not want to be treated as a second-category citizen," said Leon.

THE FISHES:

Szymek, brave Szymek, thought he could do everything at once. He was already married when he was accepted to study at the Department of Electronics at the Wrocław University of Science and Technology. His wife, Małka Wajman, a computer programmer, was pregnant. And, a stroke of good luck, in his second year, he was offered a well-paying job. He took a Dean's Leave of Absence from college, figuring school could wait. He'll work for a while and cushion their future with savings. And then came March.

The entire Electronics Department was dissolved. After a few days, most people were automatically reinstated except for the few Jewish students who were told to register once

again – a procedure which heralded the coming divisions and humiliations. Some were readmitted, others not. "I was at work and simply didn't know I had to re-register. They summoned me to the main police station on Podwale and grilled me for many hours… accused me of being one of the planners of the student campaign. And A BOMB: no longer protected by student status, I WOULD BE DRAFTED INTO THE ARMY for compulsory two-year service. I didn't have to wait long – in April, I was already in uniform. Our son was two weeks old then."

Szymek, now in artillery, took the whole thing hard. "**I thought Poland was my country; this is where I belong. And all of a sudden, this turned out to be a lie**." College plans seemed distant; he worried about Małka. He often contemplated suicide. His three-day furlough – two days on the train and one day at home – resulted in another pregnancy, and soon they had two little ones, both born premature and often ill.

At home, Małka struggled as well. Her boss, Mr. Sztajer, was a vocal antisemite who would love to get rid of her but, by law, he could not fire the only breadwinner in the family. The children were not entitled to kindergarten care since she lived with her parents, whom the government claimed were responsible for looking after them. But her parents, Leja and Mendel Wajman were ill and required care themselves—her father had suffered a serious stroke, and her mother was bedridden with severe asthma. There was never enough food. Coal was expensive, and she never had enough to heat their apartment to a comfortable temperature. Repeated efforts to get Szymek released from the army failed, even though fathers of small children were usually exempt. "I don't wish such experiences on anyone," says Małka.

Finally, in November of 1969, the most painful decision: she asked her parents to leave her and emigrate to Israel. Her oldest sister, Bertha, was already there and could care for them, and medical care was available. In Poland, with grandparents no longer there, her kids would be allowed to attend kindergarten.

The Wajmans left. Małka never saw her father again. She wasn't allowed to go to his funeral. But, through a clandestine route via Denmark, she managed to go to his shiva.

Szymek returned from the army on January 31, 1970. He was a trained electronics technician with a year of University of Science and Technology studies and two years of army practice. After a long search, he was hired by the rail system, and his position paid 1,000 zlotys a month. "Ridiculous," says Szymek. "Wrocław was the capital of Polish electronics; everyone was excited when I submitted my resume – and soon offered their regrets." Meanwhile, Małka lost her job since she was no longer the only breadwinner in the family. Their phone was tapped. They were harassed and threatened by security services. All their friends have, by then, emigrated. They were often hungry. They had to wait two full years before they had the right to apply for emigration since Szymek had alleged security knowledge from the army. Afterward, their application to leave the country was denied four times. Finally, in 1973, they received permission to leave for Denmark.

Even there, for years, they felt the reach of wrath. Szymek, a championship table tennis player, organized a series of competitive tournaments between his club in Copenhagen and his former club in Poland. The Danes visited Poland five times in the exchange, and five times, Szymek was denied the visa to travel with his club to the country of his birth.

EDWARD BARAL:

Late 1970s. Edward Baral, a docent at Radiumhemmet, the Oncology Department of the Karolinska in Stockholm, was a rising star, already with an international reputation.

"There is a guy firmly parked at your door; he has no appointment but refuses to leave," announced his nurse one day. Edward recognized "the guy" – it was the General Consul of Poland. Quite recently, he refused to extend the stay in Sweden for a sick person for whom Edward intervened. Now, the Consul explains, a certain important patient is sick with cancer in Poland. He wishes to extend an offer for Professor Baral to immediately come to Poland for a consultation.

An awkward welcoming committee greeted Edward at the Warsaw airport and walked him through all the controls — without any control at all. He didn't even have to show his Swedish passport or open his overnight bag.

Meanwhile, around the same time, Joanna Stahl, Adam Konski, Ewa Bober, and Inka Kantor were denied permission to visit their dying parents.

Edward stayed for three days. During the farewell supper in Warsaw, one of the doctors complemented Edward on his fluent Polish. "How wise of your parents to teach you your mother tongue in Sweden," he commented. "Actually," answered Edward, "Polish was the only language in our home in Bytom until '68." Silence. Curtain. End of the evening.

The patient was transferred to Edward's care in Stockholm

and recovered.

FROM THE MILITARY; "STORIES OF ILLUSION":

The Six-Day War in Israel underscored for Polish leadership that the two countries are now in opposite political blocs. In case of an armed conflict, a loyalty dilemma could arise for Jewish officers who had "two souls and two homelands." On July 6, 1967, on purely speculative charges of pro-Israeli sympathies, the Polish army dismissed national air defense chief General Czesław Mankiewicz, General Tadeusz Dąbkowski, and General Jan Stamieszkin. All three were retired within a year. A classical move by a dictatorship – to punish for what one THINKS. There were rumors in the ranks about cooperation with Israeli intelligence, a Jewish conspiracy in the military and civil authorities, and even financing of the Israeli army by Polish Jews and sympathizers. At meetings and rallies, soldiers demanded that Jews be dismissed from the army. And so, in the summer of 1967, following strictly racist Nurembergian criteria, the military one-by-one dismissed approximately 150 high-ranking Jewish officers. The charge was "taking a political stance inconsistent with the position of the party and the PRL government, and the loss of moral and political values binding an officer of the People's Army of Poland." Those who subsequently emigrated to Israel were deprived of officer rank "due to lack of moral values" and demoted to the rank of private (IPN BU 2174/3308, sheet 19). They also lost their military pension.

The ugliest part of this ethnic cleansing is that since the 1950s, the Military Internal Service has carefully maintained information about Jewish members of the military. They compiled dossiers on colleagues and comrades in arms. They carefully listened to any mentions of relatives abroad, bugged phones, and inspected private correspondence. They spied on "their" Jews, and commissioned studies of Jewish behavior. One such study, dating back to 1958, stated that in the period 1955-1958, 582 Jewish soldiers left Poland, including 41 officers, of whom as many as 36.2% emigrated to Israel. So when, in 1967, orders came to dismiss Jewish officers, there was no hesitation as to who they may be. The Army even established a special department to *pro forma* help the dismissed officers find other employment.

In February 1971, Maj. Gen. Józef Urbanowicz, head of the Army's Main Political Board, stated: **"We were able [...] to get rid of ideologically alien people from our ranks."**

MAJOR ADAM FERBER:

Abraham (Abysz) Ferber was a true Polish patriot. He was also a man of courage. He volunteered to the First Infantry Division of the newly formed Polish Army. He was wounded three times on his battle route from Lenino to Berlin. He was promoted to commander of Heavy Machine Guns. After the war, Major Adam Ferber became quartermaster, responsible for army provisions. He served with great devotion; he loved his service and his country. His decorations included the Knight's Cross of the Order of Polonia Restituta, Poland's second highest state award.

In August of 1967, he was unceremoniously dismissed from the army.

Afterward, he got a job as the provincial inspector of weights and measures. The work was well-paid and interesting, but Adam was irreparably hurt and injured. In 1971, not seeing any prospects for his continued life in Poland, he emigrated to Denmark with his whole family. He was full of pain and sorrow; he never reminisced about Poland, never visited, and did not maintain contact with any of his former army colleagues. He lived as a recluse.

Recognized by Denmark as a WWII veteran, he received a Danish pension. He became a member of the Jewish Congregation in Copenhagen and paid dues till the end of his life.

COLONEL ALEKSANDER STARECKI:

Samuel Storch distinguished himself as a brave soldier during WWII. He took part in the defense of Warsaw and was imprisoned in a POW camp. In 1948, his continued service in the Army's General Staff was made conditional upon a change of name to something "which sounds Polish." He eagerly conformed. So eagerly that to erase any record of his Jewish roots, he also changed the names of his murdered parents and his mother's maiden name. Obstacle removed, he then progressed quickly, graduated from technical studies in Russia, and, as Colonel Aleksander Starecki, became assistant professor at the Academy of the General Staff.

Incongruously, the closest friends of the Colonel were all Jewish: his son Henryk, recalls names such as Rozenbaum, Paweł Wilsztein, and Michal Frydman. His wife's entire surviving family lived in Israel.

He received his "thank you for years of service" letter immediately after the end of the Six-Day War, perhaps already on the 10th or 11th of June, 1967. Afterward, he worked part-time at an institution that managed parks. He still collected his generous pension and lived in the prestigious and comfortable "army" apartment. In 1968, however, his son Henryk left for Israel, and the Stareckis followed him soon thereafter. This cost the colonel both his rank and his pension (the latter reinstated over twenty years later after the fall of Communism in Poland).

COLONEL RAFAŁ LEKACH

He was born in 1925 as one of five children in a village near Vilnius. In 1943, not quite eighteen, following his father and older brother, he joined the newly forming Polish Army. Wounded in the battle for Warsaw, he was forced to stay there. After the war, he completed officer training and then earned a law degree. There was a time when he was

pressured to change his name, but his wife protested, and somehow, they left him alone. In time, he was promoted to Colonel and assigned to administrative work at the headquarters of the Automobile Service.

He was committed to the founding ideology, grateful to the Russians for liberating Poland, and grateful that his siblings in the depths of Russia survived. He was a true communist.

It was a painful personal blow when, in 1967, he was dismissed from his job and from the party. The departure gifts of a beautiful attaché case and gold watch were of no consolation. He refused the civil job in a remote outpost offered by the army, found part-time work in an enterprise for the disabled, and collected his military pension. He was still in his beloved Poland.

In 1968, following the March Events, his older daughter Joanna, a third-year student in biology, was suspended from the university. While Rafał was hurt by his dismissal, Joanna was offended. "How could they?! For what?!" She saw no life for herself in Poland and applied for permission to leave the country. Alone. She was denied – the whole family had to apply, she was told. Rafał wasn't willing. A few months later, his wife Róża lost her job at the Ministry of Commerce for the Interior.

Neighbors stopped recognizing them. His wife Róża recalls that time as "a horror."

When Rafał still refused to apply for permission to leave, Róża issued an ultimatum: "Either we all leave, or I will go without you, with our two daughters." Forced to choose between his country and his family, Rafał agreed to leave, and, in an act of ultimate grief, he turned grey in one day. They applied – and now a flip of fate. The two daughters obtained visas to Sweden and were granted permission to leave the country, but the parents were denied. Over the next few years, Rafał and Róża had to apply a few more times before they were finally allowed to leave.

Both daughters became medical doctors. One married a man from our immigration in a traditional Jewish ceremony. The other is married to a Swedish diplomat. Surrounded by children and grandchildren, Rafał eventually adjusted to a

comfortable life in Sweden. Still, for years, on the anniversary of the Russian Revolution, he and his four siblings got together by phone and raised a toast in eternal gratitude to the victorious and generous Russia.

His oldest great-grandson recently became a *Bar Mitzva*.

COLONEL DR. KLEMENS NUSSBAUM AND STANISŁAWA ZAWADECKA

They were a power couple, the quintessence of the ideological elite of People's Poland. An apartment at one of Warsaw's most prestigious addresses, Belwederska Street, numerous trips abroad, a private luxury car, and many awards and honors from state authorities. It was earned and deserved. They identified with the policy of the ruling party. They believed, and they gave it their all – so their later disillusionment was the more bitter.

Their story reads like a fable. A good fable because the central characters didn't cut corners. War gave an opportunity to an unprecedented rise of these two young people – they were only twenty-four when it was over, kids, really – he was already a major, she a captain. Both were from modest families, with no marketable skills or professions, and with little education, they stepped into life in socialist Poland full of energy, principles, and ideals. They were both dreamers and doers. He eventually rose to the rank of colonel and became deputy head of the Military College at the Warsaw University of Technology. Her ascent was meteoric — from Deputy Mayor of Warsaw to deputy member of the Central Committee of the Party and, at the absolute height, chairwoman of the Main Board of the League of Polish Women. Nussbaum never changed his name or tried to hide his Jewish roots, although it would have been easier. She refused to divorce him, although, in 1968, it would have been a lifeline. The dismissal following the Arab-Israeli War in June 1967 and the subsequent March Events were the final blow.

And then comes the James Bond part of their story – they escaped! To Israel!

Nussbaum was one of the very few high-ranking officers of the Polish Army to have escaped and likely the only one who did so without having committed a crime against People's Poland. His crime was that he was a Jew.

Their son Jerry, who, at nineteen, escaped with them, stresses that there was no financial need for them to leave. Klemens' pension alone was in multiples of most salaries; they could have lived comfortably.

THEY ESCAPED TO DEFEND AND PRESERVE DIGNITY.

And in Israel, they built a new life, void of any comforts, one which required different strengths and talents.

Klemens (Kalman) Nussbaum was born in Lviv. At home, they spoke Yiddish and Polish. He went to a public school as well as to a Cheder and, after 6th grade, started an apprenticeship with a furrier. Passionately aware of the misery of the masses and widespread antisemitism, he became a member of both the Zionist Hashomer Hatzair and the Communist Youth Union. In 1941, after Germany attacked the Soviet Union, he was mobilized to the Red Army, demobilized after a serious leg injury in the battle of Stalingrad (now Volgograd), and six months later, in May 1943, volunteered to the newly forming Polish Infantry Division of Tadeusz Kościuszko. At the end of WWII, already a major, Nussbaum was a deputy battalion commander, quickly promoted to lieutenant colonel.

In 1948–1951, he studied at the Warsaw Academy of the Army's General Staff. His superiors said: "Respected among colleagues. Politically sophisticated. Marxist-Leninist worldview, […] Reticent in speaking. No addictions. High intelligence. Analytical mind." and "Sincerely devoted to the cause of the Party and People's Poland." (AIPN, BU01251/ 697, page 112).

In January 1953, he was dismissed from the Army. The records read that "he struggled with duodenal ulcer." Jerry remembers the ulcer but states emphatically that it was by no means

the reason for his dismissal. "One less Jew in the army was more like it."

While he was out of the army, Klemens toured Israel, met with friends and family, and returned enchanted and proud. But his home was Poland and, specifically, the Polish Army. With political winds changing, he applied to be reinstated, and in 1957, he was. Again, he was quickly promoted: he became deputy head of the Military College of the Warsaw University of Technology and, a year later, ascended to the rank of colonel. It was a good time for the family; Jerry recalls that his parents enjoyed social life and had many friends, most of whom were Jewish. It was not uncommon to hear a Yiddish word during frequent games of bridge in their home. Klemens always took off his uniform when he came home; "like a miner," says Jerry, "the uniform was for work." It didn't seem to be a component of his self-identity.

Sometime in the '60s, Klemens enrolled in a two-year evening College of Journalism at the University of Warsaw, which he completed in November 1967. Providentially.

In July 1967, a month after the Israeli Six-Day War, he was called to the Ministry of National Defense. "How is your health?" the head of Human Relations began the meeting. They sipped cognac and talked for about an hour. **And in these civilized circumstances, Colonel Nussbaum was once again dismissed from the Army because "he was completely deaf," an affliction supported by findings of a subsequent military medical commission. He was forty-six. His hearing was perfect.**

A month later, he took an editor position in *"Evening Express,"* a mediocre newspaper, from where he was fired "with a thunder" in September of '68. **By then, Jews were fired "with a thunder" from everywhere.**

His wife, Stanisława Zawadecka, came from a Polish peasant family near Tarnopol. During the war, deep in the USSR, she worked as a teacher and then as a foreman in one of the state farms. She, too, volunteered in 1943 to the Polish Infantry Division named after Tadeusz Kosciuszko. She was a major when she left the army in 1946. Her career afterward was stellar. The photo from family archives shows her with (middle) Józef Cyrankiewicz, the Prime Minister of Poland, and Wladysław Gomułka, the head of PZPR, the United Worker's Party. Arguably, she was the most powerful woman in Poland's governmental structure."

It all ended in March 1968 when she was boldly accused of diverting the collected Women's League membership dues and sending them "to Dayan." The real reason was that resisting pressure, she refused to divorce Nussbaum.

At the end of 1968, the Nussbaums, who in the eyes of army brass were "A family at a high intellectual and moral level" (AIPN, BU01251/697, page 113), found themselves

unemployed, unemployable, and publicly humiliated. The antisemitic campaign was in full swing. Stasia received a secret message from someone in the know that their nineteen-year-old son, Jerry, is about to be arrested. It was also clear that with their high-profile past, it would be years before they could be allowed to leave Poland. If ever. Jerry was eager to go to Israel. "100%". **And then came the dramatic decision TO ESCAPE.**

They would start with a vacation in Czechoslovakia and, from there, somehow get to Austria. A setback: in August of 1968, the Warsaw Pact invaded Czechoslovakia, and the occupied country was now a war zone. They planned anew, and in August 1969, Nussbaum, his wife, and Jerry went on holiday to Yugoslavia. They closed the door to their apartment with all their belongings and traveled by car the long way via Ukraine. Another setback – their car, with Polish license plates, raised all sorts of flags, and their efforts to clandestinely buy Austrian license plates also failed. The Polish travel documents they carried were not accepted by the Austrian border authorities. Each of these setbacks caused them to pause and reevaluate the prudence – really, the sanity – of their undertaking. So far, they have not done anything illegal – should they return to Poland? If they proceed and get caught trying to cross the border, they'll spend years in prison. Each time, they came to the same conclusion: don't turn around – **"there is nothing for us in Poland."**

Finally, a breakthrough: three Austrian passports generously contributed by friends. Impressive; people gave their own passports to be used for an illegal passage! Each of the three passports bore a different last name, and the photos did not resemble the Nussbaums at all. They were passports good for a casual wave at the border crossing but wouldn't pass the most rudimentary inspection. Still, the Nussbaums decided to go for it – on September 24, by train, just the three of them in a sleeping compartment. In the middle of the night, a moment of true panic: they heard someone in the hallway repeatedly shout, *"Polako, polako… "* Have they been found out? Is this the end of their journey? But no one opened the compartment door; they learned later that *"polako"* means "slowly" in Croatian.

That night, they crossed the Yugoslav-Austrian border and, in the morning, reached Vienna. End of escape.

Their car remained in Zagreb; it wasn't clear if they would ever recover it, but eventually, even the car reached them. Their daughter Edwarda, who remained in Poland for a few more years, eventually entered their apartment on Belwederska and removed a few photos and personal belongings, but the bulk of furniture and furnishings remained "for grabs."

In December of 1969, they landed in Nazareth, Israel. Like most other immigrants to Israel, they started by learning Hebrew in an ulpan, which took six months. In 1970, they moved to Tel Aviv, where Klemens received a research grant from Tel Aviv University. His topic was "Participation of Jews in the organization and combat operations of the Polish Army in the USSR." It didn't take long before the ambitious fifty-year-old enrolled in a PhD program. He was driven by a burning need to start anew and to redefine himself. But now money was a problem. Stasia could not work for health reasons, and his grant was not enough to support the family, so he took a second job as a physical laborer in a bakery. He got there at 4 am and worked until 8 in scorching temperatures, dripping in sweat. He then took a shower, changed clothes into a coat and tie (yes!), and went to the university for a whole day to do his research.

He defended his doctoral thesis in 1977 at the age of fifty-six. The value of his work was extraordinary. While the scope was necessarily limited because Nussbaum had no access to Polish sources, the rare personal experience of the author, who knew this army and its people, was irreplaceable. His thesis was subsequently published in book form, first in Hebrew and then in Polish, under a changed title: "STORIES OF ILLUSION: Jews in the Polish People's Army in the USSR."

But finances were still tough. To make ends meet, Nussbaum continued to work at the university and in the bakery. From 1977 to 1978, he took a third job in the *"Nowiny-Kurier"* Polish language newspaper in Tel Aviv. He was almost 60, had a sick wife, and was working three jobs to support the two of them.

In September 1980, this time strictly for financial reasons and with a lot of trepidations, the couple emigrated to Aachen, Germany, where Klemens was employed as a community secretary (managing director) of the Jewish community. It helped that, in addition to German, he was fluent in other foreign languages, such as Polish, Russian, Yiddish, Hebrew, and Ukrainian. They lived peacefully in Aachen until '89, and two months before Klemens' death, they moved to Cologne. After he died, Stasia moved to Sweden and stayed with their daughter Edwarda's family for the rest of her life. Afterward, her remains were moved to Cologne, where she was put to rest next to her husband.

Their son Jerry and his wife, who are also March immigrants from Poland, live in Canada. Edwarda, a medical doctor, remains in Sweden.

THE PAST IS NEVER DEAD

September 10, 2010, Wrocław City Hall

My Address at our first Class Reunion organized in Wrocław

45 years after we graduated from High School

Thank you to our distinguished and generous hosts. Mr. President, Mr. Vice President, Mr. Director—it is a pleasure to be here with you in an atmosphere so different from that which surrounded our departure forty-two years ago. From the bottom of my heart, and on behalf of all of us, thank you. You are the authors of this beautiful moment. My love to you, dear classmates. We shared an innocent childhood, witnessed each other's careless youth, and our first pain and disappointments.

I BOW MY HEAD TO THE SHADOWS OF OUR PARENTS.

<u>To our hosts:</u> consequences of the 1968 March Events changed our lives forever. It was not your doing nor your fault. Yet, this difficult inheritance is our joint burden. For us, it resulted in humiliation, the challenge of unplanned emigration, the realization that with us ends the 800-year-old tradition of Polish Jews, the tragedy of our parents. You inherited something equally daunting: the weight of responsibility. Passages in history books are easy to forget, to ignore, to

rewrite, or even to delete. But firsthand accounts of individual stories, if truly heard, touch, move, and create an indelible imprint. Margaret Thatcher was right to say: "We don't want a society where the country is responsible for everything, but no one is responsible for the country." Mr. President, in your wise, moving address at the solemn ceremony of rededicating the White Stork Synagogue a few months ago, we all heard your sincere, troubled, incredulous question about antisemitism: in MY Wrocław?!

I'd like to share a few vignettes from MY Wrocław.

We parted, Wrocław and I, Poland and I, forty-two years ago. I was twenty years old then, and everything I had, everything I cared about, stayed behind. It wasn't much, but it was EVERYTHING. The chestnut tree in front of my window, which watched me grow up, the University of Science and Technology, which expelled me, neighbors, who, like vultures, circled around waiting for scraps and leftovers – perhaps something of our meager belongings will not sell and will remain up for grabs, just like after deportations during the war. I left Jacek, my first love. At the border, I also left a little tourist map of Wrocław – customs officers decided that it was a government document that couldn't leave Poland without a special permit. They also snapped off the heels of my boots, looking for God knows what inside, so I came to Vienna in boots without heels, limping in the snow.

Our last meal in Poland was in Katowice, at the hospitable home of Basia's parents, the Bobeckis. Basia was my friend from the University of Science and Technology; with so few girls in the Department of Electronics, we truly stuck together.

"Where are you going, into the unknown?" her mother sobbed in the kitchen. She had seen a lot in her life. "You know, we have a cottage in Kasinka. If things truly get out of hand, we could hide you there..."

* * *

We lived on Włodkowica Street. A Jewish neighborhood, all Holocaust survivors. I am now certain that the people who lived there were not harmonious or even normal. Pani Dora, who survived the war with a fake ausweiskarte – an ID which bore her picture but the name was invented, Polish, and she pretended to be a Catholic – Pani Dora was afraid to walk on the streets in daylight. As a child, I was afraid of Pani Żenia because she mumbled to herself all the time and pounded her head on building walls – Pani Żenia lost her children in Auschwitz. One of my neighborhood playmates was a girl named Lala Mociklińska, so fat that her sheepskin coat did not close at her midriff, only at the top and at the bottom. She came out to play with cheeks stuffed with food like a hamster, and her Mother yelled from their third-floor balcony: "Lala, swallow!" All of us kids laughed. This laughter was unkind, perhaps even cruel; my Mother said not to laugh because Mrs. Mociklińska survived the war in a wardrobe and starved for three years.

I now understand that this is what TRAUMA looks like. Such was the milieu of my childhood.

Near us, next door to the Technodent dental clinic – there is a restaurant there now – there was a kindergarten, a normal Polish kindergarten with swings and a sandbox in the backyard. Miracle of miracles, they accepted me to this kindergarten. The morning routine was common to all children: put your shoes in a designated cubby and don the provided felt slippers. I had a hard time putting on my shoes at the end of the first day; somehow, they felt too small, they pinched, and my feet hurt. I bravely got home and took off the shoes—my feet were bloody, and my shoes were filled with shards of glass. I didn't go back to kindergarten and never even had a chance to play on the swings I craved so much. **Do you know about such things**?

Our Polish neighbors spoke about us warmly, yet a bit apologetically: "Jews, but nice."

Part of my Mother's family survived the war by hiding in the family fields. Their survival was made possible by courageous peasants from nearby who were paid handsomely and delivered water, food, and blankets. And SILENCE. Among the survivors was my Grandma Sabina Haas Goldman – I am named after her. She hid instead of going to the train when ordered and, for a few years to come, cold and hungry, she shared a hole in the ground with one of her sons, Froim, and hundreds of voracious lice. They were killed after the war by neighbors in the Goldman home, where the family lived for generations, in the village of Nowosielce near Przeworsk. Uncle Zacharje, the one who is buried here in the Jewish Cemetery on Lotnicza Street, the one who lost his wife and children in Auschwitz, knew who killed them. Their executioners apparently thought they, alone, of the whole family, survived, and if they only got rid of them, then the Goldmans' house, fields, and orchards would be up for grabs.

When, as a teenager, I read the poignant poetry of Zbigniew Herbert, I thought of trying to explain to Uncle Zacharje that "those who will come after us will try to master that most difficult of arts, forgiveness," but I am not sure my Uncle would want to understand. Judaism teaches that you can forgive only for yourself, never for others, and, in any event, forgiveness for all that Zacharje lost was unimaginable. Besides, in a bit, the fields and orchards were nationalized, anyway… **Do you know about such things**?

My parents survived the war by miracle, a different miracle

each day. After the war, they worked in Poland for twenty-three years; they were simple, hard-working people. What harm did they do to anyone? They left Poland with nothing, belonging nowhere, scraping together with all their might the remainders of dignity. They left because staying was unimaginable. Old beyond years, scarred beyond comprehension. They carried a couple of suitcases each, five dollars per person, their incredibly injured Jewish souls, and me – they had me. And they lost their pensions. I understand that now it is possible to collect, but for most, for my parents, it's too late. During their 20 years in the West, they did not get a penny from Poland. Nothing. Where is that money? **Please tell this to your children.**

Such are pictures from MY life in MY Wrocław. Everyone has their own. Everyone who sits here can tell you their own. And you should know it all.

Miłosz, "Return." The 1980 Nobel Prize winner in literature spent four decades in Berkeley, more than in any other place he's ever lived – so I think of him as "my Miłosz."

"…In old age, I journeyed to places where once my early youth wandered. I struggled through the thicket where the park used to be, but I found no traces of the alley…".

And this recently. Two years ago, my friend from Stockholm, Róża Goldfarb, traveled to Poland for the ceremony of the rededication of the newly restored Jewish Cemetery in the village of Łosice near Warsaw. Her still-living Mom was born in Łosice; the plan was that they would go together, but when the time came, Mom was ill and too weak to go, so Róża went with her Swedish husband, Arne. A famous journalist and a TV crew came as well because the event was supposed to be solemn and conciliatory. The day before the opening – horror – the cemetery was vandalized. Stars of David on gallows smeared on headstones, vulgar slogans… Everyone saw Róża made pictures. Then, she, Arne, and a few others grabbed some rags and scrubbed everything clean for the ceremony. The next day, the whole village gathered: a local priest with a sermon, the main Rabbi, and the elderly lady from New York who funded much of the restoration. Not a word about the desecration. The famous journalist said later, privately, that she was ashamed to speak up. **Please tell this to your children**.

Please tell them also that they threw rocks at us on the way to school. All children in Poland had to display the emblem of their school on the left sleeve of their uniform, and everyone knew that ours- the VII Lyceum – was a Jewish School, so they threw rocks at us.

* * *

Our adopted aunt in Krakow encouraged us for years to petition for reinstatement of our Polish citizenship. "Your children may want to live or work in the EU someday." Reasonable, but I kept saying NO. I already have two citizenships, I belong elsewhere on paper, and in my heart, I have a home… It felt like the story with the German Consul in Rome.

But our friend Staszek chimed in, saying that the Consul in the Polish consulate closest to me is his friend from law school. "Just call and talk to him," he urged. "The whole thing is now a simple routine," I called, mostly to placate the whole group. The Consul was indeed pleasant and warm in conversation, saying, "Simple, you never lost your citizenship; they just said so(!)," and a few days later, an envelope containing the application forms landed on my desk. And there, in the end, "I, the undersigned, requested to be relieved of Polish Citizenship…" This had to be a mistake. I called the Consul once more: "You know that that we didn't request "to be relieved"; they demanded that we sign that paper." I have already found the Constitution of the Republic of Poland, Article. 34 clearly says: "A Polish Citizen cannot lose his citizenship unless he himself asks to be relieved." The Consul understands the dilemma: if I ask to be relieved, my citizenship is lost and cannot be reinstated. He finds a quick solution: "Then put down that you did not ask."

It was Passover; the children were home for the traditional family Seder. I sat down with them and explained that there would be no Polish citizenship. I wanted to explain why, but they didn't care. And so it is to this day: I, born in Wrocław, with generations of forefathers born and buried in Poland, daughter of a peasant from Nowosielce and a brush-maker from Lviv – I don't have Polish citizenship because it was lawlessly taken away from me and now, 40-some years later, they don't know how to smoothly give it back to me, so they suggest I lie.

Yet, our school was an oasis, and we were each other's joy and support. None of us had an extended family; aunts, uncles, or cousins were a rarity, and no grandmothers to spoil with a cookie and no grandfather to make one feel safe and slip a penny from time to time. There was almost nobody. But in school, we had each other, and that felt safe. Małgosia and I raced through Mickiewicz's *"Ordon's Redoubt"* by heart and without pause as if speed earned a prize. Leon was my companion for endless discussions about books and the existentialism of Kafka and Nietzsche. Bronka tediously drew hydras and other strange creatures in her biology notebook and stubbornly insisted that she would study medicine, which no one believed because she routinely flunked chemistry. We were the closest of friends, and we understood each other. And in school, none of us had to worry about being called a dirty Jew. Some of us had Polish friends, but that was an exception. In addition to subjects required by the national curriculum, we also studied Jewish History and, from second grade on, Yiddish language and literature. From fifth grade onward, all Polish schools had a foreign language requirement; in the vast majority of schools, it was Russian. In our school, however, the foreign language was English because, thanks to the huge number of students whose families were repatriated from the USSR in 1956-57, everyone spoke Russian anyway. And, at least then, none of us really understood why they threw stones at us; we only knew that we were Jewish and Poles didn't like Jews. I still don't understand why, in certain Polish circles, the word JEW is an offense; a Jew is "dirty" or "rotten." Why? I suspect that there, on our way to school, a child would be scolded for throwing a stone at a pigeon but throwing it at a Jew was OK.

Has this changed?

And all of us loved Wrocław. Each of us has a similar childhood photo of us in an embroidered sheepskin coat on the central city square, surrounded by pigeons. In those photos, we were indistinguishable from "normal" Polish kids.

According to the PhD dissertation by our school colleague Julian Ilicki at the University of Uppsala in Sweden, the Jewish emigration, which followed the events of March 1968, encompassed about 20,000 people. We now know that Ilicki's numbers were too high; more accurately, lower numbers became available. Our adoptive homelands see us as "strong immigrants": Well-educated, ambitious, hard-working, engaged and involved, enterprising, and void of a criminal record. We've built our lives with thunder. Małgosia, the one from "Ordon's Redoubt," sat in the box with the Danish Queen during the celebration marking 300 years of Jews in Denmark. Leon, my companion in long existential debates, is a businessman in Baltimore, Maryland. Lutek became an engineer, Staszek a lawyer, and Bella, a pharmacist. Zosia is a highly reputed chemist; she knows how to create famous

Israeli cosmetics using minerals from the Dead Sea. Leon Luks is a professor of history in Germany. And Bronka, who drew hydras and struggled with chemistry, is a well-known dermatologist in Stockholm. Our adopted countries are proud of us, and we are of them.

Neither my husband nor I had any brothers or sisters. There are five children in our blended family and six grandsons already: Ari, Lev, Moses, Solomon, Atlas, and Max. Amazing and funny – all boys. Our children live in different cities in the US and Canada; like most young people, they balance strong careers and devotion to their growing families. They have courage, education, optimism, backbone, and hearts. HEARTS. For large family holidays, for Passover and Thanksgiving, and sometimes for no reason at all, they come home, crowd around the family table, and the house brims with noise and happiness. We revived. We are ALIVE.

Mr. President, in your touching address at the synagogue in May, you apologize to us, the 1968 exiles. These are important and courageous words that perhaps need more from today's Poland than from us because we have put these matters behind us already, and Poland is still struggling. On behalf of all of us, I accept this apology with full appreciation for its great significance.

In a few hours, we will sit down together to an Erev Rosh Hashana supper and greet the Jewish New Year 5771. According to our tradition, each year, on the Day of Atonement, God forgives everyone for all the sins committed against him. But with people, it is different – each of us is responsible for settling our accounts, and each of us must correct our own trespasses and wrongdoings. God is wise and stays out of people's affairs.

I will end with Faulkner, from *Requiem for a Nun:* "The past is never dead. It's not even PAST."

EPILOGUE

Do the best you can until you know better.
Then, when you know better, do better.

Maya Angelou on *Twitter*

Somehow, unbelievably, fifty years have passed.

I moved a lot: from Detroit to Ann Arbor, then to New York and Connecticut, to Northern California, to Stockholm, Sweden, and back to California. I studied, worked, was promoted, and then promoted again. I caught wind in my sails, and there was no stopping me. "Good enough" was not good enough.

I turned out to be a gifted firmware programmer. At a small, energetic start-up in Ann Arbor, I was chosen to write the internal code for what were then the newest and most important Intel microprocessors: the 8008 and 8080 – the future of processing.

I got married; my husband was a handsome, blonde, blue-eyed American from the Midwest – my reach towards America as I imagined it and evidence that opposites attract. Soon after our wedding, I was offered the position of Director of Marketing at Olivetti Corporation of America in New York, at double my previous salary. Head spinning, I moved to Manhattan. My fluent Italian and easy familiarity with Italian culture and work habits came to use. I worked hard. Marisa Bellisario, the glamorous, iron-fisted head of the corporation, noticed me, and more challenges and opportunities followed; I became her personal poster child for successful women. I flew around the world for the first time in my life in Alitalia's First Class cabin. We bought a house in Westport, a posh town in Connecticut, on the right side of the tracks, in the same neighborhood as Martha Stewart, Paul Newman, and Joanne Woodward. My first daughter was born.

Then Silicon Valley called, and I became Director of Special Programs at a start-up, the flavor of the decade. I no longer wrote code but managed staff and resources. It was a paradigm-shifting time in technology — the beginning of a new era, the vision of 'a computer on every desk.'

Previously unimaginable options surfaced; we could hardly wrap our heads around the business and social transformation our products enabled and encouraged; we were redefining the future. I loved my work. Then came Two Way Consulting, which I co-founded with my husband; we concentrated on bringing together the exploding American technology and the established European markets and relationships. Exciting. Profitable.

A few more years later, I changed professions altogether and started yet another company, now on my own: we imported architectural stone from all over the world to California: marble, granite, onyx, travertine, quartzite, limestone. The time was right: Silicon Valley gathered steam, and economic power and wealth converged. Soon, we added another aspect: design and build. My company, SABINA Marble & Granite, operated out of showrooms and warehouses; I bought forklifts to unload containers and trucks to carry around our precious cargo. If it was stone, it was our business. Soon, we became leaders in our field, synonymous with excellent design, highest quality, elegance, prestige, and good taste. The list of our clients read like Who's Who, and not just in Silicon Valley: venture capitalists and presidents of companies, media personalities; Armani stores in the US, including the San Francisco flagship; Holt Renfrew, the most prestigious department store in Canada; the New York apartment of the American queen of home entertainment Martha Stewart; the Pacific Heights home of actor Robin Williams; founder of Apple Steve Jobs, David Packard who inherited much of the Hewlett-Packard fame and fortune. We won countless competitions and awards, including the coveted CotY — Contractor of the Year — a nationwide annual award given to the Contractor who excels in quality of work and ethics of conduct. Our showrooms were named the best and most innovative in America. At annual award ceremonies for design, I sometimes returned to the stage four or five times.

I circled the world many times: for work, for pleasure, but mostly out of curiosity. I helped my parents until the end, a lot, but not enough. They were comfortable, I think, but not happy; Detroit never felt like home to them. I visited them and translated their conversations with my husband and children. To his credit, my husband wanted to get to know them better, but language was not the only barrier. He once asked my Father how he survived the war. Tata didn't understand.

"How did I survive? Which day is he asking about?"

I buried my parents quietly, in the Jewish tradition. After Nowosielce, Przeworsk, and Yavoriv; after Siberia, the Urals, and Berlin; after Wrocław, Vienna, and Rome — and finally, after Detroit — they now rest in San Francisco, far from everything they once knew. But we will always visit them here. I bring stones from faraway places to their shared gravestone. A Jewish tradition shaped in the desert: instead of flowers, Jews

Inauguration of the US flagship store for Armani. All stone by SABINA Marble & Granite. Outfit by Armani. Giorgio sent gifts, and I wear them to this day.

San Francisco (1995)

put stones on graves. So I pick up stones in my travels, place them at my parent's grave, and weave into this humble gesture quiet stories about my life: that my daughters are beautiful people, that all of us are healthy and well, that life brings me satisfaction, that I want for nothing, that I travel and see amazing things, and that I always remember them both. I inherited from them the resilience and optimism of survivors. They taught me love. Joy I generated on my own.

My first marriage did not succeed. Opposites may indeed attract, but it's a tough formula for harmony and understanding. The proverbial bird and fish can, perhaps, fall in love, but building a home together is another story. I knew quickly that it had to end, but it took me twenty years to ask for a divorce. I didn't want my parents to know I was unhappy, so I waited until they were both gone, although I think they somehow knew it all anyway. A few years later, I met Ed, and we married, forever, free of doubt, surrounded by five children from previous marriages.

The children are fine people. All educated now, they have sparks in their eyes to tackle life with heart and backbone, courage and optimism. They live in different cities in the US and Canada and work hard at building their careers and families. When they visit, the house bursts into seams, more crowded indeed as time passes – there are three daughters-in-law now, a son-in-law, a fiancée, and six grandsons. We hope for more yet. I regret that my parents never met Ed and that they don't see this crowd and wonderful chaos around our table; they may have smiled in their sleep more than they did while they were alive.

Ed's Mother, Hela, and her husband, Martin, are buried in Melbourne. We visit their graves, and I bring stones to them as well.

For 15 years, Ed and I divided our lives between San Francisco, my home forever, and Stockholm, to where he emigrated in 1969. The Karolinska is his alma mater; that's where he defended his doctorate and earned his first professorship. Yet, in the end, we settled in California.

We feel that my debt to the United States and his debt to Sweden have been repaid. We gave a lot to our adoptive homelands in gratitude for accepting us unconditionally, for the privilege of a safe home and a place to belong, for our passports, and for endless opportunities for us and our families. My Roman lesson about identity endures: **I have no doubt who I am and where I belong.**

I learned to speak Polish again – my first language and the last one I've learned. But I don't speak Polish with Ed. By choice and without any explicit agreement, we speak English with one another — that is the language of our home, our family, and our future.

Eva and Carl were married in Detroit in 1971; I was a witness at their wedding. They live in the suburbs of Pasadena and have two wonderful daughters and sons-in-law, as well as four grandchildren. We've remained good friends and meet a couple of times each year. We are joined in these semiannual meetings by a third couple: my friend Isabelle and her husband Mark, both of whom once lived on Włodkowica in Wrocław as well. With a PhD from Technion in Haifa, Mark is a world-class expert in the desalinization of water; they live in San Diego.

After thirty years, I decided to see if there was anything still left of me in Poland. I walked around Wrocław, got lost a few times, and didn't recognize street names, many of which were changed after 1989, when Poland, with other Eastern Bloc countries, liberated themselves from the patronage of the USSR.

I felt alone in the city of my birth; no tug of heart, no tear in the eye… a place. Beautiful, but not mine. I went to what, in my time, was the best restaurant in town; I could not even dream of eating there before. I asked for a table with a view of the beautiful Main Market Square, no other table would do. I then ordered EVERYTHING on the menu, one of each. The waiter was baffled, asked me to repeat, and then, incredulously: "You will eat all of it?" "Of course not, but I want to taste it." He commented to his colleagues that there was a rich German woman sitting by the window; she spoke good Polish. Just like Herr Consul in Rome had done, he decided on my identity.

Somewhere along the way, I met Ruth, Ed's adopted aunt in Krakow. I came to love her and the people around her, and for years, we visited Krakow regularly; it's a short flight from Stockholm. Ruth Buczynska and Hela Baral forged an unbreakable bond during the war in Ternopil and remained lifelong friends. Ruth knew Ed before he was born, when Hela's big belly brought great joy and deathly fear in the dark hours underground, in the bunker, and then when it was the only tangible crumb left of Hela's husband. Ruth adopted us like the children she never had. We listened together to great music in the unfortunate concert hall of the Krakow Philharmonic, and we peeked into the Piwnica pod Baranami (*The Cellar under the Rams* – the most renowned political and literary cabaret in Krakow) with which Ruth has been associated from the beginning, we ate pierogi and "schaboszczaki" (polish style pork chops), I carried to Stockholm cheeses and sausages from the Krakow Farmers Market at Kleparz Square. It was Ruth who persuaded me to write this book; she thought it was important. Then she died. The first lady of Krakow was a brilliant attorney who argued cases in front of the Polish Supreme Court. For her skill and courage during the Martial Law, she was posthumously awarded a medal "With gratitude for freedom."

The biggest lawyer club in Poland now bears her name.

Our Krakow oasis ended with her death. We now visit her at the Jewish cemetery; I lay stones on her grave as well. There are ever more stones in my suitcase as I now circle the globe.

* * *

My feelings towards Poland are complex. I'd like to, I would truly like to look upon Wrocław and Poland with warm feelings usually reserved for one's birthplace and childhood home. I'd like to feel joy that the old chestnut tree still stands in front of the house on Włodkowica Street where I grew up. I'd like for what is happening in Poland to be important to me in an intimate way, not just as "foreign affairs." I'd like to feel a connection, a bond, and even in some small measure, I'd like to still belong there. I'd like to love my birthplace.

I'd like to—but I can't. There was a time when I hoped Poland would reach out to us, that someday I'd find a Polish passport in my mailbox and a few simple words: perhaps just "it was a mistake," or "please forgive and accept..." It would be inconsequential; nothing would change – but some dignity would be restored. To Poland.

I didn't plan to write this book. Perhaps it is the final account of my Polish life? There was a time when we lived and belonged there... Then they threw us out.

* * *

I've been to Venice many times. It is a beautiful symbol of how to live strong, age with grace, and, yes, how to die with dignity.

Our wedding. Sons, all Edwards, and daughters, both mine (1999)

*In one of SABINA Marble & Granite showrooms, with a just received national
award (2003)*

Visiting the remote Hamer tribe of Omo Valley in Southern Ethiopia (2012)

Negotiating the Sahara in Morocco, near the border with Algeria

Easter Island, Chile (2010)

Torres del Paine National Park, Patagonia, Chile (2010)

Dog sledding beyond the Arctic Circle, Jukkasjärvi, Sweden, (2011)

Sabina Baral with her oldest daughter Monica (1979)

At the Bar Mitzva of the youngest son, Robert, Winnipeg, Canada (2004)

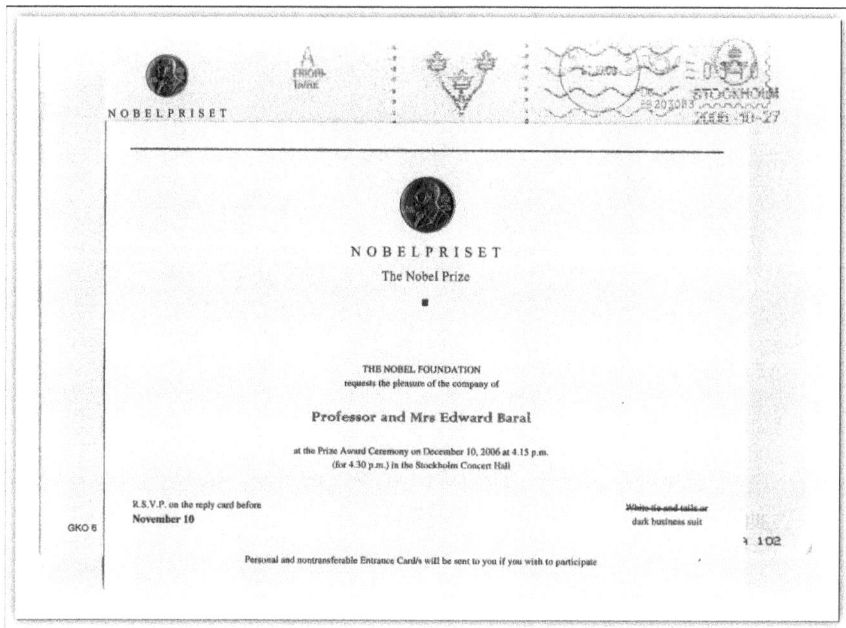

Invitation to the Nobel Awards ceremony, Stockholm (2006)

Ed (second from left) and his three sons. From left: Stefan, Fredrik, and Robert in Vail, CO (2013). There is a tradition of an annual male skiing trip in our family; even Ari, our oldest grandson, has participated already.

Sabina with daughters Monica and Vanessa (2002, at Fred's wedding in Vancouver, BC). Monica now holds a Master's Degree in Landscape Architecture from the University of California at Berkeley.

Vanessa holds a Master's Degree in Clinical Psychology from Pepperdine University in Malibu and is a California-licensed MFC. She specializes in trauma, grief, and loss

At the family home in California

s

I don't know where I am going from here,
but I promise it won't be boring.

David Bowie, 1997

www.ingramcontent.com/pod-product-compliance
Lightning Source LLC
Chambersburg PA
CBHW040802010826
48981CB00029B/156